TAKEN

CHRIS JORDAN

TAKEN

First published in Great Britain 2006
MIRA Books, Eton House, 18-24 Paradise Road,
Richmond, Surrey, TW9 1SR

© Rodman Philbrick 2006

ISBN-13: 978 0 7783 0127 1
ISBN-10: 0 7783 0127 3

58-0806

Printed in Great Britain
by Clays Ltd, St Ives plc

For Lynn Harnett, forever and always.

ACKNOWLEDGEMENT

The author wishes to thank Diane Shaw and all the good folks at Piscataqua Savings Bank for sharing details of financial intrigue.

1

FIELD OF GREEN

On a perfect day in the month of June, in a lovely field of green, my life starts falling apart. At five minutes after four in the afternoon, to be exact.

At ten of four things are still fine and dandy. I'm watching eagerly as the handsome boy with the aluminum bat steps out of the batter's box and readjusts his gloves, just like A-Rod, his big-league hero. I lean forward in the dugout, but resist the impulse to shout encouragement. My son, tall and lanky for his eleven years, doesn't mind the fact that his mom is an assistant Little League manager, but he has asked me not to shout from the sidelines like so many of the other parents. Parents who are, like, hideously uncool. His phrase. Tomas "Tommy" Bickford. My perfect, precious, truly gifted son. My amazing, maddening child. Amazing because he seems to be changing every day, sometimes from minute to minute. Maddening for the same reason, because I never know if he's going to be my sweet little boy, goofy and affectionate, or if he'll dis me with his soon-to-be-teen-stud coolness. Tommy can toggle between the two identities in the space of a heartbeat, and every time it happens it hits me like a soft blow to the belly.

At eleven he's such a guy. And somehow I never imagined my son would be, well, a *guy* guy. What did I expect him to be? Did I think he'd stay my baby boy forever? Clinging to my apron strings? And I do wear aprons. Aprons inscribed with the logo for my catering company. I also make cookies. A thousand or so a day, for the upscale delis and restaurants in my neck of the Connecticut woods.

I like to think of myself as a warmer version of Martha Stewart. Warmer and a lot less wealthy. But doing okay in my own small way. Katherine Bickford Catering books over two hundred events a year. Peanuts compared to the really huge commercial catering firms, but more than enough to keep my twelve employees very busy indeed. Average event, eighty-five plates. Average charge per plate, sixty-two dollars. Do the math and you'll discover that adds up to more than a million dollars gross. A million bucks! Of course, we showed a whole lot less than a million in profit, but still. And I really did start the business in my own kitchen. With a small, frightened four-year-old boy "helping" me sift the flour.

We've both come so far in the last seven years that it sometimes takes my breath away. Especially when I admit to myself that when we started out I was even more terrified than the four-year-old. Terrified of suddenly having to raise a child on my own. Terrified I would never get over the grief of losing Ted, the love of my life, my sweet husband. Terrified that I would simply vanish into the black hole of despair if I stopped moving or stopped mothering for even a minute.

Even now, seven years later, just thinking his name gives me a Ted-size pang of melancholy. Like a low, mournful note on a cello, quietly sounding in the deepest part of me. But the anxious fear is gone. Over time the grief has become regret, for all the things poor Ted has missed. Tommy on his first bicycle—*Don't touch me, Mom, I can do it all by myself!* Tommy on his way to first grade, fiercely insisting that he not be accompanied into the school—the bravest kid in all the world that day.

Amazing boy. For the first month or so after Ted died, he came to our bed—my suddenly lonesome bed—and slept at my side in a fetal position, reaching out in his sleep as if he thought I, too, might vanish from his life. And then one day at breakfast he quietly announced that he was "too big" to sleep in his mommy's bed. Hit me two ways, that one. Fierce pride that at four he had such a strong sense of self. And regret that he didn't seem to need me quite as much as I needed him. At least while he slept.

How many hours did I stand in Tommy's bedroom door that first year after Ted passed, watching him sleep? More than I care to admit. And yet just watching him helped me. As watching him now helps remind me of who I am. My first and most important identity: Tommy Bickford's mom. Proud to be, even if he doesn't want me shouting his name from the dugout.

What the hell, let him deal with it.

"Come on, Tommy! Clean stroke! Good at bat!"

Stepping back into the batter's box, he shoots me a glare. Also a grin, like he knows Mom can't help herself.

The pitcher, a husky kid who looks as if he's been taking steroids— hasn't, I'm sure, but he has that beefy look—peers in for the sign, flings back his arm and delivers the ball. Not exactly a fastball—I'm guessing 70 mph or so on his dad's radar gun—but straight and true and heading right for the catcher's mitt.

Tommy steps into the pitch with his bat level, swinging slightly up, and *bonk!* He's made contact. The ball carries over the short-stop's outstretched glove and rolls all the way out to where the left fielder waits, then scoops it up. Drops the ball, gets it again, makes a wobbly throw to the cutoff. Cutoff drops the ball but keeps it in front of him, very good. By which time Tommy is sliding into second—an unnecessary act of daring, but the boy loves to get his uniform dirty—and the winning run has crossed the plate.

Pandemonium. Our players throw their gloves in the air, letting out war whoops and girlish cheers, and Fred Corso, our bullnecked manager—he's also the Fairfax County sheriff—punches his fist in the air and then strides out of our cinderblock dugout.

"Yes! Way to go, Tomas! Good hit, son!"

I keep forgetting, Tommy wants to be called Tomas now. Probably hasn't reminded me more than a million times in the last two weeks, but good old Fred has remembered. Feeling a little chastened, and resisting the impulse to run out on the field and give my boy a hug, I remind his excited teammates that it's time to line up and shake hands. Congratulate the opposing team, the Fairfax Red Sox, on a game well played.

We're trying to instill sportsmanship and doing a pretty fair job of it, if I do say so myself. The losers look sheepish, slapping five without much enthusiasm, but everyone is polite and they get the job done.

I catch Tommy from behind and lift the hat off his head. Give his raven-black hair a scoodge—his word—and face him, grinning. "Nice going, Tommy! You really smacked it!"

"Thanks, Mom." But he's already backing away, afraid I'll spoil his moment of manly triumph with a kiss. Then he stops, sidles up next to me, looking deeply serious. "You know what, Mom?"

"What?"

"I think I deserve an ice-cream sundae."

I fork out the necessary money and he runs off to the snack trailer, which is parked next to the field for the games. Runs by Karen Gavner and her husband, Jake, who have twin girls on the team. Not especially gifted athletes, but good kids. Connecticut blondes, both of 'em, and studying to be heartbreakers. I've seen the way they look at Tommy, but if he's discovered girls he hasn't let me know about it. Which he might not, come to think of it.

"Meet me at the van!" I shout at his back.

He acknowledges with a bob of his head and then vanishes into the milling crowd of parents and players, high-fiving as he goes.

And that's the last I see of him.

The hated minivan. My poor Dodge Caravan has recently become the object of Tommy's scorn. Am I not ashamed to be seen in the pathetic "Mini-Vee," as Tommy calls it? What does it tell the world about me, to drive such a totally boring car? Actually, his phrase is "hideously boring," not totally boring. *Totally* was last year's favorite modifier. Everything is hideous now. Just the other day he ticked off all the reasons I should trade in the hideous Mini-Vee for a really cool Mini-Cee. Of course I bite. "Mini-Cee," it turns out, is Tommy-talk for Mini Cooper.

"You mean that funny little car?" I asked him. "The one at the circus where all the clowns get out?"

"It's made by BMW, Mom," he informed me. "It's not funny looking. It's way cool. It would look good on us, trust me."

It would look good on us. Where did that come from, the idea of a car as a fashion accessory? Of course I know exactly where it comes from. TV, Internet, magazines, the neighborhood, in roughly that order. Beemers and Audis and Mercs are the vehicles of choice in our part of the world, but I'm aware of the Mini Coopers that Tommy so admires, because there are two of them just down the street, prominently displayed in the Parker-Foyles' driveway. His and hers, color coordinated.

"No chance," I told him. "Put it out of your mind. I'm a Caravan kind of girl."

At which point his eyes rolled so high I thought they might get stuck in the back of his head. And that makes me laugh in recollection. Hey, I remember being embarrassed about the car my mother drove, too. My mother's stodgy old Ford Fairlane station wagon, how embarrassing. And shame on me for thinking so at the time.

So I lean against the van on a perfect summer evening, waiting for my son. Scanning the field and parking lot for Tommy. Not seeing him.

Waiting.

For the first few minutes I'm not terribly concerned. There'll be a line at the snack trailer. Friends to talk to. More hands to slap, kudos to receive. But then traffic clears enough for me to see the snack trailer, and there's Jake Gavner closing the window, shutting down—sold out, no doubt—and my mom radar is drawing an empty screen. Can't seem to pick up Tommy. Did he run back into the school to use the boys' room? Unlikely. We're ten minutes or so from home and I happen to know Tommy prefers to use his own bathroom whenever possible.

So I'm trying not to act overly concerned as I walk over to the closed-up snack trailer and rap my fist on the back door.

"Yo!" from inside.

"Jake! It's Kate Bickford."

The door swings open and Jake is there, flashing a quizzical smile. Nice-looking man with slight rosacea on his cheeks and a comfortable paunch he never tries to hide. Great with kids—somehow he remembers all the names, and who belongs to who.

"Hey, Kate! Dogs are gone."

"Excuse me?"

"Hot dogs. We're out. No slumming for you today."

He winks. For the life of me I can't think why Jake Gavner would be winking at me, and then I get it. The hot-dog conversation. Couple of weeks ago I was starving and ordered a dog with extra kraut. As I chowed down, we chatted about comfort food. Joking around that if any of my customers saw me eating hot dogs I'd lose business. Either that or they'd be expecting cheap tinned sausages as appetizers at the gala banquets. Wasn't exactly a scintillating conversation, come to think, but apparently something about it stuck with Jake.

"No, no, I'm fine," I tell him. "By any chance, did you notice where Tommy went?"

"Tommy? Nope. You lose him?" He looks around sharply, eyeing the empty field, the near-empty parking lot.

"He came over to get an ice cream," I tell him. "Chocolate with chocolate sauce, hold the nuts. Thought you might have noticed if he wandered off with some other kids."

"Tommy, huh? Nope. No ice cream for Tommy, that I recall."

"He never showed?"

"I'd remember, Kate. The kid won the game. I'd have comped him a sundae. Always do that for game winners, if they try to pay."

"Really? That's nice of you. Um, maybe Karen served him?"

He shakes his head. "I had the counter and the coolers. Karen was on the grill."

"Is she around?"

"She took the extra coolers home. Got to get the stuff back in the freezer, you know?" Jake studies me, senses my anxiety. "Call her. Maybe she saw him. But he probably went home with somebody else, is my guess."

"Yeah," I say. "Thanks."

And turn away thinking, he wouldn't dare. Not my son. Take off without telling me? Not Tommy. At the same time, the comment about game winners getting free ice cream bothers me. Did Tommy know? And if so, why hit me up for three bucks? Did he have other plans? Plans that included a little pocket change?

Now I'm more than uneasy. Call it anxious. Anxious but not quite ready to call 911. Or more directly, Sheriff Corso, our team coach. Because I can already hear Fred telling me not to worry. The boy was excited, okay? Getting that big hit went to his head. Enough so he forgot to tell Mom he was getting a ride home with somebody else. Some group of rambunctious teammates who wanted to praise him.

I hit Home on my cell and hear it chirping. My own voice comes on the line, suggesting I leave a message. "Tommy, are you there, honey? Pick up, please."

But I'm keenly aware that Tommy hates letting the answering machine cut in. He'll kill himself racing for the phone, even if there's no prospect that the call is for him. Bruises on his shins to prove it.

Where's my boy? And what is he thinking, scaring me like this?

I march to the gymnasium entrance, convinced he's inside using the boys' room, or more probably raising some kind of hell with his buddies. The entrance is locked, but I can see into the gymnasium. It's dim and empty. And silent. No laughing boys. No lockers slamming. Nobody home. Just silence.

I hurry to the Caravan. I'll just quick check at our house before calling Fred Corso.

I have to force myself not to stomp on the accelerator leaving the empty parking lot. Thinking, *Tommy, how could you do this to me? Make me worry like this? Is this the way it's going to be for the next five years? Scamming Mom for money, not coming home until the crack of dawn?*

Get a grip, I urge myself. One of the other mothers offered him a ride. He felt it would be impolite to say no, and they took off before he could tell me. Some variation on that. But still, no excuse. He knows I worry.

Already I've covered six blocks. Must have passed through two lights but have no recollection of it. Driving on autopilot while my frazzled mind cranks out scenarios. All of which conclude with me giving Tommy a big hug and telling him never do that again. Never make your mother think the worst might happen.

I'm held up on the last light on Porter Road. Elderly couple can't get it together to actually go when the light turns green. "Q-tips," Tommy calls them. Meaning elderly drivers with that soft white, cotton-ball hair peeking up over the seat backs. Can't recall the last time I really blasted the horn, but this time I punch it hard and the driver jerks in his seat like he's been shot and then lurches his Lincoln Town Car through the intersection. More horns, some of them directed at me.

Weaving through the confusion I've created, I cut into the intersection, get my lane and remember to use the turn signal for our street, good old Linden Terrace, coming up quickly on the left. Actually a cul-de-sac with a turnaround at the end, which cuts down on the through traffic and probably adds ten grand to the evaluation of all the homes there. Well worth it, we all agree. Not that I care about property taxes right now. Not with Tommy filling my head.

Almost there. Almost home. Third from the end. The big, cedar-shingled Cape-style beauty behind the two massive maples that have taken over the front lawn. One full acre, with commonly held woodlands behind. There's a separate three-car garage, also shingled, which came in handy when I was starting up the catering business. It was the big garage that first sold Ted on the place. *You never know when it might come in handy,* he'd said. He was thinking "boat," but for a while it held stacks of folding tables and chairs, crates of crockery. Totally against the local zoning laws, of course—no business activity allowed, not even storage—but my neighbors took pity on the young widow and looked the other way until I could afford to rent a proper warehouse. Much appreciated, that quiet act of kindness. Sometimes looking the other way is just what the doctor ordered. Better than casseroles left on the step or offers to babysit. *Give her time,* they must have urged each other, and now the garage was just a garage again and Tommy is eleven years old and giving his mother fits.

Leaving the van in the driveway, I bound up the breezeway steps, kick the screen door open and approach the inner door with key in hand. Because we always lock up and activate the alarm. Nice neighborhood, but still. Bridgeport is a mere three miles down the road, and in Bridgeport they have gangs and drugs and crime that sometimes manages to seep into suburban Fairfax. So we lock.

But the door is unlocked and the alarm isn't sounding. And that can mean only one thing. I'm already heaving a sigh of relief as I enter the kitchen area.

"Tommy?" I call out. "Tommy! I was worried sick! What were you thinking?"

No response. Pretending he can't hear me. Pretending he didn't do anything wrong. Ready with a facile fib about how he did so tell me he was getting a ride home and it must have slipped my mind. Early-'zeimers, Mom. You're losing it.

"Tommy?"

The TV is on in the family room. Low but audible. A Sony PlayStation game. It will be *Tenchu:Wrath of Heaven,* his current favorite, or maybe the new *Tomb Raider.* But game or not, the little scamp can hear me fine. And now he's starting to piss me off. He should be here in the kitchen, ready with an apology, however lame.

"Tommy! Turn off the TV!"

I march into the family room, expecting to see my son perched in front of the big-screen TV, manipulating the controls of his precious PlayStation.

But Tommy isn't there.

"Hello, Mrs. Bickford. Take a seat, would you, please?"

There's a man in my brown leather chair. He has Tommy's video-game control box on his knee, working the joystick with his left hand. His face is obscured by a black ski mask.

In his right hand is a pistol, and he's aiming it at me.

There are only five rooms in the house, not counting the basement, and Lyla searches all of them. Each room, and the basement, too, looking for Jesse. The boy must be playing hide-and-seek. A game he loved when he was five, only a little less so now that he's reached the advanced age of eleven, when boys are usually past wanting to play with their mothers.

Her Jesse is an exception. He's an athletic kid, fit and lean and tall for his age, but in some respects he's still Momma's little boy. Any moment now he'll leap out of a closet, or out from under the stairwell, with a gleeful *boo!* and her hands will fly to her heart.

You scared me, dear!

He'll kill himself laughing, holding his tummy, bent over from the sheer joy of it.

Oh, Mom, you're such a wuss!

That she is; from the first day that she held his tiny body, all she's ever done is worry. Worry, worry, worry, morning, noon and night, until it makes her dizzy with anxiety. Worry that he'll wander into the swimming pool and drown—not that they have a pool, thank God.

Worry that he'll tumble down the stairs where he likes to play mountain climber. Worry that he'll fall from his bicycle, or worse, that he'll be stolen by a child snatcher who looks, in her waking nightmares, like Freddy Krueger.

She reminds herself that there are no Freddy Kruegers in the real world, certainly not in boring old New London, Connecticut. And that Jesse has fallen on the stairs more than once and received nothing more dangerous than a bruise or two. Took a wild spill from his bike, for that matter, and wore the scabs on his knees like badges of honor, no tears and no complaints. He's a sturdy boy, her Jesse, heals quickly. Healthy as a horse, unlike his doting mom, who suffers from a variety of infirmities, not the least of which is a background hum of fear that never leaves her, not even when she's sleeping.

Fear of the world, her husband, Stephen, calls it, but it's more like fear of all the bad things waiting to ruin the lives of good people. Sensible fears, if you read the papers or listen to the news. Toilets falling from airplanes, crushing the innocent. Drive-by shootings. Mysterious diseases. Planes full of madmen crashing into skyscrapers. Fear is the reasonable reaction, is it not?

"Jesse? Hide-and-seek is over, honey. Olly-olly-entry!"

Silence in all the five rooms of her home. Silence from the basement, too.

Where is that boy? Must be in his room, hiding under the bed with all that dangerous dust and mold. Bad for his respiratory system, so they say, and Lyla believes it, as she believes every warning of impending disaster. Inhale too much dust and your child will develop asthma. Eat too much peanut butter, he'll develop allergies. She tries to warn him about such things, but he's just a boy and believes he'll live forever.

"Jesse? Come out, dear. Supper's almost ready. Your favorite, hamburger casserole."

Her son's bed is neatly made. Did she do that? Must have, he'd never fit the sheets like that, or smooth the blanket and pillow. Lyla gets down on her hands and knees, lifts the skirt of the bed. There he is, in the far corner!

No, no, only a shadow. A shadow shaped like a boy.

Closet! Yes, of course, why didn't she think of that first? He must be in the closet, watching her through the vents in the door. Naughty boy.

Lyla opens the closet door, sweeps back the clothes hangers. She has the distinct impression that Jesse was in the closet very recently. She can smell the scent of his skin, his hair. Must have slipped out while she was looking under the bed.

What Lyla wants to do is lie down in the closet and sleep with the smell of him on her hands, her hair. Dreaming that her son is close by, just out of sight, and that soon all will be well, and Jesse will be safe again. But she can't sleep, not until she's found him.

Lyla searches all five rooms again, and then ventures into the basement. Down the sturdy steps, clutching the handrail. Pulls the string on the bare lightbulb. A basket of laundry perches on the washing machine. More of his clothes, including his grass-stained uniform. The Mystic Pirates. Not for the first time, Lyla carefully takes the soiled uniform from the basket and holds it up, as if looking for clues to her son's whereabouts. The grass stains, of course, and the usual dirt on the knees, but is that splotch under the letters a bloodstain?

Anxiety thrums through her body like a jolt of electricity. Heart fluttering, she races up the basement steps with Jesse's uniform top in her hands. Wanting to show her husband this new evidence that something is wrong, terribly wrong. Something has happened to Jesse, something that made him bleed on his Little League uniform.

At the top of the stairs Lyla trips and falls to her knees, sliding on the slick linoleum.

"Steve!" she cries out. "Steve, come look! Blood!"

But the house is empty. In the oppressive silence, Lyla gets shakily to her feet. Clutching the stained uniform, she heads into the living room.

"Oh, God," she whispers. "Bring him home. Make him safe."

There on the mantel above the fireplace is a framed photograph that brings her a little peace, in the brief interval before she must begin searching again. In the photograph, Jesse's Little League uniform is clean. No grass stains, no bloodstains. He's just made fun of her for ironing the uniform—*They're supposed to be wrinkled, Mom, don't you get it?*—but he's obviously pleased by all the attention. Look at the grin on his face as he poses with a bat, taking the stance, eyes bright and fearless. Her perfect, flawless son.

Lyla collapses onto the couch, clutching the framed photograph and the soiled uniform. She will allow herself to weep, but only for a few minutes. She has much work to do, and weeping exhausts her. First she must search the house again. Five rooms and the basement. And then if Jesse still isn't there, she's going to do a thing that has been forbidden to her. She's going to use the cell phone and make the call and demand to know where her son is, and when he will be returned.

Never call, she has been told in no uncertain terms.

But no one can stop a mother from trying to contact her own son, can they?

The decision to use the forbidden number gives her strength. She gets up from the couch, still holding the photo and uniform to her breast, and begins the endless circuit. Room to room, searching for her missing child.

"Sit down, Mrs. Bickford. May I call you Kate?"

I'm frozen. Can't seem to move. The gun terrifies me but I can't stop looking at it. Easier staring at the dark and shiny gun, rather than into the glittering eyes of the man in the black ski mask.

"Obviously you're frightened." The voice coming out of the mask is low and smooth, with a tone of preening confidence that makes me hate him. How dare he break into our house? "It's okay to be scared," he continues amiably. "But if you don't sit down in that chair I'm going to have to shoot you in the kneecap or something, and that will make things complicated. So sit down. NOW."

I find myself in the chair, unable to breathe, unable to stop staring at the gun, which seems to be pointing right into my eyes, or beyond my eyes, into my brain.

"Better," says the man in the mask.

"Who are you?" I manage to say. "What do you want?"

"Better and better. Take a few more deep breaths, would you, Kate? Feel better? Good. Put your hands on the arms of the chair, where I can see them. Excellent. Now, stop looking at the gun and look at me."

I force myself to look at the mask. I've seen pictures of guys dressed like this, snipers or SWAT guys or whatever. Never expected to see one of them in my own house, a living nightmare perched on my favorite chair. The mask has a big hole for the mouth, so he's speaking clearly, unmuffled. Very white teeth. Capped or bleached, hard to say. The mouth is neither old nor young. My age, more or less.

"Good. Better. Just try to relax and we'll get on with business."

"Where's my son?" It bursts out of me, much higher-pitched than my normal voice. As if some other, younger me is crying out.

"Tomas? Not to worry, Mom. Tomas is in a safe place." A sneer on the lips. Very pleased with himself. But the gun never wavers. Very steady hands. Hands that scare me almost as much as the gun. Hands that must have touched my son.

"Where?" I demand. "Where is he?"

"That's enough," he says. "No more questions."

"If you hurt him...! If he's been harmed in any way...!"

The man in the mask leans forward, bringing the gun closer. "Shut up, Kate. You want to be a good mommy? You want the kid back in one piece? Then shut up and listen."

I start to reply, then stop. Part of me, the small, unpanicked part, understands that I must do what he says.

"Fine," he says. "Very good. Must be a terrible shock, huh? Coming in and finding a stranger in your house. Hate to tell you this, but your security system sucks." He takes a deep, satisfied breath and settles back into my chair. "Okay, you want to know what this is about? Go on, ask away."

"Yes. I want to know."

"Excellent. And you haven't panicked yet. Which is good for both of us. Shooting you would make things ugly. Trust me, you don't want that. What this is about, Kate, is very simple. It's about money. Your money. Which is soon to be my money."

"How much?"

"Good question," he says, smiling with approval. "Here's my answer. All of it. Every penny. You okay with that, Kate? Is the kid worth wiping out your bank accounts?"

"Yes."

"Good answer, and I like the way you didn't hesitate. We're going to get along just fine, you and me. For the period of our brief acquaintance. And if we don't get along, if you don't cooperate, you know what I'm going to do?"

He waits. My mouth is so dry it's hard to form a word.

"What?" I finally ask.

"I'll cut out Tommy's heart," he says. "I'll cut out his heart and give it to you in a plastic bag."

The man in the mask puts aside my son's PlayStation controls and pulls a knife out of the sheath on his ankle. Gun in one hand, never wavering, and now, glittering, a knife in the other.

"This is what I'll use," he says very softly. "My trusty K-Bar. And it won't be the first heart I've ever cut out." He pauses, studying me. His lips twitching slightly. "Do you believe me, Kate?"

"Yes," I manage to say.

And I do.

The mind, I discover, is a funny thing. Much more capable than I had imagined. For although part of me, a sizable, shivering part of me, remains terrified, a cold place in my brain seems to be processing information, making decisions. Guiding me, even as I quiver in fear. The fear not so much that I will die, but that my son will die if I don't do the right thing. If I don't think and behave rationally.

Don't give him a reason, that part of my mind tells me. Meaning no sudden moves, no hysteria—that state of supposedly female panic that has always repulsed me in others—no fountains of tears. *The man with the gun may be a psychotic killer—he wants you to believe he is—but he's been in your life for less than five minutes and he's already told you exactly what he wants. You might call that progress.*

He wants money. And if money is what he wants, then money is what he'll get. At the same time, access to the money is my only leverage. How best to use that leverage? Not to defy him—he's not a man I'd care to defy, under any circumstances—but to make sure that Tommy is okay. To make sure that he'll be returned to his home, and to his mother, in one piece. Undamaged.

"How do I know—" I begin. Then stop to work some moisture into my parched mouth. "How do I know my son is...okay?"

He puts the knife back in the sheath at his ankle. A move so delicate and smooth and practiced that it makes my breath catch in my throat. Something about the way he does it makes me believe he could slip the knife into flesh just as adroitly. And with as much physical pleasure.

He smiles and clicks his white, white teeth together. "Bad Kate," he says. "She didn't ask permission to ask a question."

"Please tell me my son is okay."

"No begging, Kate. Here's the deal. You want to ask me a question? Pose it this way—'Permission to ask a question, sir.' Got it?"

For him this is a kind of game, obviously. And humiliating me, or toying with me, is part of that game. I have no choice but to play along.

"Permission to ask a question, sir."

The mouth in the mask grins. "Permission denied. For the time being. Sometime in the next few hours you will be allowed to speak to Tommy on the cell. He'll be a little woozy because he's been drugged—"

"You drugged my son!"

He moves so fast I don't even have time to react. One moment he's seated in the chair—my chair—and the next the gun is pressing against my forehead like a cold steel finger, pushing me back into the cushions.

Can't help it, tears spill from my eyes and run down my cheeks. He's inches from me, his breath coming in snorts. I can hear his teeth grinding. I can smell him, the sharp scent of his maleness, his anger. It's all I can do to keep from peeing my pants, that's how much he frightens me. The last time I was this scared was as a five-year-old, imagining a monster under my bed, waiting to reach up through the mattress and grab me. I'd been too terrified to scream then. This fear is even more visceral.

"Never, never," he says, whispering his hot breath into the side of my face. "Never, ever defy me. Never raise your voice. Is that understood? Nod if you can't speak."

I nod, feeling the barrel of the pistol pressing hard into my forehead. Terrified that a bullet will explode me into the darkness, leaving Tommy without a mother.

Slowly, he stops panting and his breathing becomes regular. I haven't been this close to a man since Ted died, and it gives me a sick feeling. Makes my skin crawl with revulsion.

At last he backs up a step, and the pressure on my forehead lessens. His hand cups my chin, holding my face. He squeezes until I whimper in pain.

"Kate, Kate. What are we going to do about you, huh? I thought you wanted to cooperate. Play the game. Get your kid back."

"You're hurting me."

He responds by squeezing harder, then suddenly his hand is gone and my face is burning with shame.

"Where were we?" he says, his voice weirdly amiable again. "Oh right. You want me to prove your son is still alive. Understandable. Of course we drugged him, Kate. Had to. Did you want me to coldcock him with this gun? No? Drugging the target is the safe way, Kate. You'll just have to trust me on this. We have a method. The method works."

We, of course. There has to be more than one person involved. Are they all monsters like the man in the mask? Or is he the designated heavy, selected because he knows how to instill fear?

Oddly enough, the idea of Tommy's abduction being part of an organized activity is something of a relief. Maybe there are saner minds at work. People who understand there is nothing to be gained by killing my son.

My eyes are still blurred with tears, but I can tell that he's back in the chair. A wave of dread sweeps through me, as if soaking into my bones, producing a new flood of tears. I hate this, crying, hate how it makes me look weak. But I can't stop it from happening. There are times for me when crying is as involuntary as breathing. Times when it is better not to fight it, just to get it over with, to get beyond the tears. As, eventually, I did when we lost Ted.

Suddenly, something hits me in the face. Something soft and light. It falls to my lap. My hands find a little wad of thin cloth.

A handkerchief.

"Wipe your face. You have snot running down your lips."

I do as he says, thinking, what sort of man carries a hankie these days? And then it comes to me. A man who makes women cry. A man who has done this before, and is ready for every eventuality.

"The method, Kate. The method is your friend. Let me explain how it works."

He's interrupted by the chirping of a phone. Sudden and shrill, it sends a jet of cold blood through my heart. With the gun still aimed at my head, he reaches into one of his pockets and extracts a cell phone. Angrily snaps it open and checks the display.

"I told you, never call this number!" he snarls into the phone. "Never, never, never! No, it's not possible! Okay, okay. Stop crying and listen to me carefully. Are you listening? Good. I promise you, he's alive. Your son is alive. That's all you need to know at this time. And if you do exactly as I say, if you follow my instructions, you'll see him soon. Very soon."

He snaps the cell phone closed, slips it into his pocket, and calmly stares at me with his dark, glittering eyes. As if daring me to say something.

I remain silent. But I've discovered something important. Mine is not the only child who has been kidnapped.

The white panel van is unmarked, but it will almost certainly be mistaken for a phone company van, or a vehicle dispatched by one of the many utility companies that service the area. Which is precisely why it was selected. A white panel van in a suburban neighborhood is as close to invisible as a solid object can get.

Some minutes before Mrs. Katherine Bickford enters her home on Linden Terrace, the white van parks next to a street-surface utility access on Beech Terrace. Two men wearing generic work clothes and tool belts exit the van, place three incandescent orange cones near the manhole cover and return to the van.

The white van is positioned in such a way as to afford it a clear view through the common, toward Linden Terrace and—no coincidence—the target home, a shingled Cape with a large garage. This common area, which abuts three cul-de-sac streets in the development, is known as "the green," to local residents.

A full two-acre swath, the green is a popular dog-walking area. No resident would think of walking a dog there without a pooper-scooper in hand. It's that kind of neighborhood. By mutual agreement foliage is kept low, no more than twelve inches in height, so as not to provide cover for any nefarious activities that might arise. Drug dealing, teen drinking, whatever. Residents are in the habit of glancing toward the green whenever they exit their driveways, because children play on the green, kicking soccer balls, playing laser tag, or fluttering Frisbees. So far there's never been a problem with strangers or suspected pedophiles, but by common consent all the residents keep an eye on the green, and are prepared to report anything unusual.

The white van with the orange cones is not unusual and will therefore not be reported. Likely it will not even be noticed.

Inside the van, two men, both approximately thirty years of age, drink from a silver thermos of coffee. Both men are trim and physically fit, and seem at ease with each other, as if they are well suited to working as a team. From the outside, a passerby might suppose the two men are listening to the radio as they pause for a coffee break—Rush Limbaugh, perhaps, or maybe G. Gordon Liddy—but in reality they're monitoring an audio feed from the target home.

"Fucking guy," says Hinks in a tone of admiration.

"You gotta hand it to Cutter," says Wald. "He's got a way with women."

"Fucks he do it?"

"Language, Hinks. We're working for the phone company here. They have standards."

"They can kiss my ass," says Hinks, sassing him back.

He's known Wald for nine years now, eight in the military when they held the same rank in a special ops unit commanded by Captain Cutter. This is their first foray into a civilian mission, and so far it has been interesting—and potentially much more lucrative than any of the boring jobs either man has been offered since being discharged. That the assignment is highly illegal, and laden with danger, makes it all the more appealing.

Their banter is interrupted by the intercepted cell call to Cutter, currently inside the target home. Upon hearing the substance of the call, the two men exchange glances.

"That woman is out of her ever-loving mind," comments Hinks. "The lovely Lyla."

"Piece of ass," agrees Wald, "but definitely missing a few crucial marbles."

"Violating protocol."

"Cell's scrambled," Wald points out. "No harm, no foul."

"Still. The woman is a loose cannon. What if she goes to the cops? Think they'd believe her?"

"Cutter will handle her. Just like he's handling this Bickford bitch."

Hinks pauses, listens to the feed. The boss dispenses with the cell call and is now laying it out for the Bickford bitch in no uncertain terms. Less than twenty minutes inside and she's eating out of his hand. Eager to obey.

Truly an amazing talent.

Out in the field, the special ops rule of thumb was ten hours. That's how long it would take, on average, to break a typical target. Scare the shit out of 'em, strip away the ego, leave 'em so empty they have no choice but to cooperate. Of course, this is a civilian situation, totally different, but even so, good old Captain Cutter is impressive. Has it down to a science. His so-called "method," which the unit had used in numerous special ops situations. The idea, Cutter bores in on the target with that crazed-psycho routine of his, keeps it up until their eyes bug out with fear, then he backs off just before they start screaming. Hinks had witnessed Cutter pulling the same bullshit act in a bar in the Philippines. Mindfucking a couple of rowdy jarheads who, had they realized it, could have torn Cutter into small pieces. And yet he had prevailed by convincing the dumb-shit marines he was crazy enough to want to die and take them with him, just for laughs.

The man was convincing. So convincing that now and then Hinks wondered if it really *was* an act, but thus far Cutter had always been able to snap back precisely when the situation required. The cap ever got to the point he couldn't turn it off, they'd probably have to frag him. But that was theoretical—so theoretical he and Wald had never even discussed it—and for the time being Hinks was content with the situation. Working for Cutter was way better than sorting letters for the postal service or sitting on his butt as a security guard. There were risks to Cutter's method, of course—very serious risks—but the rewards were commensurate with the risks. Cutter's words. Cutter's method. For right now, for today, Hinks was in with both feet.

Wald, not exactly a deep thinker, tended to follow Hinks's lead. It had been that way since basic, and so far Hinks hadn't steered his bud wrong.

"You think he'll do her?" Wald wants to know. "Kind of hot, for a oldie."

"Oldie?" Hinks chuckled. "The Bickford bitch is thirty-four. That's only a few years older than we are."

"Nineteen is my target age. I like 'em fresh. As you well know."

"Think of it this way. When you were a freshman she'd have been a senior."

"Yup. And I'd have waited a year until she was nineteen. That's when they're ripe."

Hinks shakes his head. "You're a wack job, Wald."

"I just know what I want."

"Total wack job." It was said with some affection. Wald's wacky humor made him interesting.

For instance, this time on a night patrol in Takrit, trying to sort out the Saddam sympathizers from the general malcontents, Hinks had seen Wald suddenly wheel around and shoot an unarmed camel jockey in the head. Guy had been standing there with his hands empty, glowering at the troops but not resisting while the unit conducted a search for concealed weapons. Without warning, Wald dropped the son of a bitch like a side of meat. After which he turned to the rest of the unit and said, "What can I say? I could read his mind. Fucker was thinking evil thoughts."

Later it was determined that Wald's victim had indeed been a former member of Saddam's Baath party. Even if he hadn't been carrying grenades at that particular moment, no doubt he really was directing evil thought waves at the American soldiers, just like Wald said.

"So," says Wald, "the question remains. Will Cutter do her? He gonna bone the bitch or what?"

Hinks shrugs. "Doubtful. He never did much fooling around I ever saw, not even in Thailand. Also, it's not part of the method."

"Fuck the method. If she's in my range, *bam.*"

"Not how the captain operates," says Hinks.

"So far."

Hinks checks his watch. "Twelve minutes, we have to move the vehicle."

"I got ten bucks says the captain will have her licking his ice-cream cone by then."

"You're on."

Safe bet. Hinks is convinced that Wald is projecting his own adolescent fantasies, what he'd do if he was the one inside the target home. Cutter is different. Cutter will remain in control not only of the target but of himself.

That's what Hinks thinks. And so far he's been right on the money.

The idea that the man in the mask might want to rape me rattles inside my head, bouncing around like a malevolent pinball. Can't quite grasp what I will do if he tries. Saving my son remains the primary concern. The only concern, really. My physical well-being doesn't concern me at the moment. All that matters is getting Tommy back.

It's like this: if cutting off my hands would make this man go away and return my son to my bleeding arms, I'd do it. No hesitation. That's the kind of bargain I'm willing to make.

"So you're a widow," he's saying, waving the gun at me like a wand. "Must have been tough." He pauses, tilts his head. "You may respond."

"It was tough," I concede.

"But you bounced back," he says, sounding weirdly, creepily cheerful. "Did very well for yourself, Kate."

I remain in the chair, palms sweating, heart slamming. I can still feel the impression the barrel made on my forehead. Meanwhile, the man in the mask acts like it never happened, like we're having a normal conversation. There he sits in my best leather chair, confident and pleased with himself, as if he's an honored guest in my house. It makes me hate him. Makes me think that if I had the gun I'd use it, no hesitation. Which is something of a shock. Never having imagined I was capable of such a thing.

Oh, but I am. And yet I dare not make a move. The man in the mask is much stronger than I am, much quicker, and it's clear he won't hesitate to kill me if I give him reason to.

I'm sitting here in a cold sweat, thinking about nightmares. How vivid and real they can be. But nothing like this. Nothing like the dread that has settled into my bones. A dread that comes from the realization that there's nothing random about what has happened. It has all been planned, down to the last detail. Consider: the man in the mask knew exactly where Tommy would be. My son was taken from a crowded parking lot without anyone witnessing the snatch, not even me. My home-security system was breached, no problem. And the cell-phone call that pissed him off seems to be connected to *another* kidnapping. Tommy has been drugged and taken away and I will eventually be allowed to speak to him over the phone, supposedly. All of which confirms that others must be involved. The man in the mask is part of a team. A team of professional kidnappers using proven terror tactics to enrich themselves.

That's the real nightmare.

Despite all the mall stories about bogeymen, all the sad-looking kids on milk cartons, I'd always assumed real kidnappers were rare, opportunistic predators. Sick loners who stole children for their own twisted sexual purposes. The notion of teams of professional abductors, terrorizing families for money, that was supposed to be a third world phenomenon. Something that happened in Mexico or Colombia or the Philippines. Not here. Not in suburban Connecticut. Not in Fairfax.

But it *is* happening. Facts on the ground, as the shouting heads on TV like to say. Nothing I can do to change what has already occurred. My mind has been racing with what-ifs. What if we never went to the game? What if I never let Tommy out of my sight? What if I'd called 911 from the parking lot as soon as the first pang of worry quivered in my gut? What if? What if?

Too late, Kate. Deal with it. Find a way.

Part of me remains convinced the man in the mask intends to kill me no matter what I do, or how much money he gets out of me, that erasing the victims is all part of the plan. But I can't allow myself to give up hope. Not as long as there's a chance, however small. Imprinted in my brain is the promise he's made, that he will put me in contact with my son. Presumably before I get him the money, however that is to be accomplished.

My bank, I know, is closed for the day. Five o'clock they shut the doors. And it's now well after six. The thought of waiting until tomorrow makes me physically ill. I can't stand it that long, can I? My heart will stop if I can't speak to Tommy soon, assure myself he's okay.

"I can see your mind racing, Kate," says the man in the mask. "You're wondering how we're going to do this. How you get the money and exchange it for your son."

I keep my mouth shut, knowing he'll tell me.

"Very good," he says, amused. "You're learning not to respond without permission. We knew you were a smart lady, Kate. That's why this is going to work, once you learn the method."

A phone bleats, jolting me in the seat. My phone this time. He pauses, cocking his head. "Let it go," he instructs. "Your voice mail will get it. Then we'll see who it is."

The phone rings six times and then goes silent.

"Two minutes," he says, settling back in my chair. "Relax."

I'm watching the digital clock on the VCR. Never thought a second could take so long to elapse, as if time itself has become molten. *Tick, tick, tick*—but of course there's no actual sound. No comfort from an old-fashioned clock.

When a little more than two minutes has passed, the man in the mask stands up. He moves a few steps to his left, the gun pivoting as he moves, unerringly aimed at my heart. He retrieves the nearest phone and returns to my chair. Settling in, getting comfortable. Mocking me with a small, satisfied smile. With his left hand he thumbs a number.

"Surprised?" he asks. "I know your voice-mail code, Kate. I know everything."

He pauses, listening to the prompts, thumbs a button on the receiver, listens some more.

"Somebody named Jake," he says, disconnecting. "Wants to know if you located Tommy. Would Jake be the guy at the snack trailer by any chance?"

I wait.

"You may respond," he says.

"Yes."

He tosses the phone at me. It hits the middle of my chest, right between my breasts, and falls into my lap. "Pick it up," he says. "Call him back. Tell him the kid was at home when you got here. All is well."

I scroll to Jake's number, am about to key it in.

"Wait," says the man in the mask. "This is your first test, Kate. Convince him. Convince me. If you fail, if you try to get cute, end of story. You and your son are both dead. Got it?"

I nod.

"Proceed."

The connection opens almost immediately. "Jake Gavner."

The phone is so slippery with my own sweat that I have to grip it with all my might. "Jake? Um, this is Kate Bickford returning your call. Just wanted to let you know Tommy is fine. He was here when I got home, playing a video game."

"Great. Give him my best."

"Thanks, I will."

"Helluva a game he had."

"Sure was. Helluva game."

"Hey, put him on. I'll tell him so myself. Maybe give him a rain check for that ice-cream sundae."

For an awful moment my mind goes totally blank. I'm aware that the man in the mask is studying me with interest, as if curious to know whether I'll pull this off. Whether I'll live to make another phone call. The studied indifference is a pose—it has to be—but it says he doesn't care one way or another. Live or die, my choice.

"Sorry, Jake. Sent him to the shower."

"Well, don't be too hard on the kid. Isn't every day a boy gets a game-winning double."

"I'll be sure to tell him that. And thank you, Jake. I appreciate it."

"Next time the dog is on me. With extra kraut."

"Thanks. Bye."

A moment after disconnection the phone slips from my nerveless hands. With a deft move the man in the mask retrieves it, checks to make sure I've really disconnected.

"I'm impressed," he says. "You're good. Even I believed you."

The flood of relief makes tears come, but I fight it. Determined never to weep again in the presence of this vile man. This monster in my house, sitting in my chair, holding my phone. Holding my son.

"You should know that every call to this address is being monitored," he says. "So if you tried something silly, I'd be informed. If, for instance, your friend Jake had said he'd like to drop by for a little post-game nooky with the widow Bickford, I'd know about it."

Nooky. A word so sly and ugly that it makes my jaw clench. I'm not a prude, but certain words have that effect on me. *Get over it, Kate, I urge myself. Do not react. Don't allow him any more control over you than he's already got.*

"As you've no doubt already figured out, we can't transfer funds until your bank opens tomorrow morning. What I have in mind requires a personal appearance from the account holder. You, Kate. All prettied up and looking happy and relaxed because you're buying a condo in the Cayman Islands. So pretty that soon I want you to get some sleep, Kate. Think you can do that?"

I shake my head no. Is he crazy? Sleep? Not a possibility. "My son. You said—"

"Shh."

I shut up.

"Better. You had a little relapse there, speaking without permission. You're forgiven this time, Kate. I'm in a forgiving mood because you did so well with the phone call. Tell you what, before beddy-bye we'll call your kid, okay?"

I nod furiously.

"Before we get to that, I need to do a little walking around in your beautiful house. Check out a few things. So I'm going to cuff your ankles. Put your feet out in front of you and hold them together."

I do as instructed and a moment later my ankles are cuffed together with a thick, white plastic strap.

"Can't be released," he informs me as he straightens up. "All it can do is tighten. If you don't want the circulation cut off to your feet, you'll leave it alone. I'm going to be out of the room for five minutes, tops. If you leave the chair, I'll know and you'll be punished. Very unpleasantly."

In a blink, he's gone. Out of my line of vision and prowling somewhere in my house. When I realize what it might mean, that the man in the mask has pressing business elsewhere in my house, my heart starts to race. Hope rings through my body like a gong. Tommy is right here in the house! He's been here all along! He's in the next room, unconscious but alive!

I leap to my feet, fall over with a thump. Facedown on my own plush carpet, I think, *Don't be a fool, he'll hear you.* He'll punish you, and worse, he may punish Tommy.

Cautiously, silently, I get up on my knees and begin to crawl. A kind of bunny hop because I can't move my feet. Hop, hop, hop. Dragging myself along with my hands. Making a line straight for the door where the man in the mask vanished. Leading me to my son.

Tommy is in his own bedroom, I'm thinking. Yes, yes! He was there all along and I never looked! Must be there, why else would the man leave me alone? Why else would he say, "I want to check out a few things"? Couldn't be anything that important, with one exception. My precious son.

Even before I get out of the family room, I'm already thinking about how to get up the stairs. Should I make a diversion for the kitchen, find a knife, cut the ankle cuffs? No time. *Follow the man to Tommy's room. See with your own eyes that your son is alive and safe in his own bed.*

I crawl to the stairs and prepare to ascend. My baby is up there in his own bedroom and he's in danger, terrible danger.

I make it as far as the first step. That's when the man in the mask emerges from the downstairs bathroom with his pants around his knees.

"Son of a bitch!" he exclaims, hastily yanking up and zipping his fly. "Can't a man take a piss around here?"

Then he's on me in a heartbeat, boot stomping into my back, forcing me down off the bottom stair, grinding me into the floor, forcing the air from my lungs.

Breathing heavily, he towers over me as I groan and roll over, trapped between his legs. "Kate, Kate," he says with a sigh of disappointment. "What were you thinking?"

"Tommy!" I blubber. "In his room. You were g-going to ch-check on him!"

And then I weep convulsively. As I did the morning after Ted died, when I awoke thinking he was in the bed next to me. The awful disappointment crashing through me, rending me to pieces, dissolving me in tears and phlegm and shuddering misery.

The man in the ski mask kneels next to me, making soothing noises, stroking my back as it convulses with grief. "Shh, shh. Go on, let it all out. Do you good to cry, Mrs. Bickford. You thought your boy was here, in the house, huh? So you went to him. That was really, really stupid. We never keep the package in the target house, Mrs. Bickford. We're very organized. We have a method." He strokes my forehead, his rough thumb tenderly tracing the imprint of the gun barrel. "Do you understand? Am I getting through to you?" He pauses, dark eyes staring at me from out of the mask. "You may answer."

"Y-yes."

"Good. Now you must be punished."

He reaches behind his back. Something glitters in his hand. Then he plunges a needle into my shoulder. Blackness flows from the needle, making my arm numb, oddly warm. A pulse of warmth carries the numbness into my head. Before I can organize my thoughts and fight it, I'm swirling around a drain, a dark hole in the center of my brain, going, going.

Gone.

where's jesse? **7**

Cutter uses a key and lets himself into the foyer of his boxy little house. Only five rooms, but then he's never been a man who needed a lot of space. Hell, he practically lived in a Hummer once, for five very long weeks. Calmly but quickly he punches in the disable code to the security system—real state-of-the-art, unlike poor Mrs. Bickford's pathetic excuse for a security system. An item he'd liberated from the depot at Fort Dix, last time he passed through. Actually on the way out the door. *Sorry to see you go, Captain Cutter. Here's your hat, there's the door.*

Assholes. After all he'd done for the army, for the country, for the unit. Risking his life, time and again. Shedding blood for the so-called greater good. One small screwup and he was no longer wanted, no longer a valuable member of the team. Should have demanded a court martial instead of letting them shoo him away with an honorable discharge, but he'd had other things on his mind at the time.

"Lyla? I'm home."

He hears her slippered feet shuffling on the linoleum as she wanders in from the kitchen, wringing her hands. Actually wringing her hands, as if trying to remove something from her skin. Invisible blood, perhaps, like Lady Macbeth?

The idea makes him shudder.

"Where's Jesse?" she asks, her gorgeous gray eyes twitching. Not really focusing on her husband, but aware of his sudden presence in the house. "I looked in his bedroom. I looked in the basement. I looked everywhere. Where's my son?"

"He's away for a little while. You know that."

Lyla hasn't been eating lately and her weight, always petite, has dropped to less than a hundred and fifteen pounds, but her grip on his arm is unnaturally strong. Fierce with her anxiety. "Jesse needs his mother. How could you forget that?"

Cutter gently pries her fingers from his arm. "Go lie down," he tells her. "Take your medication. Jesse is fine."

Her big eyes suddenly lock onto his. "You're lying! What have you done to our son? Where have you taken him?"

Times like this, Cutter isn't sure if he wants to hold her in his arms or slap her beautiful, haunted face. Knock some sense into her. Not that he's ever raised a hand to her. She can't help it, and he knows that. He's known for years that Lyla has what they both carefully refer to as her "bad spells"—intervals where she drifts into her own reality—but the desperate situation with their son, Jesse, seems to have completely un-hinged her. She hasn't eaten in days, hasn't slept. Prowls the house like a ghost, searching for the boy, as if her will to mother him will make him reappear. It's all very sad and pathetic, but Cutter hasn't got time for it now. Once he has handled the situation, then it will be Lyla's turn. Get her some professional help, but not until the boy is back at home, safe and sound.

More than a few army and civilian shrinks have probed and med-icated Lyla over the years, but it's too dangerous to call one in now. No telling what she would say, where it would lead. The wrong word from her, taken seriously by a credulous shrink, and the whole situation could unravel. His boy might not survive, and that is the only thing that matters. Not his own well-being, and not Lyla's sanity. Just the boy.

Cutter takes his wife by the arm and leads her into their bedroom. She follows willingly, muttering almost silently, her eyes focused on some imagined distance. He seats her at her sewing table, where she sometimes works on her delicate brocades—works of art, really, as beautiful and delicate as she is. He searches for her medication, the most recent prescription. There it is on the bookcase, at eye level, right in front of him. She's always hiding her meds in obvious places, as if the mere act of touching the bottle will render it invisible. He fills a glass with water, persuades her to swallow a pill.

"I'm not crazy," she says. "You know that."

"I know, Lyla."

"I've been crazy in the past, but not now. Jesse really is gone. I've looked everywhere."

"I know you have. You must try and get some sleep. Just let me handle everything, okay?"

She's not listening to him, though. He can tell, the way her eyes drift, the way she cocks her head at an angle that seems slightly un-natural. "Maybe he ran away," she says, conversing with herself alone. "Boys run away sometimes. They always come back eventually. They come back when they get hungry, or when they want their mother."

"He'll be back soon, Lyla. Jesse will be back with us, I promise."

She turns away from him, crosses her spindly arms, hugging her-self. "My husband is a liar," she says in a kind of chanting singsong. "He lies and he lies and he lies. And he thinks I don't know. That's what's making me crazy. All the lies. I can't concentrate because of all the lies inside my head."

Cutter hopes the pill will make his wife sleep, and that when she awakens she'll be better. Not cured, but a little better. That's the most he'll let himself hope for. And this time it looks like the medication is having some effect. Her motions, previously jangled and abrupt, have become languid, as if she's adrift in her own private sea.

When her eyes begin to flutter—a good sign—he turns to leave, intent on his own very pressing business.

"I'm going to call the police," she suddenly announces, forcing her eyes open. "I'm going to report him missing. I found his uniform, you know. It has blood on it. So I'll call the police and tell them."

"Not now," he says. "When you wake up."

"You promise?"

"I promise," he lies.

The telephone line has been disconnected. And when he leaves, as soon he must, the doors will be locked from the outside. Not that Lyla will attempt to leave. Among other things, she's become agora-phobic, prone to debilitating anxiety attacks at the mere thought of crossing the threshold.

"You dropped something," she says sleepily, pointing vaguely.

Cutter reaches down, picks up the black ski mask and slips it into a pocket, buttoning the flap.

a small villa in the caymans   8

W aking up is like swimming through thick black ink. No, not swimming, exactly, more like drifting gradually upward. Expending no effort. Vague thoughts with no body attached, drifting, drifting. There comes a time when I'm aware of something cold on my face. Hmm, didn't know I had a face. Right, of course, everybody has a face. And a body, and hands and arms and legs. I'd forgotten. Now vaguely aware of my limbs. And then I begin to feel something on my skin. Drip, drip, drip. Icy-cold. I don't mind, what do I care? I'm asleep. Things happen when you're asleep. Dream-things over which you have no control. Icy-cold things. Ignore them.

Tommy.

The thought hits me like an electric shock, and suddenly I'm wide-awake and aware of light penetrating the inky dark. My eyes snap open. My vision is blurred, but I can make out the shape of someone crouching very close to me. Looming.

"Kate? Hi there. Rise and shine—0700 hours. Seven o'clock for you civilians."

I'm soaked. The man in the black ski mask has been dripping ice water on my neck and blouse. Using a spoon as a ladle, like basting a turkey. I'm the turkey. I'm shivering and I hate him. Hate waking up to fear. Hate the dread of worrying about my son. Hate the power this monster has over me.

Hate, hate, hate.

My arms swing of their own accord, connecting with his legs. He laughs and backs away. Do my legs work? Yes, as a matter of fact they do, and my feet start kicking, aiming between his legs. He dances easily away, avoiding any contact.

"You asked for it!" he announces gleefully.

A bucket of icy water smacks me full in the face, making me gasp, filling my nose and mouth. My limbs stop thrashing. Useless, anyhow. He anticipates my every move.

"You stink," he says. "Take a shower, freshen up."

I sit up, wiping my eyes. I'm already in the downstairs bath—he must have been dragged me in here when I was unconscious. What else did he do to me when I was out? It must have been, what, twelve hours? Twelve hours gone! My clothing seems to be in place, nothing hurts. Would I know?

"You're still a virgin as far as I'm concerned," he says, noting my self-assessment. "Now strip down, get in the shower. Use the soap, that's a good little girl."

"Fuck you."

I'm checking him out, looking for the gun. He must have it nearby, can I reach it first? But the mouth in the mask grins, one hand snakes behind his back, and now he's brandishing the pistol. "Don't be shy," he says. "Get in the shower. When you're beautiful again, we'll call your kid, say hi."

He backs out of the door, into the hallway, giving me room. But the door remains open.

"Go on. Do it."

I shake my head.

"I can knock you out and wash you myself. Is that what you want?"

The thought sickens me beyond anything else I might have to do while conscious. I turn my back, peel off my clothes. Every part of me is angry, but the thought of talking to Tommy, hearing his voice, it's enough to keep me moving. Once in the stall, I yank the curtain closed and turn on the cold water. Trying to clear my still-foggy head, get my thoughts in order. Keep the anger at a manageable level, girl. Use it to make you strong. Nurture it until an opportunity arises.

To calm myself, I fill my head with thoughts of my son. Specifically, that very special day when Ted and I first met the unnamed baby who would fill our lives with joy, and changed us from two to three. The baby who became Tommy the Wonder Boy was six months old at the time. We'd been through the usual adoption wringer. Opened our home to social workers, filed financial statements, divulged our bank accounts and tax returns, been interviewed together and separately. We had been investigated, stamped and stapled. Put on waiting lists. Promised babies who were not delivered. Told to wait. We paid through the nose, lawyers and agency fees, and were told to wait some more. It got to the point I refused to even look at a picture of a prospective baby. It was too painful to moon over a photograph, only to have the mother change her mind, or give her child to someone else, someone more worthy.

It was so horribly painful, and it made me feel so guilty about not being able to have a baby of my own, that I finally opted out of the whole process. Left it up to Ted. Who knew exactly what I was going through. Bless the man, one day he came home with a certain look in his eye and said, "Get in the car." And so I did, with my heart hammering like a heavy-metal drummer, and we drove north for an endless hour or two, barely speaking because we were both so nervous, and then Ted was taking me into a room and a smiling woman put a bundle into my arms and that was Tommy.

Once on a talk show I saw a panel of mothers who had problems bonding with their kids. How sad. Lucky for me, I had a problem with the fertility part, not the bonding part. Happened the instant he was placed in my arms. Wham! I was in love with the baby, body and soul, from the very first moment. Love welled from my heart, my mind, my body. I was too embarrassed even to tell Ted (who would have understood), but for the first few weeks my breasts actually ached, as if they wanted to lactate. My head swam with a love so intense it almost frightened me. For several months I had terrible, anxious nightmares about someone snatching him away, and in those dreams, losing him was like dying.

A social worker later told me it wasn't unusual for an adoptive mother to suffer from prospective-loss anxiety. After all, in a surprising number of cases, it actually happened. Adoptive mothers bonded with infants, only to have them taken away by the courts and returned to drug-addict birth mothers, or to relatives, or held in foster homes until the courts sorted it out, which might take years. The folks from the adoption agency assured me this couldn't happen with Tommy—both of his young parents had been killed in a taxi accident in Puerto Rico—but I couldn't help it, I worried. The nightmares and the anxiety gradually faded away as I settled into the new life of mothering a helpless infant, but the worry part never quite left me. Which is fine. Mothers are supposed to worry, it's part of our job.

Now the old nightmare thing is actually happening, in wide-awake real time, and the losing-him-is-like-dying part is real, too. I have to get Tommy back or die trying, that's all there is to it.

When I pull back the curtain, there's a clean towel and a pile of neatly folded clothing waiting on the toilet-seat lid. And I wasn't even aware the man in the ski mask had come into the bathroom, let alone laid out my clothing. Yet another scary thing about him—he moves like a shadow. And there he is, sitting on the stairs outside the open door, staring at me from the holes in his mask.

"Nice wardrobe," he says. "You've got taste. I picked out the Donna Karan ensemble. Black for banking."

I've got the towel around me, dressing underneath it, face averted. Ashamed of my humiliation. The creep has stripped your life bare, does it really matter if he sees you naked? Apparently it does. Because I'm blushing furiously as I wriggle into underwear, black pants, silk blouse.

Finally I drop the towel and emerge fully dressed, more or less. No shoes yet. He hasn't picked out shoes.

"Your hair," he says. "Fix it."

A glance in the mirror reveals that my hair needs attention. I keep it short so I can always blow-and-go, but a night on the bathroom floor has left me looking damaged. I bang out the dents with a brush, use the blow-dryer and my fingers, and in ten minutes I actually look presentable.

"Kitchen," he says, gesturing with the pistol.

I walk ahead of him into the kitchen, thinking about knives. I have quite a collection. Boning knives so sharp you're bleeding before you realize you've been cut. I can't imagine plunging a knife into a fellow human being, but the man in the mask isn't human. On the other hand, if I kill the bastard I may never see my son again. A thought that never leaves my mind, even for an instant.

The air is redolent of freshly brewed coffee.

"It's going to be a big, busy day, so I made a pot," he explains. "Take a seat."

I sit on a stool at my own counter. Miss Obedience. Having noticed that my knives seem to have vanished from the counter. Did he check all the drawers, too? Of course he did. He had hours and hours to get things right while I was unconscious. He's been over the whole house, checked everywhere. If I had a gun, which I don't, he'd already know about it. The man may be a monster, but he's an intelligent monster, and therefore even more dangerous.

Careful, girl. Don't lose your focus. Tommy is the focus. Do only that which will bring you closer to your son.

"You've had seven calls," he says. "Six left messages. Five are work related—you're a very busy girl, Kate, congratulations—and one was for your kid. Some girl. He's a good-looking kid, the girls must be all over him, huh? Anyhow, you can respond to the calls when we finish up our business at the bank. Go on, have your breakfast."

He slides a bowl of cereal across the counter. Milk has been added. Tommy's Rice Krispies are talking to me, reminding me of all our breakfasts in this room. Did this vile bastard know what this would do to me, hearing my son's cereal?

It takes all my will not to fly across the counter and slap that sneering smile off his ski-masked face.

"This is the schedule of events," he's saying. "First we have a light breakfast, then we call your kid, then we go to the bank. We'll return here to await confirmation of the wire transfer, and then I will leave. If all goes according to plan—if we follow the method and do not deviate—your son should be back in this house by, say, three in the afternoon, at the latest."

The rational part of me knows he could be lying—all he wants is money—but I can't prevent a flood of hope so strong, so deeply felt it almost makes me giddy.

"You're not eating," he points out.

I push the cereal bowl away. Check the mug of coffee he set out. Could I scald him? No, the coffee is lukewarm. He's anticipated the scalding thing. Or maybe some other victim threw a cup in his face and he's learned from experience.

"The method. That's what gets your kid home," he says. "See, I've made a study. Stupid kidnappers take the child, then call the parent. Ask 'em to get the money, meet them somewhere. What's the first thing the parent does? Calls the feds. Under the mistaken impression that's the smart thing to do. FBI, they screw it up nine times out of ten. Nobody gets paid off, the kid gets wasted. With this method, we take control of the parent as well as the child. Stick with the parent until the money is safely transferred. It's just common sense, that's all. Strategic positioning."

All the time he's speaking, bragging about his so-called method, he's aiming the gun at my heart. Five feet away, can't miss. He likes that pistol almost as much as he likes talking. Gives the impression he'd like to use it, given an excuse.

"You've got just under five hundred grand in a money market account. Four hundred and ninety-six thousand and change. That's what attracted our attention in the first place. Guess you must be leery of the stock market, huh? Can't say I blame you. And bonds don't pay enough to make a difference, do they? Thing is, you having all that cash just sitting there, it makes things easier for me."

It strikes me like a blow to the stomach that's it's my fault Tommy got taken. If I hadn't kept the money from Ted's life insurance in that account, if I'd put it in mutual funds like the financial managers had advised me, then I wouldn't have been such an easy mark. But I hadn't wanted to spend that money—Ted's last gift to us—so for a time I borrowed against it, letting simple interest accrue over the years. Figuring one day, in the far distant future, Tommy will inherit a very nice sum, or maybe we'd use some of it for college, but whatever the case, it would be coming from his late father, not from me. For sentimental reasons. Reasons that now seem ridiculous, if not downright stupid. Talk about making myself a target! I'm getting the impression that the man in the mask browses through bank accounts like some people browse for books. And he must have picked me because I fit the abduction-for-profit profile: single parent with a large sum of readily accessible cash.

"If you're finished with your breakfast—what's the matter, no appetite?—we'll proceed to step two. The kid call."

He produces a cell phone from a vest pocket, hits one key, is connected almost instantly.

"Put him on," he says, then nods to himself.

He slides the cell phone over the counter and indicates that I pick it up.

"Tommy!"

"Mom? Is that you?"

Tommy's voice. He's alive. Suddenly I'm weeping, blubbering, and my son is telling me not to cry. "I'm okay, Mom. I was at the game and then I don't remember. They said they gave me stuff to make me sleep. It made me forget. Then they—"

Before my son can finish telling me what else they did, the phone goes dead. Not even a dial tone, just silence, horrible silence. I want to scream. The man in the black ski mask is studying me, and he seems very pleased with himself. I throw the cell phone at him. It bounces off his shoulder and lands on the floor, skittering.

"That was interesting," he says after a moment. "I almost pulled the trigger."

"Fuck you! I want my baby back!"

His teeth click together, chop chop. "End of the day, Kate. Provided you follow the method. Now put on some makeup. You want to look good for the bankers, don't you? It isn't every day you buy a new house."

"What?"

The man in the mask sighs. "I told you yesterday. Why is it women never listen? You're buying a house, Kate. A small villa in the Caymans. Isn't that nice?"

The marble floors of the Fairfax National Bank feel spongy some-how. I'm wearing my sensible flats, not the heels the man in the ski mask picked out. My knees are watery and light—I'd be wobbling on those heels. Not a good sign when you're about to make a major transaction.

I catch sight of my image in the plate-glass mirrors near the vestibule, and am amazed at how normal I look. A not-quite-young career woman in her elegant, perfectly understated DKNY outfit. Still slim, almost wil-lowy. Small breasts, nice trim butt molded by the line of the perfectly draped trousers. Frankly, I look like a million bucks. Or a half million anyhow. Never know from looking at me that my heart is racing and my bones are infused with equal parts dread and wild anticipation.

Hoping this will all be over soon. It must, one way or another. Couldn't stand another day of this. *Follow the method and you'll have your kid back by three, the latest.* That's the deal, supposedly. So I'm being my best obedient self. What other choice to I have?

None.

Around my left ankle, concealed by the slightly belled trousers, is a plastic bracelet with a small electronic tracking device. Snapped on just before I left the house. Out of his immediate control, but not, apparently, out of view. *I'll know exactly where you are at all times. Take the wrong street, I'll know. Try to leave the bank by a back door, I'll know—and your kid will pay the price.* I tell him the ankle bracelet is unnecessary, that I'll do exactly what he has requested, but he smirks and tells me to shut up like a good girl.

The GPS tracker is backup. My team will have you in visual contact at all times. You won't see them, but they'll be there. Count on it.

In my sweaty hands is the manila folder he handed me in the garage, just before I slipped behind the wheel of my minivan. The folder contains the necessary financial information, as well as a brochure for Island Dream Villas.

"If you're thinking about making a run for it, now's your chance," he tells me as I hit the ignition key. "Just remember, there are consequences. We will not hesitate. Your son will die. Follow the method, do not deviate from the plan, and he will live. It's that simple."

"What if I have an accident?" I ask him.

"Make sure you don't."

A moment later I'm backing out of the garage. At first it feels like I'm driving drunk—I'm dizzy with anxiety—but by the time I make the first turn I'm more or less in control, and follow the agreed-upon route without incident.

Made it. Ready for the next step. To my left is the teller area, three windows open. One of the people waiting to conduct business is the beautifully coiffed owner of a downtown jewelry store, clutching his blue, zippered bag with yesterday's receipts. Can't think of his name, but we know each other by sight. What would he do if he knew? Nothing to stop me from telling him, nothing to stop me from announcing that my son has been abducted and the man behind it waits inside my house. Nothing but the fear that I'll never see Tommy again.

I march into the back area, where the loan officers work in small carrels. Find the desk marked Assistant Vice Treasurer. The woman

at the desk, another familiar face, looks up and smiles. "Good morning, Mrs. Bickford."

"Morning, um, Diane," I say, reading the nameplate.

"Have a seat, please. Now, what can I do for you?"

I lay the folder in my lap. "I was told you handle wire transfers."

"One of my many jobs. You need to wire funds?"

I nod. Mouth so dry I'm having trouble forming words. "I'm, ah,
buying a vacation home."

Diane brightens. She's about my age and similarly dressed. There
doesn't seem to be a hint of suspicion in her open, pleasant face. But
then she knows me, apparently.

"You catered my niece's wedding. Alana Pillsbury?"

"Of course," I said. "You're Margaret's sister?"

"Sister-in-law. It was lovely really. Those people you have, they're
so nice. And the food—to die for! Bill and I were expecting rubber
chicken, you know? Because I happened to know what the per-plate
price was—Margaret can't keep a secret, not about money! So we were
simply amazed when we saw the spread."

"We try," I say.

"This must be your busy season."

"Yes, we're pretty well booked until October."

"Fabulous. Now, what's this about a vacation home?"

With slightly trembling hands, I push the brochure across her desk.
"They call them villas. But it's really like a condo sort of thing. Separate buildings, but the association takes care of everything," I say, repeating the lines supplied by the man in the mask. Who has assured
me there will be no problems. All this about villas is just window dressing, a diversion. People in my "bracket" transfer funds all over the
world, supposedly. Never thought of myself as being in a particularly
elevated "bracket," but obviously he thinks so.

There is no indication that Diane disagrees, or doubts my intentions.

"Oh, my God, I'm so jealous. A villa in the Caribbean!"

"It's an investment, really. We won't be able to use it for more than a few weeks a year."

"It's fabulous, Mrs. Bickford."

"Kate, please. Here's the information." I hand her the instructions. Copied in my own hand.

Diane studies the page, looking quite serious. Now it will all blow up in my face. Surely she'll figure it out, press a button under her desk, and in a moment the bank will be flooded with uniformed police officers. Instead, she smiles and nods and says, "Sea Breeze Limited is handling the sale on that end? And this is the number for their bank?"

I nod. "They're, um, my appointed agents. That's the number they faxed me."

"And this is the account you wish to transfer from?"

I nod again, fearful that my voice will give me away.

Diane goes to her computer screen and checks the balance. "Excellent," she says. "Funds are sufficient. Almost to the penny. Do you want the wire fee to come out of your regular checking account?"

I nod again.

"Okay, now we have to be formal. I know who you are, Kate. Of course I do. But it's a requirement that we see two forms of ID."

I'm prepared for this, and produce my driver's license and a copy of my birth certificate.

"A credit card would have been fine," she says, handing them back. "But the birth certificate works, too. Okay. We're almost there. I need to print out a form, then you sign it and we'll be done."

Three minutes later I sign my name. Concentrating so that my hand doesn't tremble.

"All there is to it," Diane announces. "You understand that the IRS will be notified of the transfer? The new security regulations require they be notified for any sum transfer in excess of ten thousand dollars, or any overseas transfer, regardless of size. This qualifies on both counts."

"That's fine."

"Excellent."

"How does this work, exactly?" I'm departing from the script, but it seems like something that should be asked.

"We use Chase Manhattan. It's all electronic, of course. They notify the recipient bank that funds are due, and that bank distributes the funds. Assuming the number you gave me is correct, the transaction should be completed before the end of business. Probably a lot sooner."

"And that's it?"

"That's it," she says brightly. "We're done here."

As I stand to leave, she shakes my hand. "Congratulations, Kate! If you ever need a house sitter, let me know."

A minute or so later I'm back in the minivan. Barely have time to put the keys in the ignition when the cell phone in my purse starts ringing. It's his cell, not mine, and it takes a moment for me to get it opened.

"Any problems?"

"No. They said by the end of business."

"You did good, Kate. And now I want you to fasten your seat belt. It's not like you to be so careless."

I look wildly around. There are other vehicles in the parking lot, but I can't see anyone watching me.

"Oh, they can see you," he says in my ear, as intimate as a lover. "You just can't see them. Come on home, Kate. Follow exactly the same route that got you there. I'll be waiting."

"My son!" But the cell phone is dead.

Driving home is like a dream. Some other version of me drives while I observe, wondering how she manages to do it. Steer the wheel, tap the brakes, come to a complete stop at the intersections? It all seems so complicated. And yet I'm functioning as if everything is normal. Just another day in the life of Katherine Ann Bickford.

Am I being followed? Again, there are other vehicles behind me, but nothing sticks out, nothing announces malevolent intent. And yet clearly he knows where I am and what I'm doing. Knows whether I've fastened my seat belt or not. Knows whether I've been naughty or nice.

Turning onto Linden Terrace, I hesitate. Dreading what happens next. I've been out of his direct control for almost forty minutes and the prospect of returning to him, submitting myself to that loathsome creature, is almost more than I can bear. Never hyperventilated before, but there's always a first time, apparently, because I'm panting like I've just run a marathon. Points of light dance in my eyes. Dizzy.

I slowly brake to a stop, trying to get control over my breathing.

The cell phone chirps like an angry bird. I open it, drop the damn thing, finally fish it out from under the console.

"What are you doing!" he demands.

"Panic," I manage to say. Telling him the absolute truth.

"Get your ass back home, lady. Now! Pull into the garage and put down the door."

The other me takes over, the one who knows how to drive, the one with nerves of steel. And as the garage door clunks down behind me, the man in the ski mask yanks open my door. Reaches across my waist to unfasten the seat belt, the gun cold and hard, pressing into the soft part of my neck.

This is it, I'm thinking. *Now he kills me.*

Instead, I'm pulled out of the driver's seat—he lifts me with one arm, that's how strong he is—and placed on the concrete floor of the garage. He's over me, a booted foot on each side, pinning me in place. Then he slowly crouches, knees pressing against my chest with his full weight. Making it impossible to draw a breath. My legs begin to kick, futilely. Much too feeble. He barely notices. The pressure does not relent. Can't breathe.

"Here's the thing, Kate. It will take four or five hours for the wire to go through. That's on average. Might be sooner, might be later. Nothing we can do to hurry it up. And I have other things to do. Promises to keep. So you're going back to sleep."

He plunges a needle into my neck. Everything gets warm and dark. I have one last thought before fading away.

Tommy.

"So," Cutter wants to know, "is the package ready?"

Hinks and Wald look up from the video game. Both appear to be perplexed, which Cutter has learned are their default expressions, regardless of circumstance. Both men are competent, in a limited, military-trained sort of way, but neither seems capable of thinking outside the box. That's just fine with Cutter, who prefers to do all the heavy lifting, brainwise. Left to their own devices, the two men would be working mope jobs, maybe attempting small-time robberies, or deviant sexual diversions, on their days off.

In other words, without Captain Cutter to lead them, Hinks and Wald would be losers.

"Package is dead to the world," says Hinks, fiddling with the PlayStation controls. A gift from Cutter, who understands the need to remain occupied while enduring downtime. "Shot him up like you said."

"You checked his pulse?"

"Wald's department. He's playing doctor."

"Wald?"

"Fifty-five and steady." Wald doesn't look away from the images on the screen. Some cartoon creature with massive limbs and enough weapons to blow its imaginary world to hell.

How Wald thinks of himself, Cutter muses. Tough, durable and deadly, but controlled from a distance, by someone with a smarter computer chip.

"You made sure his throat is clear?"

"Breathing like a baby, last time I checked."

"And when was that?" Cutter asks.

Wald glances at his wristwatch, a strapped and gleaming device that notes the time in all twenty-four zones. "Thirty minutes, give or take."

"Check again."

"I'll get right on it, sir," says Wald, but makes no move to abandon his cartoon killer.

"Now, Wald."

"Favor, sir? Make sure Hinks don't mess with my buttons."

Cutter rolls his eyes. Wald puts down his PlayStation controls and pads into the adjoining room. Hinks grinning and reaching for his partner's controls. "Mind if I fuck him up?" he asks.

"Not in the least."

"We got the money?"

"We got the money," Cutter says. "Wire cleared at thirteen hundred hours."

Hinks fiddles with Wald's controls, very pleased with whatever mischief he's committing. "Mind if I ask you a question, Captain?"

"Permission granted. You may speak freely," says Cutter, using an irony that, he knows, will go through Hinks like invisible smoke.

"When do we get paid?"

"Three days. That's how long it will take to get the money back into the country."

Hinks nods, as if satisfied. Cutter gets the impression the man isn't primarily in it for the money. He likes the excitement. Not that he'd give up his cut.

"'Nother question, sir."

Cutter nods.

"Why not take out the female, sir? Why leave her alive, now that we've got the dough?"

"Are you questioning my methods?"

"Didn't say that, sir. Just wondering if it's worth the risk."

"Risk assessment is my responsibility, remember?"

"Sure, of course. I was just, you know, wondering and all."

Cutter stares at him, expression neutral. "Don't wonder, Hinks. Leave the wondering to me. But just so you're not tempted to exercise your brain, the lady has been left alive because she's part of the diversion. What form that diversion will take, you'll just have to wait and see. You'll just have to trust me. Do you trust me, Hinks?"

"Yes, sir. Absolutely."

Wald appears in the doorway. "I said no fucking around! I better be at third level, you cheating, thieving bastard!"

"The package?" asks Cutter, willing himself to have patience.

"Fine, sir. Except he pissed the bed."

"In that case you better change the sheets."

"Fuck."

"Do it, Wald."

Wald sighs, vanishes back into the bedroom. Bitching all the way.

"Two hours," Cutter tells Hinks. "Then we make our next move."

Hinks looks up from the game. "Permission to ask another question, sir?"

Cutter nods. "Go ahead."

"Did you do her, Captain?"

"Define 'do.'"

"Fuck her, mess with her naked body, whatever."

Cutter smirks. "Is this in regards to your ten-dollar side bet with Wald?"

Hinks's jaw drops.

"I know everything," says Cutter. "You should know that by now."

"I'll be damned. You wired the van!" Hinks looks amazed.

"I wired your brain, Hinks. I know how you think."

Hinks shakes his head in admiration. "So did you do her, or what?"

"Let me put it this way," says Cutter, allowing himself to preen, for Hinks's benefit if not his own. "The lady is totally fucked."

Groundhog Day all over again. What was his name, the guy who played the wacky weatherman in the movie? Waking up each morning to find he was trapped in the same day. Only, the movie was funny and this, whatever it is, is decidedly not funny, not with my cheek pressed to the bathroom floor. I'm staring at the white porcelain of a toilet, able to see, more or less, but not yet able to move. More a lack of will than any sort of paralysis, because I can feel all of my limbs, prickly with pins and needles, as if I've been lying in the same position for hours and hours, or possibly days.

Bill Murray. The guy in the movie. Brain sluggish. Feels like my thoughts are filtering through heavy oil. Why am I still in the bathroom? Isn't it time to go to the bank, wire the money? No, wait, I already did that. I recall going into the bank, speaking with a nice lady. Something about the parking lot, a feeling that unseen people were watching me. Then—*wham!* It all comes pounding back, a rush of images. My panic attack, the cell phone screaming at me, the darkened garage, the man in the mask with his knees crushing my chest. Saying he'll put me to sleep again, which obviously he did.

What time is it? How long have I been out?

Must get up, must find Tommy. I struggle up to my hands and knees, head whirling, panting with the effort. There, progress. Now I'm perched on the toilet seat, willing the vertigo to pass. Expecting the man in the mask to barge in any second. What did he say before he knocked me out—he had "other things to do"? What other things? Did other things include returning my son?

"Tommy!" I call out weakly.

Without warning my stomach decides to empty itself. Taken by surprise, I aim for the bathtub, am only partially successful, spattering my feet with flecks of watery vomit. God, how I hate to throw up. Always fought it, even as a kid. Taste in my mouth is, well, awful, but it gives me the impetus to lurch from the toilet to the sink. Leaning heavily while I fumble with the faucet. Using both hands to splash cold water on my face, into my mouth. Better, head clearing, less dizzy.

Outside, the hallway is a hidden roller coaster, the carpet undulating under my feet, but I hang on to the banister and call out my son's name.

"Tommy! Tomas, are you there? Can you hear me? It's Mom!"

Nothing. The kind of overwhelming silence that means the place is empty. My instincts have already told me that I'm alone, but my instincts have been so wrong lately, they can't be trusted. I desperately want to climb the stairs and check in Tommy's room, just to make sure—he could be napping, exhausted from his ordeal!—but that will have to wait until the roller coaster stops and equilibrium returns. Confined to the ground floor, I stagger into the kitchen. Nobody home. Slide along the wall—very clever and solid, these walls—and check out the TV room. Half expecting to find the man in the mask reclining in my brown leather chair. Messing with Tommy's video games. Wrong. Using a hand against the wall to make certain of my balance, I check my downstairs office. Looks like somebody has made a mess of my desk, scattering papers and catering contracts, but the culprit has vanished. What were they looking for? Was it a "they," or just the man in the mask? Does it matter? Not right now it doesn't. This can wait.

I take my hand away from the wall. Amazing, girl, you're walking on two legs. Look, Ma, no hands! Reminds me of Tommy toddling across the carpet, going boom-zi-day as he reaches for Ted, falling flat on his tiny face and laughing. Not crying, laughing. Like falling down was fun, a show he was putting on for his dad. Ted laughing, too, with tears in his eyes, shooting me a look that said, *We'll never forget this, will we?*

No, Ted, we won't.

"Tommy! Tomas, are you there?" Hopeless. My son isn't in the house, I know it in my gut, in my heart, in my head, in every weary bone in my body. He's somewhere else. He's been taken.

The phone rings. Not a cell phone, my home landline. I'm at the desk in a heartbeat, snatching up the receiver. "Tommy?"

"He prefers 'Tomas.' You really ought to make an effort. Names are important."

The man in the mask. I recognize his sneering voice.

"Where's my son?"

"He's not your son, Mrs. Bickford. He belongs to someone else. Always did, always will."

"Let me speak to him, please? I'm begging you! You promised!"

"You're a nice woman, Mrs. Bickford. So I'll give you some parting advice. Whatever you do, don't go into the basement."

The phone goes dead.

Don't go into the basement. The words drive me to my knees, reverberating inside my head, a kind of high, terrible keening *basementbasementbasement.* What has he done? What has that monster done to my son?

Bing, bong.

Front-door chimes. Who can it be? A wild rush of hope floods into me and I react by running full tilt through the hallway, banging my shoulder on the doorjamb as I head for the foyer.

Bing, bong.

Let it be Tomas. Let it be my son. Not dead in the basement, but alive on the front steps, ringing the chimes because he no longer has his key. I can see his big loopy grin, I can smell his hair, I can feel the bony softness of him pressed to my breast, struggling to get out of one of Mom's dreaded super-hugs.

Hands shaking, I fumble with the lock and the chain—open, open!—and then the door swings wide and sunlight spills into the foyer.

Cops. Uniformed deputies. Lots of them.

"Tommy! Did you find him? Have you got my son?"

"Mrs. Bickford, may we enter your domicile?"

I gesture them inside, momentarily speechless. Dread descending because there's no sign of my son out there, and the cops do not look happy. As if they resent being the bearers of bad news. It's enough to make me flop onto the nearest sofa, burying my face in my hands as the uniforms flood into the foyer, into the living room, into my house.

"Mrs. Bickford, look at me, please."

I look up and see a face I recognize. Terence Crebbin, one of the Fairfax officers. Sheriff Corso speaks well of Terry, refers to him as "my right arm," and more than once Deputy Sheriff Crebbin has made an appearance at the ballpark when pressing police business intruded on Fred Corso's sideline as a Little League coach. Always made an impression with the moms because he's cute, a slightly harder but no less attractive version of Brad Pitt, except that his hair remains sturdily brown, no highlights.

Terry knows me well enough to use my first name, and so the "Mrs. Bickford" sounds more than ominous, it's like a physical blow to the body. I'm cringing, waiting for the bad news. But what he says comes as a complete surprise.

"Have you seen Sheriff Corso?" he demands.

"What? No. My son. What about my son?"

"Never mind your son, Mrs. Bickford. That's none of our concern right now."

"None of your concern? But he's been abducted! That's what I'm trying to tell you!"

I've known Terry Crebbin on a casual basis for at least three years, and have always found him to be cordial and polite, if slightly distant, as I suppose any married guy is apt to be around a single mom. So there's something wrong here, some terrible misunderstanding, something my poor addled mind has failed to grasp.

"Look," I say, my voice shaky and uncertain, "what are you doing here? Who called you?"

I'm desperate to know, but Deputy Sheriff Crebbin is untouched by my anxiety, and betrays not a scintilla of sympathy. His cold, mysteriously stubborn expression makes me crazy—how dare they treat me like this, after what I've been through? What I'm still going through?

"I don't know what you think is going on," I begin somewhat heatedly. "But here's what happened. My son, Tommy, was snatched at the baseball game. When I got home his abductor was waiting. Right here in the house. He had a gun. He made me go to the bank and wire money to an offshore account. He promised to let my son go, but I think he was lying."

"Uh-huh. What makes you think this 'abductor' was lying?"

"The last thing he said was 'don't look in the basement.'"

Crebbin reacts as if he's been slapped. "Basement?" He turns to the cops who have been, I now realize, handling my belongings. Picking things up, putting them down, which strikes me as rude. "Griffin! Pasco!" Sergeant Crebbin barks at his underlings. "Take a look around the basement."

Griffin, who appears to be several years older than Crebbin, shoots him a look of concern. "Sarge, don't you think, maybe we, um, need a warrant for that?"

Crebbin cuts him off with an impatient gesture, and turns to me, his expression intense, angry for some reason. As if something about me has deeply offended him. "Mrs. Bickford, do we have your permission to check out the basement? You've already given us permission to enter your domicile, and the law permits us to examine evidence found in plain view. The basement is assumed to be part of the domicile, so in essence you've already given us access to the basement."

Why is he babbling in legalese? Nothing makes sense. Is my brain still numb with the drug that knocked me out? Why can't I make them understand that my son has been kidnapped?

"The basement, Mrs. Bickford."

"Yes, yes," I tell him. "Tell your men to go ahead. I want you to look in the basement. I want to know."

"What exactly do you want us to know?"

But I shake my head, wave him off. Can't speak of it. Too awful to contemplate. But I've been thinking about nothing else since the man in the mask phoned.

"Stay on the sofa, Mrs. Bickford. Deputy Katz? See she doesn't leave the room."

Katz is Deputy Rita, a female officer I've never seen before. Small-boned and Hepburn-thin, she stands awkwardly beside the couch with her hand on her buttoned holster, as if fearing that I'll make a run for it. And she avoids looking me in the eye. I try to tell her what happened to my son, babble something about the man in the mask, but she seems determined to avoid conversation with me. I'm not ordinarily such a motormouth, but nerves keep me yakking, as if the steady stream of words may act as barrier for whatever unthinkable thing waits in the basement.

"I thought he was here, you know? That he'd gotten a ride home with one of the other parents. From the game. Tommy won the game, he was excited. So was I. Yelling from the dugout, you know? We're not supposed to. The parents, I mean. Supposed to maintain, be supportive, but not too noisy. Other parents might get offended. Then he went for an ice-cream sundae and then he wasn't there and I was worried. Like you get when you can't see your kid. Do you have kids? You're so young, maybe not, but believe me, you never stop worrying. So I came home, looking for Tommy. Tomas, actually, that's his real name. I thought he was here in the house, playing his video games, but it was the man in the mask, waiting for me. He had a pistol and, like I said, this ski-mask kind of thing."

A door slams with the force of a gunshot. I just about jump out of my skin, as does Deputy Katz. Crebbin storms back into the room, glaring at me. I can tell he's resisting the impulse to lay his hands upon me. But why? What does he think I've done to deserve his withering contempt.

"Come with me, Mrs. Bickford."

There's no fight in me, and no point in resisting. I accompany him into the hallway. A uniformed cop rushes by, grabbing for his walkie-talkie. Then Crebbin takes my arm and leads me through an open door, to the landing for the basement stairs. My knees get even weaker. Below are lights, more cops, the low hum of excited voices trying to keep it down. Crebbin expects me to refuse, but my mother's body takes over, desperate to know what happened to my son, and I find myself descending the stairs, passing into the shadows of the partially illuminated basement.

At the bottom of the stairs, cops wait on either side, leaving an opening just large enough for me to pass through. Passively forcing me to the north wall of the basement, and to the large chest freezer that holds goods for my catering business. Cookie and bread dough, mostly.

My heart is racing and my jaw is quivering, but there's just enough of me paying attention to get the impression that these men have already looked inside the freezer but are pretending not to have done so for some reason. Maybe because whatever waits in the freezer cannot be said to be in "plain sight," and is therefore not subject to a warrantless search.

I want to scream at them to act human, stop acting like cops, like a warrant matters at a time like this, but I haven't got enough spit to open my mouth. Why are they looking at me like *I'm* the monster? Do they really think I'd kill my own child?

"Go on, Mrs. Bickford. Open the lid, please."

I stagger to the freezer on wobbly ankles, sick with dread, partially blinded by my own tears. Not really there inside my head at all, but floating outside my own body, watching poor wobbly Kate Bickford reach for the handle. Watching her lift up the spring-balanced lid, letting it fly open. Watching as she covers her mouth and screams and screams and screams.

Screams not of grief, exactly. Shock and relief, perhaps, but not grief. Because the body in the freezer is not her precious son, Tomas "Tommy" Bickford. The body in the freezer is an adult male with frost on his lips and a small purple hole in his forehead. The body in the freezer is the late Fred Corso, Fairfax County sheriff, Little League coach, and friend.

2

THE METHODS

face down on the infield grass | 12

The boy dreams that he's lying facedown on the infield grass. Around him a game is being played. He can hear the crack of the bat, the chatter of the players, but he can't see anything except the blur of grass in his eyes. The pungent green smell of it filling his nose. The boy can't move—can't make his arms and legs wake up—but he's keenly aware of an urgent pressure in his bladder and knows that if he doesn't get up soon he'll pee his pants.

Bad idea to take a nap in the infield. What was he thinking? Now he's half-asleep and can't wake up and a batted ball might hit him, but what he's really afraid of is embarrassing himself in front of the crowd. All the kids, the coaches, his mom. Eleven-year-olds don't wet their pants. Not in public, anyhow. Not when they're wearing uniforms. Plus, he's supposed to be playing shortstop. What if a ball gets hit in his direction? Can't make the play if you're lying down, can you?

Below the murmuring chatter of the players he can hear his mother's voice echoing from the dugout, exhorting him to get up. Really embarrassing, Mom telling him to wake up in front of all his friends.

How did he let this happen? What was he thinking when he decided to take a nap on the grass, in the middle of a game?

Bladder hurts. The boy has to go, badly. He's thinking if he can unzip his fly, maybe he can pee into the grass while he's lying down and no one will notice. But when he tries to move his hands, his wrists get pinched somehow. Is someone standing on his wrists? Maybe they haven't noticed him lying in the grass.

The boy concentrates on moving his hands to his waist, desperate to get his zipper down so he can relieve the pain in his bladder. He concentrates so hard that it hurts and the pain helps wake him up so he can force his eyes open.

His eyes are still blurred with sleep, so it takes a while to focus. And then when he does focus, it still doesn't make sense. There's a thick white plastic strap around his right wrist, cuffing him to a bedpost. He's not facedown in the infield grass at all, he's facedown on a mattress. A mattress that stinks of pee.

Not his bed, not his mattress. Can't see all that well yet, can't turn his head to look, but this doesn't feel like his bedroom at all. Something wrong here. Something worse than wetting your pants in public. Something so terrible he doesn't dare think about it yet, not until his head clears. Something that makes him want his mother very badly.

"Mom," he calls out. "Mom, are you there?"

Right behind him, right in his ear, so close that it almost stops his heart, a stranger's voice suddenly says, "If you don't stop pissing the bed, kid, we'll have to put rubber pants on you."

Tomas starts to thrash on the bed, fighting the cuffs, and trying not to scream.

Here in the suburbs, even the holding cells are upscale, more or less. My cell is a small, plain room, eight feet by eight feet, with no seat or lid on the commode, but the paint on the walls is fresh, and the floors have been scrubbed with pine-scented disinfectant. The bunk is narrow but adequate, rubberized and fireproof. No pillow, of course, because a distraught prisoner might stuff a pillow into her mouth and choke to death. No graffiti on the walls, no cockroaches, nobody there but me.

The lack of roaches is notable because I spend most of the first awful night on a trip down memory lane, and insects are included. One notorious Roach Motel in particular.

It happened like this. When we were first married, Ted and I drove across the country in his grandmother's Ford Crown Victoria. That was her wedding present to us, a ten-year-old sedan with unusually low mileage because she was, as she told us, the "classic little old lady who drives to church on Sundays."

In addition to being little and old, Clara was a lovely lady, and a wise one, too. "Drive until the road ends," she advised us. "See everything you can along the way. Two weeks on the road, you'll be bonded for life or applying for annulment. Either way it goes, at least you'll know."

In addition to the car keys, she gave us a thousand dollars for expenses. In other words she paid for our discount honeymoon with savings she could ill afford to lose. The Bickfords were not wealthy, or even particularly well off, and Grandma lived on her social security and the proceeds of her lifelong savings, which had already been tapped to help put Ted through college. When we protested, Clara fluttered her age-mottled hands dismissively. "I know how much I have in the bank and how long I'm likely to last. I did the math, Teddy. It's a rather simple calculation, you know. Take the money, have fun."

So we did. Piloting the boatlike Crown Vic down through the Amish farmlands of Pennsylvania and into the Ohio Valley, then swinging up for a glimpse of the Great Lakes, and on through Wisconsin and Minnesota and the Badlands of South Dakota. Where Ted insisted we go fifty miles out of our way to check out Wall Drug, whose signs had been haunting us for a hundred billboards along the way.

It was in Montana, Big Sky Country, that we came upon a bargain we were unable to resist. On a lonely two-lane not far from the Idaho border, roadside cabins were being discounted to ten dollars a night, double occupancy. Not a motel, cabins. Therefore old. Or as Ted said, vintage.

"Ever see *It Happened One Night?*" asked my film-buff husband as we opened the Crown Vic's cavernous trunk and prepared to unload our cheap suitcases. "Clark Gable, Claudette Colbert?"

"Oh, probably, on AMC or something. Can't remember."

"Then you didn't see it. If you saw it, you'd remember. Gable's this reporter, Colbert is an heiress on the lam from the press. She's hiding out by taking a bus cross-country and Gable finds her and pretends to help her get away, even though he's a reporter, too. Anyhow, the two of 'em have to share a cheap roadside cabin, so Gable ties a rope between the beds, drapes a blanket over the rope and tells Colbert the blanket might as well be the Walls of Jericho, that's how safe she's going to be."

"And was she?"

"By our standards, yes. I think they might have kissed."

"You think? I thought you had all those old movies memorized, scene for scene."

"Not quite." He grinned and hoisted the suitcases. "After you, Miss Colbert."

Inside, it wasn't so easy to sustain the mood of frivolity. When Ted put the suitcases down, they slid to the far end of the cabin. The place smelled like moldy cheese. Very old and very moldy cheese. The bed sagged as much as the cabin floor, and the shower stall had stains that looked like something out of *Psycho*.

"If the guy running this place is into taxidermy, we're out of here," he said, and I agreed with a nervous giggle.

We were honeymooners, remember, so we propped up the old bed as best we could and tried to make use of it. At the crucial moment, Ted screamed. Rather a girlish scream, too. Seems a large cockroach wanted to explore his backside. We stayed the rest of the rainy night in the big back seat of that big Crown Vic, and by morning I knew for certain I would spend the rest of my life with Ted.

Best night we ever had together, until that first nervous night with our new baby, and that was a different sort of thing altogether. Revisiting both of those special nights is what gets me through this awful night in the holding cell. Because thinking about why I have been detained is more than I can bear. Although I have not yet been charged, Deputy Sheriff Terry Crebbin has made it clear that I'm suspected of kidnapping and murder. Which makes no sense at all. Where did they get *that* idea? Why would anyone think I would steal my own son and then kill the chief of police, who, in addition to being chief, was a good friend? If Crebbin knows, he's not saying.

"Wait for your lawyer," he sneers at me, not meeting my eyes. "People like you always have a lawyer."

The way he inflects "people" makes it mean "bitch." As far as Crebbin is concerned, I'm guilty. Charges have not yet been formulated by the county prosecutor's office, so I'm to be held for the legal twenty-four hours.

"*At least* twenty-four hours," Crebbin emphasizes. "A whole lot longer than that, if I have anything to say about it."

"Fine," I tell him. "I'm not going anywhere. Think what you like of me, Terry, but could you at least contact the FBI and tell them my son has been kidnapped?"

Crebbin stares at me then, as if inspecting the aftermath of a particularly gruesome accident. It's obvious my very existence offends him. *I* should be in the freezer, not his boss. "The FBI has been notified. They're not interested in your case."

"They told you that?" I say, my voice rising. "You've been in contact with the FBI? What did they say, exactly? What do you mean they're not interested? My son has been taken! He's been held for ransom! They said they'd let him go but they lied!"

But Crebbin walks away without a backward glance, radiating malice. I've been allowed my phone call and used it to speak with Arnie Dexel, the attorney who handles legal and financial affairs for Katherine Bickford Catering. When I attempt to tell Arnie exactly what has occurred, he cuts me off, says he wants me to save the details for the criminal attorney he's going to contact on my behalf. Terrific lawyer, top of the line. He mentions that attorney's name but I immediately forget it, which will cause me great concern over the course of the long night in the holding cell. As if forgetting a lawyer's name means the lawyer will forget about me.

All I have to cling to is Arnie's promise that the lawyer, who is out of town on another case, will arrive like the cavalry by morning.

"Noon at the latest," he says.

"Can't you do something?" I beseech him.

"Sorry, Kate, but I really can't. This is way out of my field. I'd be derelict in my duty not to find you competent counsel. Just hang in there. Help is on the way."

Cavalry arrives tomorrow morning, he says. Probably be out before breakfast. In the meantime I must find a way to pass the hours without going completely out of my head. No exaggeration, my sanity feels in jeopardy. Thoughts are screaming through my brain like a runaway train. Nothing in my head makes any sense. The-man-in-the-mask, the-man-in-the-mask, the phrase pounds in my brain, making its own insane rhythm. Laughing at me. *Whatever you do, don't go in the basement.* Some line from a cheesy horror flick. Maybe that's where he got the idea of putting poor Fred Corso's body in the freezer. Because it had to be the man in the mask, didn't it? If he didn't kill the chief himself, he knows who did, and used the body to frame me, and somehow make it look like I kidnapped my own son. But that doesn't make any sense. Why would killing the chief of police make it likely that I'd invented the man in the mask? Because that's what Crebbin thinks, isn't it? That I'm making it up? Or is he holding something back, leverage to make me confess? Man in the mask, Tommy, Sheriff Corso, what's the connection? There must be a connection. It's certainly no coincidence that Fred Corso ended up in my freezer with a bullet hole in his forehead.

On and on and on, my thoughts colliding and tearing at each other, until finally I'm able to seize on the precious memories of our cross-country adventure in that great boat of a car, and so pass the night with my sanity more or less intact.

Morning brings breakfast, courtesy of McDonald's takeout, but no lawyer. And Terry Crebbin has made it clear that the prime suspect—me—has exhausted her right to the telephone.

"One call," says Deputy Katz, who has brought me breakfast in a white paper bag. She sounds somewhat apologetic, but will not budge. "Sarge says you only get one."

"Do you have any kids?" I ask her.

She shakes her head. "Wouldn't make any difference if I did, Mrs. Bickford. Sarge says no, that's all that matters."

"I'm not talking about the phone, Rita. Your first name is Rita, correct? I'm talking about my son. He's been kidnapped. He's been taken from his home, from everything he knows and loves. He must be scared out of his mind. Terrified. He's eleven years old, Rita. You've got to help me. Call the state police, call the FBI, call anyone who'll listen. Tell them what happened."

For the briefest moment I'm convinced I've gotten through to pretty Rita, but it turns out to be wishful thinking. She hasn't really been listening; she's been studying me and has come to her own conclusion.

"If you think calling me Rita is going to help, you're wrong," she says, sounding deeply disappointed in me. "We're trained to ignore stuff like that. Prisoners trying to get friendly, get you to do them favors. This patrolman in Bridgeport? He loaned his pen to this perp, thought he was harmless, perp says he wants to write a note to his mom? Perp stabs the patrolman with his own pen. In the eye. So you'll just have to wait, Mrs. Bickford. Lady like you, somebody will show up eventually."

Lady like me. What does that mean? Does this scrawny twenty-year-old really think she knows me? Did they teach her that in the academy? Lovely Rita, meter maid, how dare she? What gives her the right to judge me? Before I can pursue the matter, make her see things my way, she skedaddles, leaving me alone in the holding-cell area.

Famished, I devour the Egg McMuffin, chug down the lukewarm coffee. What does it mean that I haven't lost my appetite? Ted died, I couldn't eat for a week. Does that mean that my body senses that Tommy is still alive?

Ridiculous thoughts, impossible hopes. I cling to them until half-past noon, when the cavalry finally arrives.

My idea of the perfect defense attorney is Gregory Peck in *To Kill A Mockingbird*. Tall, handsome, confident, wise and deeply convinced of his client's innocence. Willing to face down a mob with nothing more than a firm jaw and his certainty of what is right. I don't know what the actor was like in real life, but in that movie he was God with a law degree and a charmingly wrinkled suit.

I've got the wrinkled suit representing me, but that's about all Maria Savalo has in common with Gregory Peck. She needs heels to clear five feet tall, can't weigh more than a hundred pounds soaking wet. Lovely big dark eyes, but deeply circled—she looks a bit like Holly Hunter deprived of sleep for three days.

"Sorry about this," she says, indicating the very expensive, very wrinkled Chanel pantsuit. "Slept in it last night and didn't have time to change. Probably got B.O. and bad breath, too. Waiting on a jury. Very tense. Great outcome, though."

"Innocent?"

"No, no. Client was guilty as hell and said so. This was the death-penalty phase. He got life," she says triumphantly. Seeing the look of

dismay on my face, Maria Savalo chuckles. "How to impress potential clients, huh? Show up looking like hell, talk about guilty clients.
I'm very sorry, Mrs. Bickford. Let's start over, shall we? You pretend
I'm presentable because I usually am, and I'll pretend I had a good
night's sleep because I often do."

With that she juggles her briefcase and then formally shakes my hand.
"This was your first night in jail, correct? My intention is to make sure
it's your *only* night in jail. There. How am I doing?"

I'm not sure how to respond, and the petite attorney doesn't seem
the least surprised. There are no lawyer-client consultation rooms at the
station, so we make do with the holding cell. She plops down on the
bunk, kicks off her heels and pats the space beside her.

"Take a load off your feet, Mrs. Bickford," she says. "We'll get
started. I gotta tell you, when Arnie called me I let out a little shout
when I heard your name. You catered my cousin's wedding in Greenwich! Small world, huh? So even though we didn't meet personally,
your reputation precedes you. The food, I gotta tell you, the food was
fabulous. Those little shrimp inside the pastry? Incredible! Unfortunately my cousin decided to dump that chump husband of hers three
months after the wedding, but that's not your fault, is it?"

I really don't know what to say. My catering business is normally
the second most important thing in my life, but right at the moment
I could care less. Part of me knows that life goes on, that no matter
what happens to me and Tommy, people will continue to get married, celebrate, host luncheons and banquets. They'll care about food,
and want to talk about it, no matter how many tragedies happen to
other people—it's human nature, how we survive. But right now I
don't even want to think about Katherine Bickford Catering, or what
will happen to it if I can't be there to run things.

Ms. Savalo senses my discomfort and reaches out to pat my hand.
"Sorry. Down to business. Just had to let you know."

"This is a nightmare," I tell her. "I can't seem to think straight. I keep thinking it can't be happening, that the police think I killed someone."

Ms. Savalo produces a tissue from her purse, evidently to offer me if I start weeping. I'm determined not to weep. Can't fall apart now. Not with my son still missing. Have to save my falling apart for later.

"Maybe it will help if we formulate a chronology," Ms. Savalo suggests. "Your version of events. Arnie gave me the highlights and I got some stuff out of the locals on the way in, but I really need to hear it from you."

"I'm not sure where to begin," I say. "The police don't believe me, but my son was kidnapped."

"Start with that," she advises. "The kidnapping."

I begin with the ball game and the field of green, rooting for Tommy. Who just lately has decided he wants to be called by his formal name, Tomas, and I'm sorry, but I haven't fully made that adjustment, still think of him as Tommy. Anyhow, there we are, Little League, parents rooting, kids playing their hearts out. How harmless it all seemed, how comfortingly ordinary. Seems like a century ago, before everything changed. I tell her about waiting in vain for my son, returning home to find the man in the mask in the TV room. How he tied me up, terrorized me, knocked me out, stole my money, and then knocked me out again.

By the time I get to the freezer in the basement, Maria Savalo is nodding, as if to some music I can't hear.

"No warrants, you say?"

I shake my head. "I let them in. Gave them permission to look in the basement."

"No warrant," she says, giving a little nod of satisfaction. "That's good. That's excellent. Now let me ask you a crucial question. Did you have any contact with the sheriff *after* your son was kidnapped? Did you by any chance call him?"

"No. The man in the mask, he—"

"We'll get back to the man in the mask," she says, cutting me off. "For now let's concentrate on your use of the phone. Did you call anyone at all?"

Wait. There is something. I've forgotten all about returning Jake Gavner's phone call. How did I manage to forget that?

"Not good," is her response, after I fill her in. "You say that for the duration of the call, you gave Mr. Gavner no indication that you were under duress?"

"There was a gun pointed at me," I tell her with a little heat, aware that my face is flushing.

"Of course there was," she concedes. "So you did your best to convince Mr. Gavner that nothing was wrong? You told him your son was home?"

"I didn't have any choice."

"You convinced him?"

"I must have. He never called back. Not while I was awake. Later, the man in the mask told me I had messages, but I never had time to check them, let alone answer."

Ms. Savalo purses her lips. "Tell me about that. You say you were injected with some sort of drug. Any idea what he used, this masked man?"

"All I know is it knocked me out."

"How long did it take? Before you passed out?"

"I don't know. A minute? No longer than that."

"Good. I'm going to order a blood test. See if any residuals remain."

I remember something else. How had I forgotten? What is wrong with my brain? "The police took blood from me when I came in."

Ms. Savalo looks startled. "You gave them permission? Written permission?"

"No, not written. Terry Crebbin said if I didn't stop shouting he'd have me gagged, so I shut up and let them do it." Amazing, how an incident like that had slipped my mind, until she mentions blood, then it comes flooding back. My excuse is that I'd been trying to convince the cops to do something about my son, and not really paying attention to what they were doing to me.

"This is the deputy sheriff?" Ms. Savalo wants to know. "Crebbin, right? He threatened to gag you? So you complied?"

"Can't stand the idea of being gagged."

"Had your rights been read to you, regarding the blood sample?"

"I don't think so."

"This could be very important, Mrs. Bickford. Think again."

"I'm not sure. I really don't remember." That's the truth, but how could it be? How could I possibly forget something so crucial?

"But you didn't sign anything? Scrawl your signature?"

"No."

"Sure?"

"Positive."

Ms. Savalo grins, and it makes her glow. Holly Hunter has nothing on her. "Better and better. Small-town cops. Felony murder, they get all excited. They've got a killer mom in custody, nothing else matters."

"I'm not a killer mom."

She looks at me with concern, radiating what seems to be genuine empathy. "My apologies, Mrs. Bickford. I was thinking out loud. Thinking like the cops, okay? We both know you're not a killer mom, but they obviously think so, and it clouded their judgment. Which is good for us."

I wish I felt good about it. Wish I felt good about something. As it is, the loss of my son feels like an unanesthetized amputation.

"What I still don't understand is why the cops think I'm lying about Tommy getting taken, why would Crebbin think I made my own son disappear?"

Ms. Savalo studies me with her dark eyes, gives the impression she's utilizing some sort of self-contained lie detector on me. The beam of truth. After a pause she says, "I can shed some light on that," and opens her briefcase, handing me a sheet of paper.

"What's this?"

"Photocopy of a legal document found in the sheriff's breast pocket. That's why it's so blurry."

"I still don't get it," I say, staring at the smudged image of what looks to be a postcard.

"It's a 'return receipt requested.' Proof that you signed for a legal document on the twentieth of June. Looks like the sheriff's department was serving you. Or that's how it's meant to look."

I squint. "That can't be my signature. I never signed this."

Savalo's smile is tight. "I bet you get lots of mail having to do with your business. Maybe you forgot."

I shake my head. "I never got any legal documents. Not recently, and certainly not last week. Besides, what does this prove?"

"The cops think it proves that you were aware that your son's natural mother was attempting to regain custody of her child," she says, speaking very carefully.

My hands begin to tremble and the photocopy flutters to the floor of the holding cell. "That's impossible," I tell her, my voice sounding hollow. "Tommy's mother is dead. Both of his parents died in a taxi-cab accident. In Puerto Rico."

Ms. Savalo scoops up the photocopy. "The suit was filed by one Enrico D. Vargas, Esquire, office listed in Queens. I checked. He's an attorney, duly registered in the state of New York."

"I don't understand." Thinking that should be my mantra, so many things I didn't understand.

"The petition to reassign custody was filed by a Teresa Alonzo, no address given, other than the lawyer's office," Ms. Savalo explains. "In the long run they can't prevent us from discovering where she resides, but it will take a while. We'll have to petition the court." She pauses, locks eyes with me. "Are you absolutely sure you've never heard from Enrico Vargas? That Attorney Vargas hasn't contacted you, or a lawyer representing you?"

"I've never heard of him," I respond weakly. "Birth mother? This can't be real. It can't. Tommy's parents are dead. They told us."

"Who told you, Mrs. Bickford?"

"The adoption agency. Family Finders."

"You saw the death certificates of the child's parents?"

I shake my head. "I don't recall seeing death certificates. We had no reason to disbelieve the agency. Ted checked them out before we applied, they were legit. Expensive but legal."

"So you took them at their word, that the baby was available for adoption, free and clear. Nobody trying to assert custodial rights?"

"No, absolutely not."

"Okay. We'll check into that," she says, tucking the photocopy back in her briefcase.

"What was Fred doing with that copy?"

"Fred? Oh, the deceased. No one knows for certain, apparently, but the supposition is that he went to your home to serve you with notice, or possibly discuss the possibility that you were about to be embroiled in a custody suit, or both. That he stumbled upon your plans to spirit your adopted child away from the authorities, attempted to intervene, and that you shot him. That to cover up the crime you invented a kidnapper. The man in the mask, as you call him."

I can feel my jaw drop. "Oh, my God."

"Obviously your position is that the abductor exists and that he's attempting to frame you."

My jaw snaps shut. "It isn't my 'position.' It's the truth! That's what happened. Exactly as I told you. He took my son, he took my money. I assume he killed poor Fred."

"Why would he do that? Frame you? Any theories?"

"I've been racking my brains," I tell her. "No idea. Why would they care? They've got my son. They've got the money. Why bother going to all the trouble of framing me?"

After a pause, letting it soak in, Ms. Savalo says, "That's interesting, the way you always say 'they.' I thought it was just this one guy in a ski mask?"

"He talked on his cell phone to others. Gave orders. I got the impression this was his business, kidnapping children and holding them for ransom."

"Hmm. And we have evidence of the wire transfer. Not easy to trace through the Cayman Islands, but we'll give it a shot. Okay, Mrs. Bickford. You've given me enough so I can have a conversation with Jared Nichols, the county prosecutor. Jared and I go way back, which may or may not be useful. At least he'll give me a straight answer."

She snaps shut her briefcase, slips into her heels and stands up.

"What do I do?"

"Wait," she advises. "I'll be gone an hour or two. Three at most. Then we'll see?"

"See what?" I ask.

The attorney gives me a bright, reassuring smile. "See if I can work the old Savalo magic. Hang in there. Like the Terminator said, 'I'll be back.'"

A moment later I'm alone again.

After we got back from our honeymoon trip, Ted and I talked seriously about having children. We'd been having unprotected sex for more than a year and I hadn't got pregnant, so a visit to the gynecologist was in order. I was put through a battery of tests—blood work, tissue samples, sonograms—and the results were not encouraging. Fibroid tumors. Not cancerous, but large enough to make pregnancy unlikely. I went through a long, painful procedure that was intended to reduce them in size. More than half of such procedures resulted in substantial reduction, supposedly, but it turned out I was in the unlucky half. No long-term reduction, no increase in the likelihood of impregnation. Most of the patients in my category eventually opted for hysterectomies. My option entirely. The fibroids were fertility threatening, not life threatening.

I offered to let my eggs be collected and fertilized by Ted's sperm, in hopes of finding a surrogate mother. Ted ruled that out, in no uncertain terms. He was going to make a baby with me, in the normal way, or he wasn't going to make a baby at all. Never mind all the legal and technical problems with finding a surrogate womb. And so we discussed adoption. Ted was especially enthusiastic about the idea of adopting—what did it matter of the child carried his DNA? It was raising a child together that mattered. Making a family.

As it turned out, finding an adoptable infant was nearly as difficult as dealing with the whole surrogate-mom issue, but of course we didn't know that when we started. It helped that we weren't insisting on a blond, blue-eyed baby. Hispanic origins were fine with us, although Ted was uneasy with the agencies who specialized in South American babies. Too many stories about poor women being more or less forced to sell their newborns, or having them stolen away and sold to intermediaries. Best to stick closer to home, where U.S. law applied. Eventually we found an agency with connections in Puerto Rico, were put on the list, and at last the great day arrived and baby Tomas came into our lives.

Could his mother still be alive? Had a woman calling herself Teresa Alonzo hired the man in the mask to take him back? But it didn't make any sense—why hadn't I been notified? Obviously if his birth mother wanted to reestablish contact, we could have worked something out. I wouldn't have been so selfish as to deny my son contact with his birth mother. Would I?

Honestly, I don't know how I would react. The notion that a birth mother might be involved is strangely reassuring, because if true it means that he's still alive. But why empty my bank account? They'd have had no way of knowing that the money was intended for Tommy's use eventually, would they? The man in the mask could access my accounts, pry into all my records, but he couldn't read my mind, could he?

Truth is, I'm not sure of anything. I've never felt so lost, not even in those first nightmare days after Ted passed. Nothing is what I thought it was. The world is upside down, or inside out, and I've no idea where I fit in the scheme of things.

Except for this. I raised him, nurtured him, loved him to pieces, and this one thing I know: I'm the only mother Tomas "Tommy" Bickford has ever known.

what he lives for | **15**

After an eternity—nearly four hours, by my later reckoning—Maria Savalo returns to my holding cell with a smile on her face and a bounce in her step. She's carrying her briefcase in one hand and a shopping bag in the other.

"The good news is you're getting out of here," she announces brightly. "The bad news is you can't go home. Not yet."

She hands me the shopping bag, which contains my personal effects, meager as they are, with the exception of my purse. Ms. Savalo explains that my purse, a simple black Coach bag, was specifically mentioned in the search warrant that was issued after I was taken into custody, and will be retained for "further examination," whatever that means.

"What do they hope to find?" I ask, bewildered. "A letter of confession?"

"They didn't say. They never do. The important thing is, the county prosecutor's office has decided not to file charges 'at this time.'"

I let that sink in. "Meaning they might still arrest me?"

Ms. Savalo shrugs. "Can't know for sure. My instincts tell me there's still a strong possibility an indictment will occur, assuming they can develop the evidence, link it together."

She goes on to explain that as far as the prosecutor is concerned, there are problems with the police theory of the crime. Not the least of which is how a woman of my size and strength managed to hoist the body of a 248-pound man into the freezer. Plus, anything the deputies discovered upon entering the house might come under "fruit of a poisoned tree"—Ms. Savalo's phrase—because they entered and searched without a warrant.

"Real sticky problem for them is what to do about the phone call," she explains, plopping down on the bunk.

At first I assume she's referring to my call to Jake Gavner, when I lied under duress and convinced him my son was safe and sound at home. But no, it seems there was another phone call, one I had nothing to do with.

"Think about it, Mrs. Bickford. What were the police doing knocking on your door? Had to be something that alerted them to you. That something was an anonymous call to the 911 line, which means they have it on tape. So far they haven't let me listen to the call—they will eventually—but from what I was given to understand by the prosecutor's office, the caller implicated you in the disappearance of Sheriff Corso. Why Deputy Sheriff Crebbin didn't apply for a search warrant at that point, I don't know. Certainly on the basis of the call, one would have been granted. But what happened is, as soon as they got the call they raced over to your place and knocked on the door. Guess maybe he thought Corso might still be alive."

"They were close friends," I tell her, feeling ill, despite the good news of my impending release. "Terry must have been frantic to find him."

"Whatever," says Ms. Savalo, somewhat cavalierly. "The point is, who made the call? Leaves the prosecutors with an unknown quantity, and they hate that."

"Must have been the man in the mask," I suggest. "He called me just before they knocked on the door, and made sure to mention the basement."

Ms. Savalo shrugs. "All this will be sorted out eventually. We have more to discuss, but first I'd like to get you situated. Your home is still a crime scene, so I took the liberty of booking you a motel room for a few days. Nothing fancy, I'm afraid. Just four walls, a shower and a bed."

"Anything, I don't care." I'm in desperate need of a hot shower, having been stuck in the same clothes I had on when Terry Crebbin and his deputies hustled me down to the station. Clothes I'd already been passed out in for who knows how many hours.

Ms. Savalo pauses, studies me. "There's a reason it's nothing fancy. I'm not really worried about spending your money at this point, Mrs. Bickford. But we've got a situation outside the station and we have to come to an agreement on how to handle it."

"Situation?"

"A media situation. They've obviously gotten wind that you're about to be released. I counted five TV-news vans. Cable and local affiliates. This is your chance, Mrs. Bickford, if you want to take it."

I'm confused not only by what Ms. Savalo is saying, but by her whole attitude, which has shifted. As if she's in the process of judging me, much to her regret, and expecting the worst.

"What are you talking about? What chance?"

"Your fifteen minutes of fame. You can hold a press conference as soon as you walk out that door. Proclaim your innocence on camera, and there's a very good chance the footage will be carried by Fox News and CNN, as well as every local station in the tristate area."

I bury my face in my hands. Whatever muted euphoria I'd been experiencing at the idea of getting out has just been extinguished by the prospect of a media swarm. Strangely enough, I hadn't even considered the possibility. Too many other things to obsess on. But the very idea of appearing on TV at a time like this makes my skin crawl. Never really understood why so many victims of crime, or those accused of it, are so eager to exploit face-time on TV. Hi, your infant daughter just drowned in your swimming pool, would you care to say a few words? Sure thing, but let me do my hair first, and while I'm at it, hire a media consultant.

Ugh. Revolting.

A wave of nausea doubles me up in stomach cramps. Gorge rising as I imagine microphones being shoved in my face by leering reporters. Hey, Killer Mom! What have you got to say for yourself!

"You've got to get me out of here," I tell her, gasping back the bile in my throat. "Is there a back way?"

"You don't want to speak to the media? Appear on TV? Tell your story?"

"Please help me," I say, involuntary tears rolling down my face. "I'm begging you. Can't you make them go away? Please?"

All of a sudden Ms. Savalo's tight smile relaxes and turns warm. She reaches out, patting my arm, reassuring me. "Of course there's a back way out. There's always a back way out, but I had to know your intentions."

"I don't understand," I tell her. "What's going on? Why are you acting like this?"

She sighs and stands up from the bunk. "Come on, Mrs. Bickford, our chariot awaits." Leading me from the holding cell, she explains: "There are two kinds of defense attorneys. Those who want to bring it to the cameras and those who don't. I never bring it to the cameras if I can help it. My opinion, it's almost always the first sign of a weak defense, or a guilty client. That creep who chopped up his wife and his unborn child in California? His lawyers kept that front and center on the cable talk shows for months. Not because they were convinced their client was innocent, but because they were afraid he was guilty. Their only strategy was to try and taint a jury. Sow some doubt, muddy the waters. I don't work like that. Just a personal preference, really. I'm much more comfortable working behind the scenes. Using my contacts, making my best case directly to the cops and the prosecutors without filtering it through Fox News."

We come to a hallway in the rear of the station. There's no sign of Terry Crebbin or any of his men, but Deputy Katz is waiting there in full uniform, a heavy, holstered revolver on her slender hip. She won't meet my eyes, but she's willing enough to look at my lawyer. Indeed, I get the impression they know and respect each other.

"We all set, Rita?" Ms. Savalo asks.

Deputy Katz nods, hands her a set of car keys.

"Thanks, Rita, I owe you one."

The rear exit to which we've been guided connects directly to the employee parking facility. Police cruisers, civilian cars, a tow truck. And the beautiful thing, no access to civilians, including the media.

"Deputy Katz loaned you her car?" I ask, astonished, as we hurriedly head for a five-year-old Honda Civic purposefully positioned not far from the exit door.

"Offered her five hundred bucks. She wouldn't take it."

We get into the car and I hunker down instinctively, expecting to be assaulted by boomed microphones at any moment.

"I don't understand," I say. "Is she a friend of yours?"

Ms. Savalo shakes her head as she fires up the engine. "Nope. Never met her before. I just explained the situation and asked for her help. She complied. Nice kid."

I'm amazed, considering how lovely Rita had been treating me. As if firmly convinced of my guilt, and repulsed by my very existence. Makes me think that Arnie Dexel has steered me right, finding a defense attorney who can "explain the situation" and get the cops—or at least one cop—to cooperate. I start to babble something to that effect and Ms. Savalo cuts me off.

"Get down in the seat. Doubt any of these jackals know who I am yet, but you never can tell."

I scrunch down, aware of the musty interior of the Honda, the coffee-stained upholstery. Never do see the TV vans congregated around the front of the station because Ms. Savalo has gotten directions that take her through an adjacent parking lot, and then onto a one-way street, avoiding the main access road altogether. A few minutes later she gives the all clear and I sit up, somewhat tentatively.

We're on the street, in light traffic, and no one is paying us the least attention.

"If you'd wanted to speak to the press, I'd have helped you set it up, advised you on what not to say," she says conversationally. "Then I would have arranged to get you other representation. Somebody you've seen on TV. Some glamour-puss like Roy Black or maybe even Alan Dershowitz. Both of them are terrific, by the way. It's just not my scene."

"Nor mine," I confess, my voice shaky.

"Good, we're on the same page. Lay low for a few days, they'll be on to the next story."

"You really think so?"

She nods. "It's a game, Mrs. Bickford. An understanding between the hunter and the quarry. Once they get the message that we're not playing the game, seeking the publicity to advance my career or yours, they'll find another, more cooperative victim."

We've merged onto a road that runs parallel to the highway, not far from the Bridgeport line. At the traffic circle Ms. Savalo checks the rearview mirror, appears satisfied, and then pulls in to an aging motel complex. She avoids the front office, which faces the traffic circle, and goes directly around to the rear parking lot, out of sight from the road or the traffic circle.

"Not exactly the Waldorf," she says, shutting off the engine, "but it will have to do."

"I told you, it doesn't matter."

"Good. Because you'll need to save your money so you can afford my fee."

We haven't discussed that yet, nothing about cost or fees, but I know enough about what lawyers charge to assume her retainer will be enormous. I start to quiz her on the subject, thinking she wants to get into it now, and once again she cuts me off.

"Let's get you out of sight first," she says, grabbing a small suitcase from the trunk of the little Honda.

Given what she's accomplished so far, I wouldn't dream of arguing with her. Walking more quickly than I would have been able to on heels that high, she leads me up the stairs to a room on the second floor. Produces a tagged motel key from her bag and quickly opens the door.

"Here we are, Mrs. Bickford. Your home away from home."

Standard American motel, of the era Edward Hopper made famous in his melancholy paintings. Therefore dated, if not timeless. Sealed window with the curtains drawn, paneled walls, a queen-size bed that looks a little splayed. Formica-laminated bureau, table and chairs, sink area in the far corner, a poorly vented, windowless shower stall. Battered TV on the bureau, looks like it might tune in *Leave it To Beaver* or *I Dream of Jeannie,* and I don't mean on the TV Land channel.

Ms. Savalo tosses the suitcase on the bed, sets down her briefcase and rubs her hands together. "There," she announces, "mission accomplished! I put a couple of outfits together," she explains, indicating the suitcase. "Nothing fancy. Jeans, tops and underwear from Target. You won't have access to your own clothes for a couple of days. Also an inexpensive handbag."

I'm so grateful I feel like blubbering. But something tells me not to blubber in the presence of my new, very feisty attorney. So I sit in one of the chairs provided, and fold my hands and wait.

"Coffee? They've got one of those little machines."

"Coffee would be great."

She busies herself by the sink and soon produces two cups of luke-warm, coffee-flavored liquid. I gulp it greedily, and Ms. Savalo settles into the chair opposite.

"You're wondering what happens next."

I nod, clutching the plastic cup.

"We put together a formal agreement, you sign it. Right now you're being billed at my usual five hundred per hour. That's on the high side for hourly billing, but I'm worth it. If you're indicted, God forbid, there will be an additional fee, somewhere in the range of fifty grand. That will cover me, a research attorney and whatever fees we pay to the investigators. Expenses extra. If it goes to trial, God *really* forbid, be ready to pony up another hundred K." She pauses, waits for my reaction. "Are you shocked yet?"

"I'm beyond being shocked, Ms. Savalo. Finding the body of a friend in my freezer, that shocked me."

"So you're okay with the money?"

I shrug. "I don't have that kind of cash. The five hundred thousand in that account was Tommy's inheritance. It wiped me out. But there's plenty of equity in my house. Some in the business, too. I'll cover it, one way or another."

"Good. Then I'll be taking a lien against your property. Standard procedure, I'm afraid."

I get the impression she's expecting me to argue about the fees and the lien, and that she has her counterarguments ready to go. I'd like to skip past all of that, and say so.

"Fine with me. Most people get freaked about the money," she explains.

"I'll get freaked about it later, if you don't mind. Right now I want you to tell me what to do about my son. Can you put me in contact with someone at the FBI? Maybe they already know about the man in the mask. I think he's done this before."

Ms. Savalo puts down her plastic cup, then places her briefcase on her knees and thumbs the lock open. "I took the liberty," she says. "Put a call in to the local office in New Haven this morning, shortly after we first spoke. They haven't got back to me yet, which is no surprise. I caution you not to expect much help from the feds."

"Why is that?" I ask plaintively. "I just don't get it. Terry Crebbin already told me they weren't interested in helping me, but it doesn't make sense. Isn't that what the FBI does, handle abduction cases? Even if they think the police are right, and that I abducted my own son, wouldn't they want to investigate?"

Ms. Savalo sighs. "Time was when they'd have been all over it. Pushing the locals out of the way, taking over. But they have other fish to fry now. Homeland security and all that. I'm not saying they won't assign an agent or two, check it out, but like I say, don't expect what you see on TV. This isn't *Without a Trace,* or even *Law & Order.* Especially if the local cops are dumping on the idea, telling them it's a custody case. Feds hate to waste manpower on custody abductions."

I want to weep in frustration, but manage to contain my tears. Determined not to break down or show weakness in front of this implacable woman. The thing is, I'm not sure if I actually like her or not—would we lunch together, in other circumstances? But one thing is abundantly clear: I need her help. Desperately.

"What can I do?" I plead. "If the FBI won't help, what do I do next? How do I go about finding my son?"

From out of the briefcase Ms. Savalo produces a business card. "This is your man," she says, handing me the card. "He's a bit eccentric—hell, he's a *lot* eccentric. But he's the best in the business."

"What business is that?" I ask, studying the card. All it shows is a name and a telephone number. No office indicated, not even an e-mail address.

"He finds lost children," she explains. "Abducted children. That's his specialty. That's what he lives for. Sometimes I think that's *all* he lives for."

when his knuckles brush the ceiling | 16

Shane. That's the name on the card. Randall Shane. Sounds vaguely familiar, but I can't think why.

Soon after giving me the card, Ms. Savalo locks her briefcase and prepares to leave, eager to return the borrowed Honda and, no doubt, to get on with her regular life, whatever that might be. I've no idea if she's married (no ring, but that's hardly conclusive) or if she has children of her own. She's given no indication of any desire to share personal information, and I'm not inclined to pry. For all I know, she lives in a file cabinet and pops out when innocent clients are framed for horrible crimes. Which is fine by me, so long as she continues to pop up whenever I need her.

Last thing she does before leaving is promise to arrange a car rental for me. It seems my minivan has been impounded, and will not be released for several days, assuming they don't find any evidence linking it to Fred Corso's murder.

"You don't want to be driving a vehicle with known plates anyhow, not for a few days," she says. "The media folks aren't geniuses, but they know how to run plate numbers."

"I thought there was a law against that."

"You're joking, right? That's good. When bad things happen to good people, you need a sense of humor."

"So you think I'm a good person?" I ask, really wanting to know. "You believe I'm innocent?"

Ms. Savalo pauses at the door, looking up at me, considering my question. Even with her high heels, our height difference is a crucial inch or two. "It's not important what I believe about a client's guilt or innocence," she says. "But in your case, actually, yes, I do believe you."

I fumble in the purse that has been returned with my personal effects. "You'll want a credit card," I tell her. "For the car."

She shakes her head. "We'll take care of it and bill you later. The vehicle will be in someone else's name, but will be valid for your driver's license."

"Oh." I shut the purse.

"I always use Enterprise," she says with a wry smile. "Because they deliver."

"You've done this before."

"Standard procedure for keeping a low profile. Look, Mrs. Bickford, you've been through a lot in the last few days. Try to get some sleep and call Randall in the morning."

I'm at the point of asking her to stay—the prospect of being left alone in this dreary motel is suddenly daunting—but realize that's silly, not to mention inconsiderate. So I thank her yet again and then lock and chain the door when she's gone.

I can always call a friend. It's not as if I don't have girlfriends galore, right? Okay, maybe not a go-to, call-in-the-middle-of-the-night best friend. But I'm on friendly terms with all the Little League moms—well, most of them—and there's Connie, who runs the day-to-day operations for the catering business, and who must be totally flipped out by what she's no doubt heard on the news. At the very least I should give Connie a call, tell her what has happened, my version. But I can't bring myself to call her for the same reason I can't call closer friends: because I'm ashamed to tell them what has happened. As if I've somehow brought this upon myself. As if part of me wants to take the blame.

Totally absurd. But that's how it feels. Deeply shameful and humiliating. What it boils right down to is, the only person I really want to talk to is Ted, and he's no longer available, at least not for a normal two-way conversation. I still tell him things in my head—surely everyone who has lost a loved one does that—but if anything, it only makes me feel more alone. And I've never felt so alone in all my life, not even in the empty-bed days that followed Ted's passing. Of course, I had Tommy to hold and comfort, and that helped. My son who may have a birth mother out there after all, one who wants him back. What would he think of such a thing? Would he want to see her? Or, and here's a terrifying thought, has he already met her and decided to abandon life in the suburbs with boring old Mom?

The line of thought is so painful I attempt to banish it from my mind. And fail, of course. Thinking that a distraction might help, I turn on the television but find I can't focus on the images. I see them clearly enough, heads yakking, cars crashing, more heads yakking, but can't make sense of the story, if there is one.

Switching off the TV, I take a quick shower in the mildewed stall. After toweling my hair more or less dry—I look like a water rat, no doubt, but lack the courage to check the steamy mirror—I lay back on the ruptured bed and close my eyes. And keep seeing my son in his uniform, and the frost-burned face of poor Fred Corso, the two blurring together until I want to scream myself unconscious.

Sleep is out of the question. I have to do something.

Randall Shane. What is it about that name?

One way to find out. These are hardly normal business hours, but recovering abducted children isn't a normal business, is it? Anyhow, that's my excuse for dialing the number on the card.

Rings three times. Answering machine with three words, *Leave a message.* I hang up and then decide to try again, having formulated a message to leave on the machine.

This time, much to my surprise, an actual voice responds.

"Randall Shane. State your business."

Now I'm really flustered, and therefore speaking too fast, rushing the words. "Um, Mr. Shane? My name is Kate Bickford. My son, Tommy, has been kidnapped. Tomas, really, that's what he prefers, but I can't seem to stop calling him Tommy."

"Who gave you my number?" he responds, making it sound like an accusation.

"My lawyer, Ms. Savalo. Maria Savalo. She, um, said you could help me."

"Address," he says abruptly.

"Excuse me?"

"Where are you, Mrs. Bickford?"

Lions have kinder growls. He sounds like he wants to come right over and rip the phone out of my hands. I'm trying to make my hand hang up the receiver when he snarls, "Tell me where you are, lady! How am I supposed to help you if I don't know where you are?"

I search around for something that will give me the motel address, can't seem to find anything relevant. No pens, notepaper, or match-books. Feeling helpless and intimidated by the rudeness in his voice, I manage to describe the motel, its location near the traffic circle.

"I'll find it," he says. "What room?"

That much I do know.

"Ninety minutes," he snaps, and hangs up.

For the next hour or so I contemplate going down to the front desk and asking to change my room. At about the same time, my brain solves the riddle of the familiar name. *Shane* happened to be one of Ted's favorite movies. You know, mysterious gunslinger protects a boy and his homesteader family from a hired killer, mostly seen from the boy's point of view. Alan Ladd and Jack Palance. In the end, having gunned down the really creepy bad guy, Shane rides off into the sunset, mortally wounded perhaps, but not wanting to let the boy see him hurting.

I never connected with the story quite the way Ted did, but I loved to watch him watch it, if only to glimpse the ten-year-old boy inside the man I loved.

I'm not sure what to expect of Randall Shane, but after being a victim of his rude and abrupt phone manner, I'm not expecting a hero in a white hat, that's for sure.

An hour crawls by. Sixty seconds to the minute, sixty minutes to the hour. No wonder it takes so long to get through an hour. We pass ninety minutes and head toward two hours. The son of a bitch has stood me up. How dare he?

One hundred and four very long minutes after the abrupt hang-up, a fist rat-a-tats the motel-room door, causing me to jump about a foot in the air, my heart slamming. Scared and angry, I undo the chain and yank the door open. Ready to give him hell if he so much as raises his voice.

Standing in the doorway, looking more sheepish than intimidating, is a tall, rangy, slope-shouldered man in his midforties. Before I can speak—not that I know what to say—he removes a Red Sox baseball cap, revealing close-cropped gray hair, and apologizes profusely.

"Mrs. Bickford? Randall Shane. Really sorry to keep you waiting at a time like this. I had trouble finding a cab. Said they'd be over in ten minutes, it was more like thirty."

"Cab?" Seeing the deep sadness that emanates from his faded blue eyes, I feel my anger drain away.

"Maria didn't tell you? I don't drive. May I come in?"

I'm thinking that if Clint Eastwood had a neatly trimmed salt-and-pepper goatee, he'd bear a passing resemblance to Randall Shane. That is, if Mr. Shane could be persuaded to stand up straight. Dressed not in faded denim but slightly wrinkled khaki pants, long in the leg, moccasin boat shoes, and the kind of loose, buttoned shirt that fishermen favor, with multiple pockets. His hands, I can't help noticing, are large, blue-veined and strong. The kind of hands that can palm a basketball or make a powerful fist.

Having been ready to dismiss him out of hand, after a bad first impression, my inner compass instantly swings one hundred and eighty degrees. My Shane is not the hero from the movie, perhaps, but he's half again as tall as Alan Ladd, and looks plenty capable of handling himself in a difficult situation. Looks, indeed, as if he's been handling difficult situations all his life.

That, I'm thinking, may be exactly what my situation requires. What I require. Because the man in the mask continues to scare me stupid, and I can't seem to shake the fear.

"I see you've got a coffeemaker," Shane says. "Mind if I make myself a cup?"

I offer to do it for him. I am, after all, a professional caterer, and ought to be able to play gracious host, even in a dump like this. But the big man shrugs me away. "Always make my own coffee," he says. "One of my quirks."

I think it a trifle odd that he doesn't offer to make me a cup, too, (not that I want one of the tasteless things) but then recall that Ms. Savalo said he was eccentric. Maybe his eccentricities extend from not driving to not sharing beverages.

Right away he sets me straight on the latter point. "Thing is, you look shaky as hell," he says, bring his cup over to the little laminated table. "I'm guessing you haven't slept in at least twenty-four hours. No caffeine for you."

I open my mouth to tell him I'm perfectly capable of monitoring my own caffeine intake, and then think better of it. What do I care? All that matters is that he's capable of finding my son. If he can do that, and wants me to walk ten paces behind him, eyes averted, I'll gladly comply.

"How do you do it?" I ask him. "How do you find kids who've been abducted?"

He shrugs, sips quietly at his coffee. "Depends on the situation. Tell me all about it, then I'll have some idea of how to proceed."

Once I get rolling, Shane doesn't interrupt and he doesn't take notes, he just sips his coffee, his eyes directed at the floor, as if fascinated by the variety of stains in the carpet. I tell him what I told Ms. Savalo, trying my best to include all the details she had to pry out of me. When I get at last to the body in the freezer, he puts his empty cup down and levels his sad blue eyes at me.

"The bastard," he says, sounding appalled but not terribly surprised. "Had you thinking it was your boy in the freezer, didn't he?"

I nod, a lump in my throat. Exactly right. Exactly what I'd been dreading when I lifted the lid. And no doubt why my hands are shaking now. Because even thinking about it still scares me. No, not "it," my fear is not centered on dead bodies, but upon the man in the mask. Because an essential part of me is convinced he's still out there in the shadows. Maybe right there in the parking lot, waiting to pounce, waiting to put me under his control.

Randall Shane picks up on my anxiety—anybody would, I suppose—and probes me for the specific symptoms.

"Just thinking of this man gets your heart racing, right?" he asks. "Brings on a cold sweat? Weakness in the belly and knees. Trembling?"

I nod, feeling deeply ashamed.

"Got an idea," Shane announces, sounding utterly confident. He folds his large hands and places them under his chin, as if posing for Rodin's *Thinker*, the khaki-clad version. "Just go with me here, okay?" he says. "I want to try something."

I've no idea what he has in mind, but nod my assent.

The big hands have folded themselves together, as if in prayer. Indeed, Shane is staring up at the ceiling, as if in prayer. But he does not, as I'm half expecting, invoke the name of God. Not even close.

After a pause, he says, "What's the most harmless name you can think of? A man's name. First harmless name that comes to mind, Mrs. Bickford. Give me a harmless name."

I shrug. "Bruce?"

Shane grins, exposing teeth that have not been laser-whitened or capped, which is oddly reassuring. "I know a couple of macho Scots would take mortal offense at that choice, but Bruce it is. From now on, until we establish his identity, that's what we'll call the man in the mask. Bruce."

"Bruce?"

"Bruce is a bastard, but he's not all-powerful, okay? He's just a man. One who probably had military training in how to intimidate a victim. Wants you to fear him because his training teaches him that fear makes victims weak, makes them not pay attention to what he's really doing. Does what I'm saying make sense?"

"I guess so. Sure."

"Are you offended by vulgar language, Mrs. Bickford."

"My son listens to Eminem and 50 Cent. I've gotten used to it."

"Good," he says, as if I've helped him arrive at a decision. "Now repeat after me—Fuck Bruce."

"Excuse me?"

"Humor me, Mrs. Bickford. I'm sure Maria told you I was eccentric. Probably told you worse than that. So repeat after me—Fuck Bruce."

The thing is, and this may sound silly or even prissy, but *fuck* is not a word I use. Lots of women in my age group and social class swear like sailors, but since I'm always meeting and greeting potential customers, I'm careful to avoid language that might be offensive.

"Come on, Mrs. Bickford. Give it a try. Fuck Bruce."

I take a deep breath and go for it. "Fuck Bruce."

"Good. Now say it like you mean it."

"Fuck Bruce!"

He grins again. "Now we're getting somewhere. Bruce is not a monster, he's a man. Therefore he makes mistakes. We don't know exactly what mistakes yet, but I'll find out, starting first thing tomorrow morning. The mistakes will lead us to Bruce, and from Bruce to your son."

"Why can't we start right now?" I want to know.

"I'm afraid it can't be 'we,' Mrs. Bickford. I'll handle this on my own, in my own way."

"You said you don't drive."

He shrugs. "True. I'll hire a driver."

"I'd be paying for the driver, correct?"

Another shrug. "I suppose so. Eventually you'd recompense Maria's office and she'd recompense me."

"Then I'm hiring a driver. Me."

He studies me, sees that I'm serious. "We'll discuss this in the morning."

"Why wait until morning? Why not start right now?"

"Because we start with a lawyer, and his office won't be open at this hour."

"The guy in Queens?"

"The guy in Queens, exactly right." Randall Shane stands up and stretches his long, lanky frame.

I really like the fact that his knuckles brush the ceiling.

what the pastry chef said | **17**

T he rental car arrives at 9:30 a.m., delivered by a neatly dressed young man with raven-black hair and soulful, chocolate-brown eyes who introduces himself as Mohammed. He cheerfully presents me with the key and a business card, should there be any problems with the car.

"Ford Taurus very reliable," he assures me. Then quickly slips into an almost identical sedan that followed him to the motel, driven by another dark young man who could be Mohammed's brother. A moment later they leave the parking lot without a backward glance. Mission accomplished.

Elapsed time, less than one minute. I'm thinking there are certain things we still do pretty well here in the good old U.S.A., and no-muss-no-fuss car rentals is one of them.

Wheels. I'm feeling a little more in control of myself and my fractured world, and that's good. Actually got about nine hours' sleep, which is amazing, considering. The same can't be said for Mr. Shane, who shared my funky room for the night, having volunteered as bodyguard to alleviate any anxiety I might have about the man in the mask returning. Excuse me—Bruce.

"He won't be back," Shane had assured me. "But just in case, I'll be here."

With that, he borrowed a pillow, laid his long frame out on the ancient carpeting and proceeded to stare at the ceiling.

"I'll be fine," he said, sensing my concern. "Good floor."

It seems that Randall Shane doesn't sleep, at least not in a normal way. He confided that he hasn't slept normally for many years. Some sort of sleep disorder, although he's been somewhat vague about the specifics.

"Best I can do is achieve a kind of meditative state," he said, as if describing an affliction as ordinary as tennis elbow or a bad back. "I kind of zone out, but my eyes are usually open."

"Are you serious? That sounds horrible!"

"It is," he admitted. "I've been hospitalized for it twice. Went through the whole course at a sleep disorder clinic. Flunked it, too. Only way I can achieve a full unconscious state is by taking powerful drugs. Not sleeping pills, the stuff they use on horses. Can't tolerate the side effects, so I don't use it. And in any case, the drugged state isn't refreshing. Because it isn't a normal sleep."

"My God."

"Praying doesn't work, not for a sleep disorder. Tried it."

"It must drive you crazy."

"It does," he said from the floor. "Humans need to dream—most animals do, apparently—and I can't, so my brain sometimes produces hallucinations. That's why I can't drive. Might see something that isn't there. Or not see something that is."

He's still examining the ceiling, so he can't be aware that my jaw has dropped. It seems that Ms. Savalo's description of him as "eccentric" is no exaggeration. If eccentric covers those who suffer from waking hallucinations.

"Don't worry," he assured me. "I'm perfectly sane. I don't see people who aren't there, or hear voices. Just images. They tell me it's retinal firing, whatever that is. My brain attempting to sleep when the rest of me is wide-awake. That's the theory, anyhow. Nobody really knows."

"But you can work?"

I must have sounded concerned, because something in my tone made him sit up and meet my eyes.

"I can work just fine," he said. "Just can't drive. So normally I hire a car service."

"Not this time. I'm driving."

"No way to dissuade you?"

"No."

"Could be dangerous if I stumble on to something," he points out.

"That's why I want to be there. In case you do."

"How about this?" he says. "How about we take it one day at a time."

"If you find my son, I have to be there. However many days it takes."

Shane sighs. "Okay," he says. "I'll find your son, Mrs. Bickford. Go on, get some *z's.*"

"Can't."

"Sure you can. Sleep for both of us."

I remember undressing under the covers, and then nothing until seven in the morning, when a ray of sunshine came through a broken slat of the venetian blinds. With waking came a brief spasm of total panic. Where am I? Where's Tommy? After sorting that out—yes, it all happened, it wasn't a bad dream—I notice that Shane is gone.

"Randall?"

Instantly the door opens. Shane tilts his head into the room, a cell phone up to his ear—he's stepped outside to make or take a call, that's all—and whatever relief I feel is deflated by the reminder that I find myself in need of a bodyguard-slash-investigator. Not to mention a lawyer.

After a quick shower, I put on the new underwear, jeans and T-shirt. Shane is waiting for me outside, hair still damp from his own shower, and as we walk down to breakfast he explains that he's just completed a lengthy phone consultation with Maria Savalo. Discussing legal and investigative strategy. A petulant twinge makes me wonder if I'm paying for both ends of the conversation. Of course I am, but what does it matter?

"Maria says she'll speak to you later today," Shane tells me, as we walk into the shabby little motel restaurant. "I told her our plan for the day—or at least, my plan—and that we'd keep in touch. I didn't mention you'd be driving me. She wouldn't approve, to put it mildly."

"He's my son. I'm going to be there."

Shane nods.

After breakfast—not bad, really, considering what the place looks like—we go back to the room and wait for the rental-car delivery. Making polite conversation but not discussing the situation, as if by unspoken assent agreeing to let our food digest before returning to the grim reality.

Now, finally, we're on the road.

"I need to stop at work first," I tell him, accelerating into a gap in the traffic circle.

"Work?"

"My catering business," I remind him.

"Oh. Right. I thought you ran that out of your house."

"I take calls there, and have a home office, but the actual food is prepared elsewhere. I've got to speak to Connie, my floor manager."

The warehouse is only a few miles from the motel, and traffic is light, so we're there in less than ten minutes. Shane suggests I cruise past the place, make sure no media hounds are baying for my blood.

I recognize most of the cars in the lot, in particular Connie's new lime-green Beetle, with the small bouquet of real cut flowers she always keeps in the vase bolted to the dash. She loves that little car, and it makes me ache with wanting to explain what has happened. God knows what she's heard on the news, or via local gossip.

"You want me inside?" Shane asks.

I kill the ignition and take a deep breath, heart pounding. "Better do this myself," I tell him. Not at all sure that I'm capable of explaining Randall Shane to anyone, let alone a group of anxious employees.

Inside the warehouse, I hear a buzz of voices coming from the industrial kitchen down the hall. First person I see upon opening the door is Sherona, our pastry chef, and when she spots me her chubby brown face actually pales. "Oh!" she squeaks. "Oh!"

"Hi, Sherona. Hi, Connie. Hi, everybody."

"Oh, my God!" says Connie, hands to her mouth. "We heard you were in jail!"

I plop down onto a stool, next to the rack of ovens. Which are not being utilized, I can't help noticing. The day's work has not yet commenced. Perfectly understandable, considering that the boss has just been unveiled as a killer mom, or at the very least a suspect in a murder.

"Okay, people, if you'll listen up, please. I only want to say this once, and hope you'll understand if I'm not my usual charming self." That produces a guffaw from Sherona, and suddenly there are a few tentative grins showing on the concerned faces. "I was in jail, but no charges have been filed."

"What happened, Kate?" Connie wants to know.

Connie Pendergast, six feet tall in her flats, is lean and angular, with great cheekbones and what my mother used to call a "strong" nose. Profile a bit like Virginia Woolf, come to think, or maybe Nicole Kidman playing Woolf. Someone trying to be unkind might describe Connie as "horsey," but I'd argue that she's handsome. Beautiful gray eyes that glow with intelligence, and a clear, tightly pored complexion make her look at least a decade shy of her forty years. Connie is twice divorced, currently paired with Mr. Yap, her pathologically spoiled Pekingese, and is one of the few women I know who play chess seriously.

As a manager, she happens to be so utterly competent I've been toying with the idea of making her partner. Or at least giving her an interest in the business. Haven't mentioned it to her yet, and this isn't the time. No guarantee the business will even survive, given the current state of affairs.

"I can't go into all the details right now," I continue, trying to sound more confident than I feel. "So here's the short version. My son, Tommy, was kidnapped three days ago. I paid the ransom but he has not been returned. The kidnappers, or someone in league with them, killed Fred Corso and left his body in my house. Evidence implicating me was placed on his body. The police consider me a prime suspect but have not yet indicted me. I've no idea what they're going to do."

"What are *you* going to do?" Connie wants to know.

"I'm going to find my son. I've hired an expert on recovering abducted children. He thinks we've got a good shot at finding Tommy alive. Obviously, I won't have time to be here, looking after the business, so I'm going to rely on all of you to get the job done."

They all looked stunned, maybe even a little frightened. Most of the employees I know very well, having worked with them every day. A few are recent hires, less familiar to me, and my next statement is really for them.

"Here's the deal—stick by me and I'll stick by you. Or stick by the business, if you want to think of it that way. For now, everyone gets paid. If the catering dries up because my reputation is ruined, I'll sell off the assets and divide them among the employees. That's my promise. In return, I ask that you not discuss me or my son or this business with anyone from the media. Will you all agree to that?"

Twelve somber faces nod agreement.

"We need to talk privately," I say to Connie, and she follows me into the small, stacked-with-can-goods room we share as an office.

When the door is eased shut I hand her a box of tissues and say, "First thing, I want you to stop crying."

She weeps, blows her formidable nose, keeps on weeping. "Poor Tomas," she manages to say between blows. "I can't stop thinking about him. He's such a sweet kid. He must be so scared."

I take back the box of tissues and blot away my own tears. "Great," I say. "Now we're both weeping."

"It's just so horrible."

"I really need you, Con. The kidnappers got all my cash. The lawyer is taking a lien on the house. God knows what the investigator is charging, I haven't had the courage to ask him yet. So the business needs to make money for as long as we can, okay?"

"Okay," she says, making one last honk into a wad of tissues. "Phone has been ringing off the hook. I switched it to voice mail."

I nod. "When I leave, switch it back. What are they saying?"

"They're worried we won't show up. For most of them it's too late to find another caterer."

"Anybody cancel?"

"No," says Connie, looking shocked. "Why would they do that?"

"Oh, I don't know. Maybe they don't want their wedding catered by a kidnapping killer mom?"

"Nobody thinks that!" Connie says vehemently.

"What did you hear on the news?"

Connie gives me an odd look. "You don't know? You didn't watch?"

"Didn't have the guts."

Connie sighs and shrugs. "Lots of alleged this and sources said that. Something about a custody fight for Tomas and poor Fred got in the way. Nothing very specific."

For the last year or so I've been leaving the planning and preparation to Connie and the crew, and concentrating my own efforts on corporate sales. Obviously, that's not possible right now. We'll go with what we've got and worry about the future when it gets here. If it gets here.

"We're booked solid for two months, right?"

"You know we are," Connie says with a small, satisfied smile. "We're the best, my dear. Clients check with us before they set wedding dates."

"They do, don't they?"

"Darn right they do. And a lot of the invitations I see include the phrase 'refreshments provided by Kate Bickford.' Not even Katherine Bickford Catering. Just your name. That's how well known you are."

"How well known 'we' are," I correct her. "I haven't baked a pie or a cookie in two years."

"Doesn't matter. People trust us to bring them great food. And that won't change."

"Thanks, Coach. This is exactly what I needed to hear."

Connie responds by giving me a hug. Making me feel small and safe because she's so much taller than I am, and because I can sense the strength radiating from her angular frame.

"You are not to worry about the business," she tells me. "Worry about Tomas, or the cops, or the lawyers, or whatever else you have on your mind, but do not worry about the business."

I pull away, wiping my eyes. "You're the best, Con."

Connie smiles. "I really am. Now beat it. Go find Tomas."

I'm out of the warehouse and on my way to the parking lot when a hand touches my shoulder. Hits me like an electrical zap, but when I turn it's only Sherona, looking appalled to have frightened me.

"Sorry," she says meekly. "Didn't mean to scare you."

"What can I do for you?" I respond, dreading that she's about to give notice. We've been through four pastry chefs in five years and Sherona is by far the best, and the most reliable. A bit rocky for the first few months, but since she settled in and developed the necessary confidence her work has been superb.

"Just wanted to say, ma'am, doesn't matter if you did it, not to me."

I'm so stunned I can't think of how to respond.

Sherona, aware of my discomfort, begins to speak faster and faster. "I mean, it's like what I'm trying to say is, I'm sure you didn't do it and you're innocent and everything, but even if you did do it you must have had a reason. Maybe that cop got physical on you or something, you had to defend yourself."

The look of intense concentration on her normally angelic face reminds me of something I'd put out of my mind, since Sherona herself never brought it up after she started work. According to her résumé, and several letters of recommendation, her training as a pastry chef had taken place at the Bridgeport Sanctuary, a shelter for abused women. So she undoubtedly knows a thing or two about threatening males, and the fear they instill in otherwise strong and self-reliant females. And she's assuming I may have had a similar experience.

She's right, in a way. But I can't let her think that my old friend the sheriff deserved to be killed.

"Fred Corso was never abusive to me," I tell her, "or to the kids, or to anyone that I know of, okay?"

"If you say so, ma'am."

"The only man who ever abused me is still out there, and he's got my son."

"You gonna find him, though."

"I'm gonna find him."

Sherona smiles, relieved not to have offended me. "When you do find that sucker, the kidnap man, you want to pop him in the oven or something, you call on me."

"I will, Sherona. Thank you."

On the way to the rental car I'm thinking, pop the kidnap man in the oven. Not a bad idea. Not a bad idea at all.

The boy comes awake very slowly. The first thing he's aware of is the inescapable fact that he's wet the bed. Again wet sheets, the stench of his own urine. Then the feel of the gag in his mouth—it tastes like throw-up. A moment later he becomes aware of the tight, tingly numbness of his wrists and ankles. White plastic straps securing him to the bed. He remembers the straps from the last time he woke up, and the sneering voice that threatened to put rubber pants on him. Rubber pants like a baby.

Bastards.

He remembers calling out for his mother, too. This time he won't make that mistake. Obviously Mom isn't here, or none of this would be happening. Still, he searches his mind for the most recent memory of his mom. Was it standing in the dugout, cheering him on? Maybe. No, no, after the game. Giving him money. Ice-cream money. But he never got the ice cream. Something happened. What was it exactly?

Choking. A hand covering his face. White van. No, the white van was first. Then a door sliding open. Shadow behind him. Then the hand on his face, a whiff of something powerful. Dizzy darkness. Next thing, his bladder hurting. Voice of a stranger, threatening him.

Kidnapped.

Tomas had heard scary stories about strangers who steal children, but the stories never had anything to do with him. Scary junk about sickos, or vampires, or slimy monsters from outer space, they were all the same really. Just stuff to make you shiver. Not real.

This is real.

Not fair, he's thinking. A sense of unfairness so deeply felt it feels like heat spreading from his belly. The heat overwhelms the cold knot of fear, melts it away, and that makes him feel stronger. Not strong enough to break the thick plastic restraints, but strong enough to let him think.

First thing, what does he know? Tomas makes a list in his head. He knows he's been kidnapped, taken away from everything that's ever been familiar. He knows he was put to sleep somehow, and that it has happened more than once. He knows he's facedown on a bed not his own, in a room not his own. He knows there are men nearby, because if he screams they come into the room, threaten him, and put him to sleep.

Tomas knows he doesn't want to be put to sleep again, no matter how tempting that might be. He must stay awake. He must think. Mom is always telling him to use his brain. If she were here, he knows she'd want him to find a way to escape. Probably she wants him to do that anyway, no matter where she is.

He sure hopes his mom is okay, but he can't let himself think about that too much or he'll cry, and if he's crying he's not thinking.

First thing, he has to do something about the straps on his wrists and ankles. In the movies guys always fray the rope and get free. But this isn't a movie and there's nothing to fray the plastic against. Nothing but damp sheets. And when he tugs, the straps just get tighter. He tries willing his wrists smaller but that doesn't work. And he can't really see what's going on with his ankles, tangled up as they are in the ruined bedclothes.

Think. *There's always a way, if you use your brain, young man.*

Tomas is thinking as hard as he can when a door opens behind him and footsteps come softly into the room.

"Dammit!"

The boy steels himself for a blow. Instead, a dark form appears in his peripheral vision. Can't quite focus, but this man, like the others, conceals his face with a kind of mask.

"I told them not to let this happen," the voice says. "My bad, Tomas. You deserve better than this."

Something shiny near his face. A knife. The boy flinches, squeezing shut his eyes.

"Shh," the voice says. "Easy now. Here's what I'm going to do. First I'm going to cut away the gag. You must promise not to scream. No one to hear you anyhow. Then, I'll free your hands and feet. You promise not to scream?"

Tomas nods.

The blade slices through the gag and he can breathe through his mouth. He takes great, gulping lungs full of air. Then coughs, because the stench of the ruined bed is so acrid.

Suddenly his hands and feet are free. Didn't even feel the knife slicing through the plastic straps. Which makes him even more afraid of the blade, what it can do.

"Roll off the bed onto the floor," the voice commands. "Sit there."

Tomas slides off the bed, away from the blade. He's dizzy, not sure if he could stand even if he wasn't so afraid of the voice and the knife it wields.

"We're going to treat you better, Tomas," the man says. "There will be a new mattress, fresh clothes. No more drugs. I want you to be healthy. Do you want to be healthy, Tomas?"

Tomas hates that the voice knows his name. He's afraid to look up at the man with the knife.

"Answer me, son."

He hates that the man calls him "son." But he's afraid not to answer. "Yes," he says.

"Yes, what?"

"Yes, I want to be healthy," he says, speaking into his hands.

"Good. Excellent. You're going to do me a big favor, Tomas," the man says. "You know what the big favor is? Can you guess?"

"No," the boy says.

"It's very simple, really. You're going to make things right."

There's something about the highway, about getting the show on the road, that makes me feel almost optimistic. Maybe because I'm finally doing something, making decisions, taking action.

Today is the day, I'm thinking. The day I find my son. The day Tommy comes home.

Have to think like that or I'll fall apart.

Ted used to joke about potholes on 295 that were big enough to swallow Hummers. And that was long before military vehicles became the new station wagons. As I'm discovering, the pothole thing hasn't exactly improved over the years. On the approach to the Throgs Neck they have the look and feel of bomb craters, and once or twice my passenger's head comes close to smacking the underside of the car roof. Not that he's complaining. Nothing less than an exploding land mine would break his concentration on the coffee he's been sipping since we got on the thruway heading south.

Earlier, explaining his sleep disorder, he'd mentioned "zoning out." Apparently that means staring at the dashboard with unfocused eyes as his right hand robotically feeds a steady dose of Starbucks caffeine into his system. Several times I've attempted to initiate a conversation, but his response is limited to noncommittal grunts.

I've owned dogs that were more responsive to my queries.

Shane snaps out of it as we begin our descent from the bridge. Suddenly his eyes brighten, his posture changes, he's back in my world. "Little nap," he says, yawning happily. "I feel much better."

"That was a nap?"

He shrugs. "My version. Not refreshing, exactly, but it helps."

Traffic opens, I find the right lane, slotting us into the flow for the Cross Island. After we successfully negotiate our way onto the parkway, Shane suddenly announces, "I've been thinking about motivation."

"Motivation?" I'm at a loss. Is he about to bring up the so-far unmentioned subject of his fee?

"There's the money extorted from you," he says. "Half a million bucks is plenty of motivation. But if they have that kind of access into bank software, it's a good guess they could have drained your accounts without having to risk a child abduction. Not to mention killing a cop."

"You just said 'they,'" I say, interrupting. "So you really think I'm right? There's more than just, um, Bruce?"

"I do," he says. "An abduction that involves ransom or extortion almost invariably requires teamwork. I'm assuming Bruce is team leader."

"Okay," I say, keeping my eyes on the fleet of battle-scared cabs that have suddenly surrounded us. "Sorry for interrupting, you said something about motivation."

"Yes. There's a strong possibility this wasn't just about the money."

"And that's good?" I ask hopefully.

He shoots me a wary look. "Can I be blunt?"

"Go ahead."

"Once Bruce had the money, why not kill you? From his point of view, you've served your purpose. Why leave you alive and go to the trouble of planting evidence implicating you in a murder?"

"How about this?" I say vehemently. "Because he's a sadistic monster. Because he's a sick, sick son of a bitch."

"No doubt," Shane agrees. "But he's a sick monster with a very specific and well-planned agenda. I'm assuming the whole thing of setting you up for a murder, making it look like you're in a custody dispute, all of that is an elaborate diversion from his actual purpose. He's creating a lot of light and smoke, making sure the major law enforcement agencies aren't treating this as a straight-ahead child abduction. He's got something else planned."

"And taking Tommy is part of his plan?"

"Yes. He's buying time. Which means, whatever he wants to accomplish, it isn't over yet."

"And that's a good thing?"

"Absolutely. Everything Bruce has done so far convinces me your son is still alive."

A horrifying thought: Shane has been searching for a reason to believe that my son is alive.

"What about this woman who claims to be his birth mother?" I ask somewhat lamely. The air now definitely out of my optimistic balloon.

"We'll know more by the end of the day," Shane assures me. "But my experience is that birth mothers rarely kidnap children after so many years have elapsed without contact. Your son is what, eleven years old?"

"Eleven, yes." I get a flash of his last birthday party—total chaos of screaming boy-monsters—and feel a lump forming in my throat.

"A distraught birth mother might change her mind and take drastic action after a few months. Possibly even a year or two," Shane says, nodding to himself. "But after a decade? After that long, why not just go through the courts to establish shared custody, or visitation, or whatever? Why risk a felony conviction—a very serious felony conviction—when the child is going to be legally of age in two more years?"

"Legally of age? What are you talking about? In two years Tommy will only be thirteen."

"Exactly," Shane says. "And at age thirteen, most custodial judges will defer to the child. All things being equal, they'd let him make up his own mind regarding who has custody, or at least who he lives with. It's actually a practical application of the law, because by the time they're teenagers, unhappy kids run away, or find their way back to the parent of choice anyhow, no matter what the law or the social workers decree."

The whole subject of a possible birth mother makes me feel very unsettled. Not quite skin crawling, but close. Reminds me of how relieved I'd been when Ted told me the parents were deceased, that we were adopting an orphaned child. Which also made me feel guilty, for benefiting from a tragedy. Guilt that was swept away by the flood of joy when I took the baby in my arms and felt his little heart beating. *He's afraid, too,* I thought, and then, *but I can fix that.* And I did fix it, by a simple act of love. Proving to myself that I could mother a child not my own, and in that way make him as much a part of me as if he had been conceived with my own DNA.

Or so I thought at the time. The idea that his birth mother might be alive changes everything, throwing me back into a deep unease about my place in Tommy's world. Unease somehow separate from my anxiety about his current well-being.

Every minute, every hour without my son makes me more uneasy, motherwise. Anxious not that my love for him will ever abate—no chance—but that he will no longer feel the same way about me. Knowing there may be another Tommy-mom in the world changes everything, doesn't it?

"So how did you get into this crazy business?" I ask my passenger, if only to distract myself.

Shane studies me, as if unsure how much information should be shared with a client. "I was with the bureau," he finally admits. "The FBI. After I took early retirement, I needed something to do."

His hesitant tone makes it sound like he's far from certain about his own motivation. Or at the very least unwilling to discuss it with me. But I'm not ready to let him off the hook. I glance over—one eye for the traffic, one for the passenger—and ask, "So this is what you did in the FBI? Located missing children?"

Shane rubs his chin, stroking his trim little beard and grimacing slightly. "No, no. At least not like what you see on TV," he explains. "I was a special agent with an expertise in fingerprint identification. Really not so much the prints themselves, as our system for accessing prints and connecting them with perpetrators. Which means linking up with other systems, worldwide. Software stuff."

"You were a computer geek?"

"Sort of. It's not that simple. Because in addition to the prints, I also worked cases like the other agents. Mostly interviews, surveillance, wiretaps. Sometimes pure abduction cases. But I was never part of an official child recovery team."

Clearly he wants to take the conversation elsewhere, but I decide to bear down. "So you take early retirement," I say. "And then what, out of the blue you decide to set yourself up as a child recovery expert?"

A glance reveals that he's wearing a slightly bemused expression. As if letting me know that an intrusion into his personal space will be tolerated just this one time. "Not exactly," he says. "I just retired, period. Never to work a full-time job again, or so I thought. Fooled around going to sleep disorder clinics for a while, to make myself useful, you know? For research? That's where it happened."

"Where what happened?"

"Kid got snatched from the clinic day care. This technician, Darla, she brought her two-year-old to work, left her at the day care. And

Darla's sicko boyfriend, who was not the little girl's father, took her. Had a pass, so he just picked the kid up and walked out with her."

"And you helped Darla get her little girl back?"

Shane nods, studying the traffic, his hands, anything but make eye contact with me. "That's what I did. The boyfriend was trying to 'loan' the little girl to another pedophile he met on the Internet. I found out where the handoff was going to take place and recovered the child."

"What happened to the boyfriend?"

"He's doing thirty years in Leavenworth."

"Nice work, Mr. Shane."

"Thank you."

"So you recover the little girl, then you decide to make a habit of it?"

"More or less. Darla, she's very religious, she said I'd found my true calling."

"Is she still a girlfriend, Darla?"

The very idea makes Shane chuckle. "Darla? Hardly. Never was. Darla likes her men short, round and brown. I lose out in all three categories."

"Guess you would at that. Mind answering one more question?"

"Won't know until you ask it."

"What are you charging me?"

His looks surprised or bemused, or possibly both. "Haven't thought about setting a price," he says. "We'll see how it plays out."

"You don't have an hourly rate like lawyers?"

"Nope. My fee depends on what happens."

I let that soak in, absorbing the implications. "You mean your fee depends on if you get the child back alive?"

"Among other things, yes," he admits. "Is this our exit?"

He doesn't even flinch when I lay into the horn and cut over to the lane for Grand Central. This much closer to the city, the parkway is jammed with honking, flatulent vehicles. We find ourselves trapped behind a smoke-belching freight truck, visibility pretty much zero. I'm worried about missing the exit onto Queens Boulevard, but Shane spots it before I do.

Twenty minutes later we're in a day-rate parking garage a block from our destination. Haven't been to this part of Queens in years, but it looks like business is booming, with folks hurrying along sidewalks that are as crowded, if not quite so wide, as Fifth Avenue.

After shutting off the rental car, I turn to Shane and say, "Ready?"

Shane clears his throat awkwardly. "I've been thinking maybe you should stay in the car, let me handle the lawyer."

"No way," I say, opening the door. "If this guy won't tell us what we want to know, I'm going to get all medieval on him."

"Excuse me?"

"Tommy likes that expression. Now I know why."

Shane grins. "It would probably be better if you don't actually threaten his life."

Somewhere deep in the garage, wheels are screeching. The sound is like a jagged fingernail inside my brain.

"We'll see," I tell him. "I'm not leaving his office without Teresa Alonzo's number and address."

The woman who claims to be Tommy's birth mother. Oh yes, I do remember her name.

lawyers, guns and money | **20**

Enrico Vargas's office is located in a seedy brick building that houses, among other enterprises, a video-rental outlet calling itself Entertainment Express, hiding behind a blocked-out, street-level window. Porno for sure. Shane shrugs, as if to say he expected no less: low-rent lawyer in low-rent location. Inside the foyer we stop to check out the listings for office suites, and find Vargas advertising himself as "Attorney to the People—Free Consultation," which makes me expect to find a waiting room full of scamming whiplash clients.

The dingy hallway actually lifts my spirits. I'm thinking a cut-rate shyster hasn't got the resources of, say, a midtown law firm. Which from my point of view is a good thing.

"What if he's not in?" I ask, needing to fret about something. "What if he's out staging a fender bender?"

"He's in," Shane assures me as we mount the stairs to the second floor. "I took the liberty of making an appointment."

"And he agreed to see us?"

"He agreed to see a man who thinks he has a case against a local McDonald's. Second-degree burns from hot fat on the French fries."

"You lied to him?"

"I gave him a reason to be here," Shane says with a grim smile.

Strange how my perceptions have changed. A few days ago the idea of a man lying for me would have been repugnant. Now it pleases me.

As it happens, Attorney Vargas does not occupy one of the euphemistically listed office suites. He simply has access to a so-called conference room, in reality a bare, beige-walled cubicle barely large enough to contain a battle-scared table and several heavy chairs. No waiting room, no gum-snapping receptionist and no shifty-eyed clients faking injuries from accidents that never happened. No windows, even. Just a briefcase, a tablet of yellow-lined paper, a cell phone and Enrico Vargas himself, slitting open his mail with a chromed letter opener.

Vargas, I must admit, is more impressive than I anticipated, given the modest surroundings. He's a handsome, heavyset gentleman in his midthirties with an unruly mop of thick, dark hair, cheerful brown eyes that beam with intelligence and a very engaging smile that shows off his white and perfect teeth. His dark blue suit isn't quite of Armani quality, but he wears it well, and it's a far cry from the off-the-rack sacks favored by ambulance chasers, at least those I've seen depicted on television cop shows.

"Welcome, I think," says Vargas, eyeing us with a kind of resignation, as if he's used to deceitful clients, and reluctantly prepared for every eventuality. "I'm looking for a bandage, Mr. Shane. Don't see a bandage. Burns require a bandage."

"I'm a quick healer. May we sit?"

"Sure, sit." He lays the letter opener carefully on the table, nudging it away with his plump pinkie finger, as if afraid it might bite like an ungrateful client. "Is this Mrs. Shane?" he asks, directing his high-beam smile at me. "Are you a quick healer, too?"

"My name is Katherine Bickford. Sound familiar?"

Takes a moment, but he recognizes my name.

"Aw shit," he says, affecting to be terribly disappointed in us. "Either of you carrying a concealed weapon by any chance?"

"I am," says Shane.

"You going to use it?"

"Not unless provoked. We're just after a little information, Mr. Vargas. Nothing that should trouble you."

"My friends call me Rico."

"We're not your friends."

Vargas sighs, resigned to whatever trouble we're bringing to him. "You never know. I'm quite lovable once you get to know me. First let me apologize for the humble surroundings," he says, indicating the small and dreary room. "I pretty much live in the courthouse and work out of my briefcase, so why waste all that money on an office?"

"You're a criminal lawyer," Shane says, making it sound like an accusation.

"A good one, too," Vargas says. "Mrs. Bickford, you find yourself in need of another attorney, keep me in mind. I'm licensed in Connecticut. Probably bill a whole lot less than whoever you've got now."

The offer has me nonplussed—can he be serious? Shane sees me about to stammer and interjects, "Mrs. Bickford already has very adequate counsel, Mr. Vargas. As I'm sure you're aware. We're here to ask a few questions about the custody suit you filed on behalf of Teresa Alonzo."

"Sorry," Vargas says lightly. "No can do. Shane, are you a cop? I get this cop feel about you."

"Licensed investigator," Shane responds in the clipped, don't-mess-with-me tone he hasn't used since our initial contact on the phone.

"Investigator used to be a cop," Vargas decides, continuing to study him the way a wary zoo attendant studies a caged tiger. "Not a beat cop, either. You're more the cerebral type. Feds, was it?"

Shane shrugs, as if he doesn't want to waste time trading guesses.

"You can check me out later, Mr. Vargas. I'm sure you've got your sources. Right now the subject is you. How a guy who stands in the back of night court hoping for a Public Defender assignment gets himself involved in a kidnapping scheme."

"Kidnapping?" Vargas looks like he's suddenly developed intestinal distress. "You serious?"

"Let me guess," Shane says, leaning his long arms on the table. His splayed-out hands no more than a few inches from the attorney's plump, manicured fingers. "This lady calling herself Teresa Alonzo comes out of nowhere, drops a nice little fee in your briefcase. Says all you have to do is file the papers."

"Whoa. Back up. You just said *kidnapping*," Vargas says. "That's a very ugly word. Please explain."

"You're part of a conspiracy, Mr. Vargas. That's my explanation. Maybe you don't know the details—maybe you didn't want to know—but now the shit has hit the fan and you're in it up to your size seventeen neck."

Vargas touches his collar and sighs. "Go on," he says. "Insult me all you want."

"The custody suit you filed? It's part of a kidnap/murder. Mrs. Bickford's boy was snatched at a Little League game. She was held against her will. Her bank accounts were ransacked. A cop got killed. Her son is still missing. And there's an excellent chance that the papers you filed are part of a conspiracy to divert the investigation for a few crucial days. When they get around to checking out Miss Alonzo and find out she's no more the birth mother of Tommy Bickford than I am, you'll be hung out to dry. All for what? Five hundred? A thousand? I bet the paperwork was already done, all it needed was your signature. A service you provide for certain clients. Clients with cash, I'm betting."

I get the impression Rico Vargas isn't listening very intently to Shane, not to the particulars. Something is clicking over in his nimble brain, calculations based on one or two of Shane's details. If I'm not mistaken, the look in his eyes betrays worry, if not outright fear. "I think you should both leave now," he announces. "I really can't discuss these matters."

"Give us Alonzo's street address," Shane demands, sounding very much like a police detective who won't take no for an answer. "Give us her address, and we walk."

Vargas shakes his head regretfully. Wanting us to think he'd really love to help, were it not for his deep moral conviction that he can't betray a client. "No can do. I'd be breaking confidentiality. I'm afraid we have nothing further to discuss."

"Give it up, Mr. Vargas," Shane suggests, not bothering to disguise an air of barely restrained menace. "Any way you want. Write us a note. Walk out of the room and leave your briefcase behind. Say it in pig latin. Whatever method salves your conscience. But we're not leaving without her address."

Vargas sighs deeply, theatrically, and then has the nerve to look to me for support. "Please tell him, Mrs. Bickford. Threatening me will only get him in trouble."

Something has been bubbling inside me for the last few minutes, a kind of outrage at the whole bantering conversation between the two men. How dare they quip and posture when the underlying subject of their conversation is my missing son!

"Tell him yourself, you son of a bitch!" I demand, waving the letter opener in front of the lawyer's chubby, self-satisfied face. "That woman may have my son, do you understand! Tell us what we want to know, or so help me God I'll poke your lying eyeballs right out of your head!"

Both men are shocked, but then, so am I. Who is this woman threatening a two-hundred-pound man with a sharp weapon? Has she lost her mind? I don't even remember picking up the opener, so how did this happen?

The scary thing, the really scary thing, is that if I thought assaulting Vargas would get me back my son, I'd do it. Do it in a heartbeat.

Vargas has backed his chair against the wall, eyes clocking the waving blade of the letter opener. Ready to duck if I lunge.

"You're a witness," he tells Shane, pleading. "Your client has threatened to blind me."

"It's not exactly a switchblade, Rico."

"Yeah? For your information people get killed with office implements all the time. I had a client once who murdered a guy with a tape dispenser."

Shane shrugs calmly. "My advice, Rico? Take her very seriously. Think about it. How would you feel if it was your kid got snatched, and some fat shyster wouldn't give up the name of a possible abductor?"

Something about Shane's reasonable tone makes me lower the blade and toss it on the table, where it clatters like a cheap toy.

Vargas sighs in relief, then slyly retrieves the blade, slipping it into his briefcase.

"The address. I want to talk to this woman. I want to ask her about my son."

Vargas stands up, as much to keep out of my range as to impose his size on the room. "I wish I could help, Mrs. Bickford. I really do. But I can't."

He's about to add something else when his cell phone rings. He picks it up, flips it open with the dexterity of a man who lives and dies by phone connections. Raising a practiced finger to indicate that he simply has to take this call, and he knows we'll understand. "Attorney Vargas," he says, giving me an apologetic, just-be-a-minute smile. "Yeah, yeah," he says into the phone. "Funny you should ask. No, of course not. Right here with me, yes." He pauses, listening for a few beats, and his expression grows somber. "Uh-huh," he says. "I suppose that's a possibility." Then he snaps the phone shut and stands up.

"I may have something for you after all," he announces. "Wait right here. I have to return this call."

"So return it here," Shane suggests.

"Sorry, no, Mr. Fed. Has to be a secure location. Meaning I have to be able to talk freely without being overheard. I'm sure you understand."

"We'll come with you," Shane suggests.

Vargas shakes his head, dislodging a thick lock of dark hair. "Not if you want any further information from me. That's the deal. Five minutes."

"Five?"

"Wait here. If you follow me, I can't take the call."

Shane glances at me and shrugs. "Five," he says.

Vargas snags his briefcase, gives me a wink that implies my troubles will soon be over, and strides from the room, leaving the door ajar. He has that comfortable, fat man's agility that suggests he'd be a good dancer, nimble and balanced and graceful. His feet pad down the hallway, seemingly in no particular hurry, and then he's gone.

Vargas hurries. Some edge to the voice on the phone puts urgency into his normally measured pace. He's keenly aware of how he looks in motion, preferring to glide into a room, using his bulk to impress, not to inspire smirks. Nobody likes to see a big man go too fast, unless they're looking for comic effect, the old high-speed waddle perfected by funnymen from Fatty Arbuckle to John Candy. Vargas loathes the very idea. Thankfully the dimly lit hallway is vacant and nobody can see his blubber shifting from side to side, distorting the cut of his fine, Italian wool suit.

As he moves down the hallway he's calculating whether or not to hit the mysterious Mr. Smith up for another fee. Vargas had been aware from the start that the custody suit wasn't exactly kosher, that the custody filing was either a smoke job or a mindfuck of some kind. Smith had assured him that nothing would come of it—certainly he'd never have to appear in court—that the purpose of the suit was simply to intimidate Mrs. Bickford into settling out of court.

All along, Vargas had been assuming that the man who called himself Smith was the biological father, although he'd never claimed to be. Never said word one about why he was involved, or why he was acting for the mysterious Ms. Alonzo. Personally Vargas had his doubts that the woman really existed. Not that he really cared. Five grand in cash to file papers? Easy money. Now it didn't look quite so easy, not with an investigator nosing around. Certainly not with the mother showing her face. And he absolutely had not envisioned that the filing might somehow have triggered a felony murder, or any felony whatsoever, other than the rather ordinary, everyday felony-intent he'd committed by pocketing Smith's cash with no intention of reporting it on his Schedule C.

As Vargas backs into the communal bathroom he already has his cell phone in hand, ready and waiting for Smith to call back. His idea of a secure location is somewhere he can't be overheard by the hard-eyed investigator. What was his name, Shane? Ought to be Shame, for fibbing to set up an appointment.

The big man stares at the tiny little cell screen, willing the phone to trill. Can't simply call back because Smith, who must be some sort of paranoid, has a blocked number. "Come on," Vargas says to the silent cell phone. "I haven't got all day."

A toilet flushes. Vargas's beefy heart does a flip-flop. Mother of God, he hadn't checked to make sure no one was in the stall. And now he's been caught talking to himself. He's about to back through the door, find a closet or an unoccupied office, when the stall door opens and Smith himself steps out.

"Hey, Rico."

Vargas is aware that he's blushing. His face is hot, and tiny beads of sweat have begun to form along his hairline. That's always been his response to being taken by surprise, which is just one more reason why he hates to be surprised, and orders his life to avoid the experience.

"You said five minutes, you'd call back," Vargas protests.

"I thought this was better," says the man who calls himself Smith.

"You were already in the building? Why didn't you just say so?"

"Try and keep your voice down, Rico," Smith suggests.

The smaller man slips behind the lawyer, throws the bolt on the door.

"This won't take too long," he says.

"I didn't say a word to them, if that's what you're worried about."

Vargas glances uneasily at the shot bolt. Not that he's physically afraid of the man who calls himself Smith. The guy is in shape, no question, but Vargas outweighs him by at least fifty pounds, and he's no slouch musclewise. Besides, there's nothing threatening about the man's posture or his tone of voice, which sounds utterly reasonable. Actually, thinking about it here, it makes sense to bolt the door. For all he knows, the pushy investigator has a weak bladder, and might come calling.

"I'm not worried," Smith is saying, leaning casually against the sink. "I trust you, Rico. That's why I selected you. Two dozen drug dealers can't be wrong, huh? You never ratted any of them out."

"Hard to stay in business if you rat on your clients," Vargas says.

"Hard to stay alive, too, am I right?"

Vargas shrugs. "Drug dealers never threaten me. Only people who ever threaten me are prosecutors. What is it you want, Mr. Smith?"

"I wasn't entirely straight with you, Rico. I'd like to make it right."

Vargas stands with his arms folded across his bulk, his back against the door, weighing his response. His money antennas are tingling, and that makes him feel good, from the top of his hundred-dollar haircut to the balls of his well-shod feet. "Okay," he says. "The case is a little more complicated than we both anticipated."

"You put it so nicely," says Smith. "Guess that's why you're a courtroom genius and I'm not."

"I try to avoid courtrooms," Vargas tells him truthfully. "Better to get it done before you go to court."

"Couldn't agree more," Smith tells him. "I need you to stand tall, amigo. Cops start asking you about Teresa Alonzo, you refuse to respond, even if it means problems with the judge or the bar association."

"I never met the lady," Vargas points out. "Can't reveal what I don't know, whatever any judge may say."

"See how easy this is going to be?"

"You said something about making it right."

"Money isn't a problem for me at the moment," says the man who calls himself Smith. "I can afford to be generous with my friends. So as a token of friendship, I'm going to give you an additional five grand, for having to deal with nosy cops."

"Guy's not a cop," Vargas explains. "He's just an investigator. Can't compel testimony of any kind. Don't worry about him, he's not a problem."

"Good, good. So will five grand make it right between us?"

"That's very generous, Mr. Smith. Although, come to think of it, I might have to bill you more than that if I get brought up on ethics charges."

"Is that a possibility?"

"It happens," Vargas says, trying to exude concern. Actually, he's not particularly worried. He's been brought up on ethics violations before and easily prevailed. Bogus custody filing shouldn't be a problem, since it will be almost impossible to prove he hasn't met the lady in question. *Miss Alonzo took off, what can I say, Your Honor? Had no idea the custody suit wasn't valid. Crazy clients, what's a guy to do?*

"Whatever is fair," the man who calls himself Smith is saying. "I'll make it worth your while."

"I better get back," Vargas says. "Tell Mrs. Bickford I'm sorry, but I can't help her."

"Be nice about it," the man suggests. "She's been through a lot."

"I'm always nice. By the way, when can I expect the additional fee?"

"Got it right here," says the man who calls himself Smith. "In my pocket."

the boy scout | **22**

"Don't get your hopes up," Shane warns me, shortly after Vargas leaves the room, supposedly to find a "secure location" for his phone call.

"He said he might have something for us," I remind him. "That was her on the line, wasn't it?"

Shane shrugs. "Maybe, maybe not. He could be messing with us, Mrs. Bickford."

"But we give him the full five minutes."

"Sure," Shane says. "Why not?"

He leans back in the chair, staring at his hands.

"Can I ask you a question?" I say, before he zones out to wherever it is he goes.

"Go ahead."

"You really carrying a gun?"

He shakes his head. "Were you really going to poke his eyes out?"

"If I thought it would work," I tell him.

Shane smiles. "You're a peach, Mrs. Bickford."

I don't feel like a peach. I feel like the top of my head is going to spin off. Skin clammy, mouth dry with anticipation. This could be it.

A connection to Tommy. Somewhere to start. My rational self knows that Shane is right, I shouldn't get my hopes up. But my hopes are already up there, Everest high, and there's nothing I can do about it.

Tommy. Have they hurt him? What's he thinking, what's he feeling at this precise moment? Can he sense that I'm reaching out to him with every ounce of my being?

The idea of what my son must be going through makes me ache so deeply that I feel capable of making any sacrifice that might lead to his return. Scratch out an attorney's eyes, throw myself in front of a bus, anything. The chaos of emotions makes me so dizzy that it's just as well I'm sitting down.

If Shane senses what I'm enduring, he gives no sign of it, and resumes staring at his hands. Not with me, here in this fetid little room, but elsewhere. Planet Shane, where no one sleeps, and dreams come to the wide-awake.

He's zoning out. Meanwhile I'm fretting, checking my watch every thirty seconds. Thinking it all comes down to this, a crucial phone call. A name. Something to work with. A place to start.

After a century or so, five minutes have passed.

"Shane?"

His tall, rangy body shudders slightly as he awakens from his trance. Blinks his eyes, clears his throat, checks his own watch. "Right. Wait here, I'll check on Rico."

"No way. I'm coming with you."

"Suit yourself. But I expect he's pulled a Copperfield, made himself vanish."

The dingy hallways are empty, which seems odd, considering that this is a very busy, vital part of the borough. Even the cheesiest real estate must be expensive, or as Connie likes to say, even the low-end is high-end. But we appear to have the place to ourselves. No sign of Vargas, no sign of anybody.

Shane strides purposefully along, methodically trying doors, finding all of them locked. Nothing furtive about his actions, either. He behaves as if he has a perfect right to try doors, as if he's been poking into places much like this his whole life and pretty much knows what to expect. Which, in turn, gives me confidence that I've latched on to the right person, the man who can help me find my son.

"I'm thinking our new pal Rico has access to another one of these rooms," he explains. "One for interviewing clients, another for the private stuff. Calling his bookie, checking in with his parole officer or whatever."

"Parole officer?" I respond, startled. "You're kidding, right?"

"I'm kidding. Savalo checked him out for us. Enrico Vargas is a member in good standing of the New York State Bar. But I also made a few inquiries of my own, from different sources. Word is that Vargas has an unsavory reputation for getting deep into the pockets of his lowlife clients. Suspected of passing on jailhouse instructions to criminal enterprises, possible money laundering, and so on. Most of his paying clients are midlevel drug dealers."

"You think he's personally involved? That he already knows where they've got Tommy?"

"Nah," says Shane, rattling doorknobs. "I think he's being played. And I think he's worried, which should be in our favor. Assuming we can locate the son of a bitch."

The last door in the hallway is labeled Restroom in both English and Spanish, and there's no need to rattle the lock because the door is propped open with a wastebasket.

"Must be unisex, huh?" Shane wants to know. "As well as bilingual."

"I guess."

"So it doesn't matter who looks inside."

"I'll do it."

"No, no," says Shane. "I'm the designated bathroom-looker."

He shoves aside the waste can and steps inside, letting the door shut behind him. A moment later a muffled curse erupts and I decide to follow him inside.

The bathroom has one plywood stall, well inscribed with graffiti, and a single urinal bolted to the wall. There must be a sink, too, but at the moment I don't notice one because Enrico Vargas is giving me the evil eye. The pupil of one of his handsome brown eyes is hugely dilated, and somehow fierce, while the other eye appears disinterested. He sits on the floor with his back against the wall, seriously endangering the seat and cuffs of his well-tailored suit. His mouth is open, as if he's about to say something but can't quite think of the word.

Before he can speak a tiny drop of blood exits his left nostril and lands, *plink!,* on his crisply pressed shirt collar, and that's when I know he'll never think of the word, or anything at all, ever again.

Shane crouches, getting a better angle but keeping physically clear of the body. "I'll be damned. You can barely see it at the back of his neck, under all that hair. An ice-pick handle."

On TV when people come unexpectedly upon a corpse they always seem to throw up. Even TV cops start gagging. But I feel nothing. Nothing in the form of a great, flat numbness, as if my whole body has been injected with Novocaine. Plus, I'm really, really angry at Rico for screwing up. He was going to be my connection, the facilitator of my own personal mother-and-child reunion.

Next thing I know Shane has me around the shoulders and he's making me face the other wall so I can't see the dead lawyer and his stupid evil eye, the pupil dilated by an ice pick inserted deep into his brain.

"We have to move fast, so I want you to concentrate and listen to me, okay, Mrs. Bickford?"

"Call me Kate, please." Now I'm feeling giddy, which is totally inappropriate. What have I got to feel giddy about?

"Huh? Okay, fine. Kate. Kate, you're going to go down the stairs and out the door and turn left. Go to the end of the block and you'll see the garage where we parked. Get the rental car and leave the area. Don't even think about what happened here because you were never here, you never met Rico Vargas."

"I never met him. Okay."

"You drove me into the city, dropped me off at a subway stop, and then you drove home."

"I drove home?" I ask. The numbness makes everything he says seem slightly silly.

"You will. You'll drive back to Fairfax. Go to the motel and wait for a call, either from me or Maria Savalo. You got that, Mrs. Bickford? Kate?"

"You want me to go back to the motel."

"Right now. The cops are probably already on the way. You can't be here."

"What about you?"

"I'm fine, Mrs. Bickford. Leave. Right now. Don't look back."

"He doesn't look dead, does he?" I say. "Except for the funny eye."

Shane gently but firmly pushes me out the door and guides me to the stairwell.

"We killed him, didn't we?" I ask. "By coming here, asking him questions?"

Shane shakes his head. His manner is firm, unwavering. "Poor Rico was dead before we got here," he says. "He just didn't know it."

Normally, I'm one of those people who can always recall where the car is parked. Normally, I'm focused, oriented. But normal left my world the minute Tommy vanished, and for the life of me I can't re-member where I parked the rental, or even what it looks like, exactly. Ford Taurus, okay, Ford Taurus very reliable, but what color? Silver? Gray? I wasn't really paying attention when the kid handed me the keys. And I'd been following Shane when we exited the garage, keeping up with his long strides, concentrating on how we'd handle the lawyer.

Right. Handle him to death.

Stairs. I recall coming down a flight of stairs. *Concentrate, Kate, this couldn't be more important. You need to get out of here before the po-lice arrive. Failure is not an option. Failure means getting locked up, end-ing any chance of finding Tommy before the unthinkable happens.*

Concentrate. You're getting out of the car, leaving the garage. What do you see?

Right, you came down a flight of stairs. You parked on the first level above the ground. And the rental car is no more than fifty feet from the exit door, you can see it in your mind now, you can retrace the path. Find the car, you'll be gone in five minutes. Less if you run.

I run up the concrete stairs, burst through the door, lungs heaving, and find myself in the murky half light of the garage. Take just a moment for my eyes to adjust, and then I'm off. Keys in hand, I hit the button and hear the rental car honk, the lights flash, and a spasm of relief floods my body.

I'm almost at the car, hand outstretched for the handle, when a movement catches my attention.

I'm not alone. At the other end of the garage, ten rows away, a man is hurrying for his vehicle as I am hurrying for mine. Can't make out his face or any individual features in the perpetual twilight, but there's something about the way he moves. A kind of coiled, athletic grace. He's got great posture and balance, an inner gyroscope that keeps him precisely vertical.

I know that walk. Saw it up close and personal.

"Hey!" I yell. "Hey!"

Of course I could be wrong. My mind playing tricks, turning every innocent pedestrian into the man in the mask. Not that this man is wearing a mask. A ball cap that casts a shadow over his face, but no mask.

Could be him.

"Stop!" I find myself screaming. "Wait!"

The figure turns, looks in my direction. Freezes for the time it takes my heart to clunk once, and then he slips away so swiftly it's as if he's not there.

Slipping like a furtive shadow between the rows of parked cars.

Two options. I can give chase on foot, or get into my car, lock the doors and attempt to follow him. Decide there's no way to catch up to him on foot, and if I do, then what? Threaten to attack him with a letter opener no longer in my possession?

There's a third possibility, much more likely. That yelling like an idiot has not only alerted him to my presence, but made me a target of opportunity. That he's slipping through the shadows right now, heading my way.

Get in the car, Kate. Now.

Inside the rental, I attempt to lock the doors with the switch and succeed in making the horn sound. Good move, let him know exactly where you are. Reaching over, I slam down all the locks and then the engine is running and I'm screeching backward out of the space, the wheel spinning in my hands.

Never burned rubber in my life. Always a first time. As I jam the brakes and force the transmission into drive, a big silver SUV fishtails around a corner and bears down on me like a fear-seeking missile.

No place to go. I'm unable to turn in any direction without putting myself directly in the approaching vehicle's path. Backing up will only force me into a parking slot, pinned on both sides. I'm trapped, frozen like Bambi in the headlights.

As the SUV draws even, a strange thing happens. The tinted side window slides down. From the dark interior an arm slowly extends. For one horrifying instant it looks like the arm is holding a gun, cocking a trigger. Shooting me between the eyes. But the hand is empty, the barrel of the "gun" is an index finger firing icy slugs of terror into my brain.

The SUV glides away, accelerates around a corner, and is gone.

Total duration, no more than a few seconds on the clock. An eternity in my heart.

Cutter merges the stolen Explorer into the traffic on Queens Boulevard for a few blocks before finding his way to a less congested parallel street. If an alert goes out for a silver Ford Explorer, good luck, he's counted ten similar vehicles in three blocks. Besides, any responding cops are likely to assume a fleeing perpetrator would use one of the Long Island expressways. Whereas he has an appointment in Manhattan and will proceed in that direction at a leisurely pace.

Tooling along with his left arm in the window, catching the summer air, he reflects upon his encounter with Mrs. Bickford. She had caught him by surprise. He'd not expected her back in the garage so soon, and certainly had not anticipated being recognized. What was it that gave him away? His profile? General size and weight? Something about the way he moved? Whatever, it hadn't been his face. He'd never been unmasked in her presence, and she could no more have made out features than he could. Indeed, at first he hadn't realized who was hailing him. Thought it might be a woman looking for help—dead battery or whatever. Not that he could have stopped to render assistance at that particular time.

'Scuse me, miss, I'd help you but I just killed a man and have to make a getaway. Cutter smiles to himself. Amazing how effective an ice pick can be as a means of execution. Quiet and effective, but particularly useful when it comes to eliminating the splatter effect. Slice a target's throat and you get covered with DNA markers. Whereas an ice pick to the brain stem is remarkably clean, if considerably more difficult to execute correctly. In that sense, mission accomplished. Not that Cutter had taken any pleasure or satisfaction in executing the lawyer. It was a thing that had to be done, to keep the plan on track. Vargas hadn't known all that much, no more than a suspicion that the custody petition was somehow bogus, and the ability to identify Cutter by face, if not by name. That was enough to seal his fate. Mrs. Bickford's actions simply made the inevitable happen sooner rather than later.

Good old Mom. Still in there swinging. In the end, all she'll accomplish is digging herself deeper and deeper into his trap, until the authorities have no choice but to charge her, even if some of the planted evidence looks, well, planted. By then it will be too late—his mission will have been accomplished. Still, you have to admire her nerve. First thing she does when she gets out of the clink is hire a freelance heavy to put the screws on witnesses. Tall, rangy-looking dude with a cool, confident way of moving that gives Cutter pause, but not so much that he's prepared to alter his plan. No need at the moment.

If they get close, ice picks are available at any hardware store. Not that he'll need to make an additional purchase, since he already has another just like it in his possession.

Always be prepared—he learned that in Boy Scouts. Except he wasn't prepared to silence Mrs. Bickford, not yet. Not while she's useful. Tells himself there's no sentimentality involved, it just makes sense to keep her front and center as a suspect. And yet, to be truthful, there's something admirable about the woman. She's braver than she thinks she is, frightened but still able to function, which is the battlefield definition of courage. Also, he's grateful that she's done such a fine job of keeping her adopted son in good health. Sickly boy would have been no use to him. Tomas will need his strength for what comes next.

We'll all need our strength, Cutter thinks. *Me, Lyla, the boy.* Very soon the next phase of the operation will be put into motion, and that's when things are likely to get a little dicey, a little edgy. No way to predict exactly what will happen next. He does know the ultimate goal—it burns in his brain like a hot gold disk—but how exactly he'll get there has yet to be determined. At this stage it's crucial that he remain flexible, not get locked into any particular scenarios or details.

All of his training has taught him the importance of flexibility, of being able to think rationally in irrational, unthinkable situations. What he has in mind is not so far removed from war, after all. In a battle the only thing certain is uncertainty. You have to accept that— accept that things will change, that events may spiral out of control— and go with the flow, always keeping your goal in mind.

Cutter's goal is simple enough. He wants his family back.

Considering what has transpired, the tragic events that have clouded poor Lyla's already delicate mind, the task of reassembling his little family is more than merely daunting. Some might conclude it impossible. Not Cutter, though. He doesn't know the meaning of impossible. He's incapable of accepting defeat. He'll win at all cost.

Hooah and all that clichéd, chest-pounding shit. The point is, he'll never give up.

That's what Cutter learned in the Boy Scouts, and later in service to his country. No matter what crap the world heaps on you, never, ever give up.

That's what he keeps telling himself now, in this desperate hour. And at the core, in the animal parts of his brain, in the marrow of his bones, in the muscles of his heart, he believes it.

Tomas has a plan. He has no idea how long he's been here, in the white room. At least a day. Maybe longer. He's tried to figure out what time it is from the TV, but the tuner doesn't seem to have a timer, at least not one he can find. And there's no cable or satellite access, just a stack of DVDs and a player. Mostly lame-o family-rated fare like *Finding Nemo* and *Agent Cody Banks,* and a dumb but fun movie called *Faster* that Mom would never let him see because of the R rating. Hot cars and girls with big butts. He'd seen it three times so far and it still doesn't suck, although he thinks it's really stupid how the guys keep doing stupid things to impress the girls. Making cars leap over cliffs and stuff, this one guy actually paragliding from his flaming car just before it smoked into the ground like a guided missile. Wicked good explosion though.

It was a scene in *Faster* that gave him the idea for his plan. It wasn't the same because there were no heavy glass vases in the white room, but he'd come up with his own variation. Tomas has no real confidence that his plan will work—these are big strong adults and he's a kid—but it gives him something to do, something to think about other than how his mom must be worried, and what the man in the mask will do to him once he stops pretending to be nice.

Tomas concentrates on imagining his escape. Picturing himself outside the white room. Getting away and being celebrated as a hero. Standing up on a podium with all the cameras strobing and the big-butt girls hugging him and stuff. "The Boy Who Got Away." "Star Short-stop Defeats Kidnappers." He'll have a scrapbook, other kids will want his autograph.

What will it look like, outside the room? Is this a regular house? The white room has no windows, so it must be in the center of the building, right? Or it could be in a warehouse, like in *Faster* where the gang is cutting up stolen Ferraris and turning them into super-cars that can run on train tracks down in the subway tunnels.

Tomas likes the warehouse idea because warehouses are big and there will be someplace to hide even if he can't escape all the way. The problem with the white room, aside from no windows, is not having a place to hide. There's no under-the-bed because the bed is just a mattress on the floor. No closets, no alcoves. No bathroom or toilet, even—just a stinky plastic potty-chair thing like old people use when they can't make it to the bathroom.

Tomas hates to use the potty-chair, but he doesn't have any choice. It's that or wet the bed. Or worse. But he doesn't have to go now, so he doesn't have to think about anything but the escape plan. Making it happen.

Except for the mattress and the TV, there's nothing in the white room but a small dresser with two drawers, and the drawers are too small for a boy his size. He knows because yesterday—was it yesterday?—he tried to squeeze himself into one of the drawers. Thinking he can hide in the dresser drawer and then wait until they look and think he's gone—*where's the kid!*—then he'll escape through the open door. Except he can't fit in the drawer, no matter how hard he tries.

It's the only time he's ever wished he was small for his age. Not just small. If only he could shrink himself up to the size of an insect, like in that old movie he used to like when he was little, *Honey, I Shrunk the Kids*. Or even better, a cloak that made you invisible, like Harry Potter had.

But there were no invisible cloaks and no shrinking ray guns in the white room. Nothing but the mattress, the stinky potty-chair and the cheesy dresser. Just enough for a plan.

Tomas works the drawer out of the dresser. Carefully and silently. For the first time since his abduction—since he got the hit that won the game—he feels exhilarated.

For the moment he truly believes that his escape plan will work, just like in the movies.

Cutter has a plan, too. He's not quite ready to put it into action because with this particular part of the plan, everything depends on timing. Not split-second, detonate-the-bomb timing. More like waiting for a piece of fruit to ripen and then biting into it at exactly the right moment.

Piece of very expensive fruit named Stanley Munk. Who is, at this very moment, pausing to look in a store window on West Fifty-first Street, in good old Manhattan. Trying to look like a casual shopper. Pathetic, really. Big important man, but when Stanley attempts to practice deception he reverts to adolescent behavior. Gets all cold and clammy, eyes darting around, palms sweating. Cutter doesn't know about the sweaty palms for sure, never having shaken the man's hands, but he was willing to bet they were sweating right now. Especially the hand that clutches the briefcase handle.

Cutter knows what Stanley has in the briefcase and how much it means to him. Thinks it's a personal matter, his secret life, but he's mistaken. Cutter knows what lurks in that briefcase, knows the sickness Munk has been hiding for years. Just as he knows where the Munkster is headed on this fine day. Disguised, or so he thinks, in jeans, Nikes, dark glasses and a Yankees baseball cap. For Stanley Munk, who favors designer Italian suits and handmade shoes, dressing down is a form of disguise. Not that it would fool anyone who was paying attention, who recognized Stanley's cocky master-of-the-universe strut, or the ever-so-slight sneer of preening confidence that is his default expression.

Very important man, our Stanley. Holds the fate of hundreds, possibly thousands, in his clever, capable hands. Hasn't a clue that he's been selected to play an important role in Cutter's master plan. No idea he's a target of opportunity because of who he is and what he can do. His particular skills.

Rather than follow the target, which might get him noticed, Cutter heads up the street, double-parks a hundred feet or so beyond the entrance to the Clarion, a hotel whose entrance is scarcely wider than its set of bronze double doors. The Clarion has eight narrow floors and fifty-six narrow rooms. Not exactly a hot-sheet hotel, not on this particular block, but the management tends to be discreet, and unlike most midtown establishments, will accept cash without the security of a credit card.

Cutter has been inside the Clarion, checked the joint out, although not at one of the times when Stanley is present. He doubts the Munkster would have any reason to recognize him, but it never hurts to be careful. He and Stan are going to get reacquainted real soon, but not today. Not until the situation ripens.

When the time comes, he wants Stanley Munk so off balance, so drenched with fear and anxiety, that he can't think straight.

Cutter adjusts the passenger-side mirror until he has the narrow hotel entrance in view. And there he is, clutching his precious briefcase, darting through the bronze doors. Where Cutter knows he will take a room under an assumed name, paying cash.

Thinks he's being clever and careful, does Stanley. Living his secret life. Less than a dozen blocks from the penthouse where he plays the big shot, entertaining all his influential friends, living the good life, less than a dozen blocks to the dark side of his world. If only they knew what distinguished, successful Stanley was up to, what really squeezed his juice, they'd recoil in disgust.

Dark side is going to cost him, big-time.

Cutter slips the stolen Explorer into gear, glides to the intersection and waits patiently for the light as about a thousand pedestrians churn across. People complain about driving in the city but he doesn't mind. All you have to do, take it one block at a time. Same deal with his master plan. Taken as a whole, it's overwhelming, perhaps impossible. But take it one step at a time, it's doable.

First secure the boy. Done.

Then the money for operating capital. Done.

Then silence Vargas. Done.

Then take over Stanley Munk's life, make sure he's totally under control, behaving predictably. Do that, cross all the *t*'s, dot all the *i*'s, it will all work out. The plan of action will all come together on the big day in Scarsdale. Has to. So long as he remains focused on the next step in the sequence, and doesn't get distracted by the sheer audacity of what he's attempting.

In ten minutes, fifteen at the most, he'll be out of the city and heading north. Heading back to the white room. Ready for the next move.

"I doubt they'll have anyone at the train station, but you never know," says Maria Savalo. "Just be ready to duck down."

At the wheel of her sleek new BMW 545i, my diminutive attorney has the confidence of Sally Ride piloting the space shuttle. She carefully removes her high heels and slips them into a special Manolo carry bag before starting the engine.

We're going to pick up Shane, who has been released from his lengthy interview with homicide detectives. Ms. Savalo knows all about what happened in Queens, the body in the bathroom, my encounter with the man in the parking garage. On the latter, she has expressed some doubts.

"You say all he did was point his finger at you?"

"You had to be there," I tell her. "It was him, I'm sure of it."

"I'm sure you're sure. But I'm a defense attorney, so I doubt everything, especially eyewitnesses."

"Why would he do that if it wasn't him?"

"In Queens? Are you serious? Guys point fingers at women all the time, whether they know them or not. There's a perfectly plausible alternative theory. Woman shouts at a man in a parking garage. Thinks he's someone she knows. Guy can't really see who it is, so he roars up in his big bad car, takes a look and blows her a kiss."

"He didn't blow me a kiss."

"It's the equivalent. That cute little move with the finger gun? I see it in pick-up bars all the time."

"Oh," I say.

"Not that I'm in pick-up bars all the time," she adds hastily. "You know what I mean."

My attorney is an expert driver. Keeps both hands on the wheel, ten and two o'clock, just like they taught us in drivers' ed back in the day. Must be different now that so few people use or even recognize analog clocks. I recall Fred Corso talking to the team about how ball players run the bases counterclockwise because most batters hit right-handed. The kids looked at him like he had two heads—counterclockwise? What was the old dude talking about?

Poor Fred. His death weighs on me. For whatever reason my son was taken, one thing seems certain: if Fred Corso didn't know us he'd be alive right now.

"They must be checking out this Teresa Alonzo person, right?" I ask Savalo. "She claims to be his birth mother, so she'd have as much reason to kidnap Tommy as me."

Ms. Savalo keeps her eyes focused on the road. "Who's 'they'? The locals, the state police, the FBI?"

"Any of them," I say, feeling indignant. "All of them."

"Maybe the FBI. Somebody might actually push a button there, and pull up a file on Rico Vargas and his clients. But unless they're actively involved, meaning that they believe your son's abduction was by a third party, it's doubtful."

"That seems crazy."

"No argument from me," Savalo responds cheerfully. "The ways of the bureau remain mysterious to us mere mortals. I assumed they'd be all over it, but they're not. As for the local cops, they don't have the resources for a wide-ranging investigation. So they concentrate on the target of opportunity—that's you. As for the state cops, they work with the prosecutor's office and they've got some very experienced investigators. So if Jared Nichols decides to check out this mysterious birth mother, he has the personnel to do it."

"Has he? Checked it out?"

"No idea. Sorry. He's a friend, but he's also a prosecutor and I'm a defense attorney. So there's a lot he can't tell me without putting himself in legal jeopardy. And Jared never puts himself in legal jeopardy. He wants to run for Senate."

"Great. Just my luck."

Savalo shoots me a look. "Not entirely a bad thing, Jared's political ambitions. It means he's very careful about who he charges. Suburban moms aren't high on his list for targets of opportunity. He prefers mobsters, corrupt union bosses, kiddy-porn rings—basically what your average suburban mom finds offensive."

The casual reference to kiddy porn makes me squirm in my seat. It's one possibility that I haven't allowed myself to consider: that my handsome boy has been taken by sexual predators. Even though I know it's the most common motivation for abduction by strangers. Sexual predators don't ask for ransom. Or do they?

I can't summon up the courage to raise the subject with Ms. Savalo. Not now. If the subject must be discussed, I'd rather do so with Randall Shane. He's the expert. And he made a point of telling me that it was a child molester abduction that got him into the business of looking for lost children. As if to warn me that the possibility was out there.

It's well past the commuter rush, and the station itself isn't busy at the moment. Of the half-dozen passengers who disembark the northbound train, only one is tall enough to be Shane.

As he comes loping down the stairs from the platform, I start to weep convulsively. Great heaving sobs.

"What's wrong?" asks Savalo with real concern.

"I d–don't know." And it's true, I don't. Certainly I didn't expect to start sobbing. It just suddenly came over me and couldn't be resisted, like the impulse to sneeze. And once I've started, it's hard to stop.

It's difficult to hug a passenger when you're the driver of a bucket-seated Beemer, but Ms. Savalo finds a way to lean across the console and embrace me, patting my back. "Tension," she says, her breath warm on my neck. "You're under incredible tension, Kate. Go on and cry, maybe it will help."

My nose is running and neither of us can find a tissue, despite rummaging through our purses. I'm a blubbering fool, but it's like a case of the hiccups, I can't seem to stop. Try holding my breath, but I'm still sobbing when Shane gently opens the rear door and slips into the seat behind me.

"What have we here?" he asks softly. "Mrs. Bickford? What's wrong?"

Silly questions. Everything is wrong, and that makes me bawl even harder. Crying so convulsively I can't draw a breath. Why did seeing Shane trigger uncontrollable tears? Was it because the last time I saw him he was keeping company with a dead man? Because my whole world, Planet Kate, had tipped on its axis and started spinning out of control?

Randall Shane produces a pocket-size packet of Kleenex, begins to unfurl the tissue. "It's about time," he says. "I was beginning to think you were built out of titanium. Let it go, Mrs. Bickford. Cry till you run out of tears."

I nod, take a handful of tissues, and gradually, very gradually, manage to slow my heaving chest. By the time my breathing returns to something like normal, and my eyes no longer blur, Shane has begun to recount what happened since I left him in Queens.

"There was some minor unpleasantness," he admits, leaning back in the seat. The lawyer's Beemer is a sizable sedan, but Shane's long legs take up all the available room. "Homicide in the borough, the default assumption is drug related. Plus, they know Vargas specialized in defending dealers. So the assumption is, the hit came from a disgruntled client. And I must be the hit man."

"That's your idea of 'minor unpleasantness'?" asks Savalo with obvious affection, if not admiration.

"The officers persuaded themselves otherwise, eventually. Couldn't establish any previous link between me and the deceased. Plus, I don't have a sheet and these boys in Queens, they rarely get a chance to converse with a suspect who doesn't have a criminal record."

"You were with the FBI for years. Did that impress them?" Savalo asks. Her impish expression means she knows the answer.

"Oh, yeah," says Shane. "They were awed. Probably why they failed to beat me with rubber hoses."

"I assume you told them the truth?"

Shane shrugs. "I didn't lie."

"So they know you're working the Bickford case?"

That gives me a little shock. For some reason I hadn't thought of myself as a case, or if I was a case, that it would be attached to my name.

"They know. And they know Vargas had plenty of folks who'd like to see him dead. Quite a few of them in law enforcement. I guess he defended some real scumbags."

Savalo studies him, as if trying to peel back a layer and see what's underneath, what he's really thinking. Shane, meanwhile, strokes his beard and doesn't bother to hide the twinkle of triumph in his eyes.

Suddenly I get it, that expression of his: the man has good news. Something happened. I'm almost afraid to ask him what, exactly, just in case I'm reading him wrong. Another disappointment might set me off, and I've used up all the tissues.

"They let you walk," Savalo says, homing in on him. "Why? Come on, Randall. What did you get?"

Shane folds his hands on his knees, which puts them about chin high. "They pulled the security tapes from the garage. My first thought, they'll find images of me and Mrs. Bickford, tie her to the Vargas killing. Wrong. Because the tapes are blurred."

"And that's good?" Savalo wants to know.

"Yes and no. Maybe."

"Randall! Stop being coy."

That amuses him. "Me? Coy?"

"Come on, we're dying here. What have you got?"

Shane grins, reaches into his jacket pocket and produces a video-tape. "A blur called Bruce," he says. "Once you've seen the tape you'll know why it's so important."

Tomas has been waiting for what seems like days and days. He's managed to upend the chest of drawers and position it to one side of the door. Standing on the chest makes him over six feet tall. In a movie he'd have an iron pipe or something. As it is, the best he can manage is one of the wooden drawers to swing as a weapon. Started out fairly light, now it weighs a ton.

With no way to measure the passage of time, he has no clear idea of how frequently they check on him, but it seems like some sort of regular interval. They'll come eventually.

Waiting is hard work.

He's heard the phrase "sleep standing up" but never really believed it until now. Like he's zoned out or hypnotized. Eyes open but not re-ally seeing anything, like when you freeze-frame a DVD.

The click of the hasp unlocking is so soft he almost misses it. Then he hears a voice, a man mumbling to himself, and Tomas is fully awake, adrenaline pumping.

When the door opens, the boy swings the wooden drawer with all his might, aiming for head level.

Whacks the man full in the face. The man falls, stunned and groaning, and Tomas flies from his perch. He's in a dim corridor, running like he's stealing home, hands outstretched to the plate.

What he finds is another door. He grabs the handle, yanks, and discovers another padlock sealing the heavy door. Trapped. He's kicking at the door in frustration, in a panic to keep running, to get away, when he hears the voice behind him.

The man hobbling, holding his face with one bloody hand. Reaching out for Tomas with the other. The growl of a maddened animal in his throat.

"You're dead, you little shit," the animal promises. "I'll kill you with my bare hands. First thing, I'll snap your neck."

And then the angry hands are yanking him up, lifting him into the air, and he's flying into darkness.

Approaching the exit for Fairfax, Cutter considers checking out Mom again. The delectable Mrs. Bickford. He knows where she's holed up—the seedy motel on the circle, room 227, round the back—but decides there's nothing to be gained by another drive-by, not at this time. Not with her uncanny ability to recognize him from a distance. Maybe later, if he needs to give her a tweak, or access the danger from the tall, bearded man who escorted her to Queens. Law enforcement of some sort. According to Vargas, a private investigator—the feds still assuming the position, thumbs up their butts. Which won't last forever, they'll eventually start putting things together. Even a blind squirrel finds a nut, given time. He knows this, and it doesn't worry him. By the time the feds piece it all together, if ever they do, the deed will be done. Mission accomplished.

Cutter keeps the big SUV in the travel lane, with cruise control set just below the speed limit. Mr. Careful. Joe Commuter. Left arm cocked out the side, right hand firmly on the wheel, the very picture of a relaxed motorist. If travel isn't too clotted in New Haven, he'll be at his destination in less than an hour. Have to ditch the stolen wheels soon, tonight perhaps. Let Hinks take care of it, while Cutter concentrates on the next move.

Lyla floats into his thoughts, with her sad, mournful, beautiful eyes and her endless pleading. Where's Jesse? She knows the answer to that one. The facts are buried deep in her addled mind, but she can't accept it, so she invents her own reality. Maybe the increased dose of medication will help, maybe not. Nothing Cutter can do about it at the moment.

What have you done to our son?

The only tune she knows, poor thing. Cutter's in charge of her world, has been for years, so anything bad that happens must be his fault. That's her fractured logic. So if something happens to Jesse, it must be his fault, as if he's responsible for every bad thing in the world. Nevertheless, if he can get their son back home, safe and healthy, maybe her condition will improve. It's happened before, cycling in and out of sanity, but she's never had to deal with a trauma like this before. The giant black hole of *Jesse gone,* sucking her sanity away.

He can fix it, though. He can make it happen.

My husband is a liar. He lies and lies and lies.

Unfortunately true. But only when necessary. Only when deception is part of the plan, the method.

A jackknifed truck on I-95 slows him down to a crawl for three long miles, makes him almost an hour late, and by the time he gets to the boat shed the shit has hit the fan.

Wald is out in the yard, dressed in his white painter's overalls, sucking on a cigarette and looking extremely agitated. Swings around as the Explorer enters, quick marches to where Cutter parks, his bland features contorted with anger.

"Fucking brat!" he barks, flinging the cigarette to the ground.

Right away Cutter notices the spot of blood on the sleeve of Wald's overalls. Makes him want to grab the man and slam him up against the Explorer, but Cutter forces calm upon himself. No sudden moves. The normally obedient Wald, whose intelligence is barely dull normal, is unpredictable and prone to irrational violence when angry.

"What happened?" Cutter asks as they make for the shed.

"Fucking kid broke Hinks's nose," Wald explains.

Rather than quiz him on the details, Cutter waits until they're inside the shed, out of sight.

The shed. To all appearances a modest boat-repair facility, complete with a crappy, keel-rotten old Chris Craft that came with the lease. Their excuse for renting the shed, to restore the ratty boat to its classic condition. Six-month restoration, supposedly. Shed owner happy to have the lease paid in advance, doubtful that the project could be finished in a mere six months. *Guys spend years on boats like this,* he'd warned Cutter. *Every time you take something off to fix, you find another thing needs fixing.*

However long it takes, Cutter had said. *This little sweetheart means everything to me,* he'd said, gazing with love-struck reverence at the sagging plywood hull. *She's all I think about,* he had added. *What she'll look like when we're done. I even dream about her, isn't that weird?*

Shed owner didn't think it was weird, a man dreaming about a boat.

As per Cutter's instructions, the air compressor is on. The idea being that it will mask any sounds that came from the soundproof enclosure. High-pitched screams and whatnot.

Hinks crouches by the watercooler, a wet rag pressed to his face.

"—ucking kih oke my node," Hinks manages, scowling behind the rag. Blood spatter on the front of his overalls, on the rag, everywhere.

"Where is he?"

Hinks nods at the padlocked door of the enclosure.

"Is he okay?" Cutter asks.

"Ooh the uck airs!" Hinks says through the rag. "Ill the ittle ucker, all I care."

"Wald?"

Wald shrugs, his eyes shifting away. "He'll survive."

"He'll survive?" Cutter says. Feeling his blood pressure spike. Wanting to coldcock both the morons, but keeping the impulse in check. "What happened, exactly?"

Hinks grimaces, spits a wad of clotted blood on the floor. "Hit me wid a roar," he says.

"Kid hit him with a drawer," Wald explains. "That dresser? He dragged it to the door, stood up on it and whacked Hinks with the empty drawer when he came through the door."

"The inner door?"

"Of course the inside door. Hinks locked the outer door like you said. Otherwise the brat would have escaped and I'd have had to shoot him or something."

Cutter stares at him. Under no circumstances is the boy to be harmed. Standing orders. Injured or dead, he's worthless to the enterprise.

"Just an expression," Wald says, picking at his teeth. A nervous habit indicating deception on his part.

"So you didn't shoot him."

"Nope. He's unshot."

Unshot. An expression Wald used in the field, usually when he'd beaten a civilian nearly to death. *Don't look at me, the fucking rag head is unshot! Sir!*

"You beat him?" Cutter asks, very calm.

"No way."

"So he's untouched? I go in there, I'll find him untouched?"

Wald stares right back, eyes cold. He shrugs. "Pretty much," he says. "Little smack on the nose. Like you'd smack a puppy. For what he did to Hinks."

"Hinks? Is that what happened?"

Hinks has his eyes closed. He seems to be inhaling the bloody rag. "'Eed a 'octor. My node."

"I'll fix your nose, Hinks. After I check on the boy." He turns to Wald. "Keys."

"What?"

"Give me the keys, Wald."

"Cap, are you pissed or something?"

"I'm handling the situation. Give me the keys."

"'Cause it was like a reaction thing," Wald says in his not-my-fault, never-did-a-thing voice. "I see Hinks all bleeding and everything, I see the kid trying to sneak by him, make a run for it. Which if the outer door hadn't been padlocked—following your orders to a t, sir—like I say, if it hadn't been locked, the kid was out of here."

Wald in his excuse-generating mode, spewing effluent like a broken sewer pipe.

"Keys," Cutter demands, holding out his hand.

"So, Cap, it was like a reaction thing, okay? I see the kid, I see Hinks all bloody, I give the kid a little smack. So he can't escape or nothing. That's all. We had to keep him in control, right? I grab him by the arm or something, it might have been worse. Could have dislocated his shoulder. Which I did not do. Never grabbed his arm or nothing. Always thinking, Cap. Even when it's a light-speed deal. Smack on the nose, it hurts. Like it hurts a puppy. But no lasting damage."

Reluctantly, Wald slips a hand in his overalls pocket, produces the key ring. Two keys for two padlocks. Hands it to Cutter.

"Captain? Just to be totally honest? Before you go in there? Maybe I yelled a little. To make him, you know, docile."

"I'll check him out," Cutter says, starting for the padlocked outer door.

Wald puts his hand on Cutter's right forearm. Cutter looks down at the offending hand. Wald hastily removes it.

"Thing is," Wald says, "I told him we were coming back to kill him."

"You said that?"

"I told him to say his prayers."

"You told him to say his prayers."

"Right. So what I'm saying, you go in there, he might think you're going to kill him. Just so you know."

"Just so I know."

"It was a reaction thing, Captain. Are we clear? I did no permanent damage. One little smack."

"Fine," says Cutter.

"'Octor," Hinks mumbles. Staggers to his feet with raccoon eyes. "Node," he says into the rag.

"Be right back," says Cutter.

He unlocks the padlock, slips it free of the hasp and opens the door to the small passageway. A passageway constructed to both hide the enclosure and provide a backup door should the first one be breached.

Cutter listens, ears attuned for sounds of life. Hears nothing. The passageway is illuminated by a single fluorescent tube. Blood trails are pretty obvious. Spatter from Hinks's leaky nose heading for the outer door. Spatter from the boy leading to the inner door. The boy's blood trail looks wrong. Wobbly somehow. He's not walking, he's being carried. By Wald presumably.

Palm-smear on the inner door, has to be Wald.

Blood on the padlock, too.

Blood everywhere in the passageway. More blood than can possibly come from one adult nose.

Little smack, Wald said, *like you'd give a puppy.*

We'll see, Cutter is thinking. His icy composure and self-control a bulwark against the dark possibilities. It had been a simple assignment. Two grown men to watch over one eleven-year-old boy. Trained soldiers, special forces no less, with beaucoup experience in dicey, difficult operations. And they had fucked up at the very first opportunity.

Cutter decides he'll deal with disciplining the troops after he's dealt with whatever awaits him in the enclosure. First things first.

A fuckup. A bloody damn fuckup.

Deal, he urges himself. His fingers tremble slightly as he inserts the key in the second padlock. With an effort of will, he calms the trembling. Takes a breath, waits three heartbeats, and then slips the lock off the hasp and pushes on the door.

Jams before it swings wide. Something on the floor, in the way of the door. Cutter forces the door open.

Just beyond the door, blocking it, lie the remains of the splintered dresser. Cheap particleboard and Formica. Evidently stomped by Wald in his fury. Using the edge of his foot, Cutter clears the debris away, then locks the door behind him. As much to prevent Wald and Hinks from entering as to prevent a possible escape from the enclosure.

Cutter sniffs. Strong odor of urine and feces.

The enclosure is quite small, ten feet by ten feet. Enough room for a mattress, a potty-chair, a small, two-drawer dresser with a TV on top. The dresser smashed to bits, of course, and shards of glass underfoot means the TV has been similarly destroyed. Sizable dent on the wall where Wald hurled the television. Must have been in full rampage, young Wald. Savoring that sweet adrenaline surge. Stomps the offending dresser, trashes the TV, tips over the potty-chair—and that explains the stink of piss and shit. Although not the odor of fear, very distinct to Cutter, who has smelled it many times, under various circumstances. Sometimes his own fear, more often someone else's fear. Distinctive odor that makes the air feel sharp, crystalline, dangerous.

Smacked him like a puppy.

"Tomas?" Cutter says gently.

He's aware of the lump under the mattress. As if Wald tried to cover his mess. Out of sight, out of mind. Cutter takes a deep breath, reaches down, flips over the mattress.

The boy, hiding his bloody face, trying to scuttle back under the mattress. Nowhere else to hide. Moving and therefore alive. Cutter sighs, plops himself down on the mattress, hugging his knees. No ski mask today. Mask time is over.

"Tomas? My name is Steve, Steve Cutter. Come here, I want to see how badly they hurt you."

The boy has made it to a corner of the room, arms covering his head. Not sobbing or crying. Not saying a word. Waiting.

"Tomas, I know that one of the men threatened to kill you. He won't. I won't let him hurt you again."

The boy is frozen against the wall, head and face averted. Cutter notes the white patches on the boy's bloody knuckles. Tension. Fear.

"I'm sorry this happened, Tomas. It wasn't supposed to be like this. But you're safe now. Let me see what he did to you. Assess the damage."

Cutter gets up from the mattress, edges slowly to the corner. No movement from the boy. Waiting.

Cutter crouches next to him. Smells the fear exuding from his young skin. Reaches out, strokes the boy's matted hair.

A small fist smacks him in the jaw. Not enough to loosen his teeth, but a pretty strong punch.

"Got me good," says Cutter, touching his lip. "Go on, take another punch. I won't hit you. Free punch, kid, now's your chance."

The small fist connects again, not as hard this time, and Cutter grunts. "Ow," he says. "Let's stop hitting, shall we? Let me see your face."

Small brown eye peeking through fingers. The boy would kill him if he knew how, that's what his eyes reveal. Cutter closes his hands over the boy's fists, pulls them away from the hidden face.

"Took a pretty good shot to the nose," Cutter says. "Might be broken. I can fix that, once the bleeding stops."

The boy jerks his head away, turns it to the wall, defiant.

"I'm going away for a while. Ten, fifteen minutes. Then I'll be back with warm water and soap. Clean you up. Check you out. Fix what needs fixing."

"Fuck you," says the boy, speaking to the wall.

"That guy you hit with the drawer? You fucked him up good. He deserved it. You know why he deserved it? Because he's a dumb asshole."

"You're an asshole," the boy says. Turns to look at him, meeting his eyes. Showing his courage, his strength, his defiance.

"Yes," Cutter agrees. "But I'm on your side. And that's a good thing."

sine pari **27**

Shane's place is not what I expected. Having envisioned an unkempt bachelor pad inhabited by a man who never sleeps, complete with duct-taped recliner, big-screen TV and empty refrigerator. There were sure to be stacks of empty pizza boxes, the moldy walls would be decorated with old swimsuit calendars, and the floor littered with unopened junk mail.

So much for women's intuition.

To my surprise, the modest, one-story ranch in New Rochelle feels like an actual home. Elegant but comfortable-looking furniture, accented with a hint of oiled teak. Glowing cherry floors, recently refinished, with several lovely oriental rugs that could be collectable. No swimsuit calendars on the off-white walls; instead, there are museum-quality reproductions of watercolors by Winslow Homer and John Singer Sargent, each piece illuminated by soft cove lighting. Custom-made bookcases line most of the walls, and the books themselves look not only well read, but well dusted.

My first impression is that great care has been taken to preserve order in this place. Second impression is that with the exception of the coffeemaker, the kitchen has a seldom-used look to it. For all his domestic talents, evident in the home he has created, Randall Shane spends very little time preparing food. Something in me wants to spill flour on the neatly trimmed countertops, which have never, from the look of them, been appropriately christened.

Obviously there are no women in Shane's life, or if there are, none that cook.

We've come here to view the promised surveillance tape, since my motel room lacks a VCR, and because Shane's place, unlike Ms. Savalo's Westport waterfront condo, is thus far free from media intrusion.

"Be it ever so humble," says Shane as we enter. "Coffee?"

"Not for me," says Savalo. "I'm high on life."

"I've got 'SleepyTime Tea' if you can't hack the caffeine."

The attorney shakes her head, bemused, apparently, by this domestic version of Shane.

"Mrs. Bickford?"

"Coffee, please."

Mostly I want to urge him to hurry up and show us the tape, see if there's anything on it that will connect us to finding my son. But Shane is acting purposeful and deliberate and it's clear he'll get to the viewing in his own time, and not before playing gracious host. I also get the impression he rarely has visitors and isn't quite sure how to behave, which may explain his oddly formal manner. The man has gray in his beard, and the years of sleep disorder show in his watery blue eyes, but at home he has the energetic mannerisms of a much younger man.

Savalo and I glance at each other while our host, humming contentedly to himself, brews a pot of coffee. The petite attorney rolls her eyes, makes a point of looking at her watch.

"I saw that," says Shane. "Someday your eyes are going to get stuck. Didn't your mother warn you about that?"

"Mom-warnings were mostly about men. Guys with clean houses and Mr. Coffee machines were not to be trusted."

"You'd rather I lived in a dump?" asks Shane, sounding amused.

"Just repeating what Mom said. But hey, she's on her third husband, what does she know?"

Handing me a mug of black coffee, Shane leads us to a room he calls "the workshop." Looks to me like an artist's studio, and at least part of it serves as exactly that, complete with easel and a small, wheeled table loaded with brushes and tubes of watercolors. A piece of muslin is draped over the easel, hiding whatever it is he's working on.

"Sunday painter," he says dismissively. "I'm terrible."

Somehow I doubt that—whatever he is, Randall Shane is not a hobbyist—but I don't do the polite thing and beg him to show us an example of his work because I'm focused on seeing the surveillance tape.

About half of the room is taken up by a long, sturdily built bench filled with computer gear. There are several impressive-looking hard-drive stacks, a couple of monitors, VHS and DVD recorders and players, and black boxes that may or may not be cable and satellite modems. My son, Tommy, would know exactly what they are, but my own computer expertise is pretty much limited to e-mail and online shopping. The wall above the bench is festooned with shelves and wire baskets holding various techie gadgets, whose functions can't even be guessed by the likes of me.

Shane has already alluded to utilizing the internet for research, and for hunting down suspects. I recall him saying that as an FBI agent his expertise had to do with software—was it fingerprint-identification software?—and this bench is obviously where he does most of his in-house work.

"Welcome to Geek City," he says. "Who wants the chair?"

There's only one chair at the bench, so rather than fight over it we all opt to stand. Shane slips a tape into a player, keys a control panel and switches on a flat-screen monitor.

"First tape is taken from inside the parking garage," he tells us.

The image on the screen is in black and white but very sharply focused on the entrance to the garage, from an angle inside the structure. Beyond the gate, the image brightens and flattens out into white static, as if overwhelmed by daylight.

"Here he comes," Shane announces in a hushed voice.

Sure enough, a silhouetted figure emerges from the wash of daylight and then rapidly comes into focus as he advances in the direction of the camera. A man wearing a baseball cap, a long-sleeved shirt, jeans and running shoes. He seems to be looking down at his feet as he walks, so that the visor of the cap completely obscures his face. He's carrying something in his right hand, but I can't make out what, exactly. Not a gun, though. An object small enough to be almost obscured by his hand.

Just as the figure is about to pass directly under the surveillance camera, something happens and the image is suddenly blurred.

"What did he do?" I want to know.

"Sprayed the lens with some sort of oil. Probably WD-40, available in palm-size cans in any hardware store."

"Why oil and not paint?" I want to know. "In the movies the bank robbers always spray the surveillance cameras with paint."

Shane nods. "Paint works. But oil is better if there's a chance that someone is checking the monitors from a remote location. The lens just looks like it's out of focus. No reason to assume foul play."

As we watch, the now-blurred figure walks back out toward the entrance and is swallowed up by the wash of light and static.

"Bruce?" Shane asks me.

I nod. "That's the man I saw in the garage. That's what seemed familiar, the way he walks. Plus, he was dressed the same way. You can't really tell on the tape, but he moves like a very powerful, confident man. An athlete. Maybe a soldier. Someone who's used to being in charge."

Shane nods with satisfaction. "That's what I'm picking up, too. Military bearing. Even with his head down, he's keeping his shoulders back."

"Right!" I say excitedly. "Like I told you, he talks like a soldier, too. The way he puts words together."

"As identifications go, it's not exactly a courtroom certainty," Savalo points out.

"We're not in a courtroom," I insist. "This is the guy."

"I'm going with Mrs. Bickford," Shane says. "Not only for the physical ID, but because he accosted her."

"Pointing a finger isn't accosting," says Savalo, playing devil's advocate.

Shane gives me an abashed look. "If I thought he'd be in that garage, I'd never have sent you out alone," he says. "I assumed he'd fled the scene."

"He didn't follow us there," I point out. "He was waiting."

"That's what the time log shows."

"But how did he know we were going to talk to Vargas?"

Shane shrugs. "We can't be sure. But I think he's covering his tracks. Anticipating that any investigator would likely want to talk to the attorney who filed the paternity suit. Which meant Vargas had to be silenced."

"'Scuse me," I manage, before clamping hand to mouth and hurrying from the room in a panic, gorge suddenly rising.

Shane rushes ahead of me, opens a door and flips up a toilet lid. Just in time. After the nauseating act is over, he makes me sit on the closed lid and hands me a cold, wet towel. "Hold it to your forehead."

"Sorry," I gasp. Thinking, *Great. First you dissolve into a crying mess, now you're throwing up. Wonderful day you're having, Kate. What's next? A full-scale nervous breakdown?*

"Perfectly all right," Shane is saying, looking at me with deep concern. "It's my fault. Loads of tension, combined with the fact that you haven't eaten all day. I have a bad habit of not remembering that people have to eat."

Savalo makes an appearance, peering sideways around Shane because she's not tall enough to see above his shoulder. "You okay?" she
wants to know.

"Fine," I say, despite the vile taste that lingers in my mouth. Nothing solid came up, just a few specks of bile.

"She hasn't eaten," Shane explains.

"Not that," I tell them, fighting to calm myself. "Bruce. He scares
me sick."

"Of course he does," Maria Savalo says sympathetically. She
crouches at the commode, pats my clenched hands. "He scares me
and I never, uh, met him," she adds carefully.

A moment later Shane is guiding me out to the kitchen. He rum-
mages through the cabinets until he locates an unopened box of Ritz
crackers. He puts a few crackers on a plate, pours milk into a tum-
bler. "Here you go," he says. "Force it down if you have to. You need
to put something in your stomach."

"Do you have any peanut butter?"

"I think so. Let me check."

When I was a little girl, that's how my mother treated an upset tummy.
Crackers with a dab of peanut butter. Comfort food. I'm not the least
bit hungry, but the food tastes good and the cold milk seems to make
my heart stop hammering. And then, of course, I'm reminded of Tommy
with his chocolate milk and Fig Newtons and I have to fight back the
tears.

Not going there again. Have to keep going forward or I'll lose my
balance and fall into the abyss.

"Better?"

"Better," I agree, and take a deep breath that helps to clear my head,
if not my heart. "Now, what about the second tape? There's something on it, isn't there? Something useful?"

"I can take you back to the motel," Savalo suggests. "You need to
rest."

I shake off the suggestion. "I'll rest when we've got Tommy back. What about the second tape?"

The look in Shane's eyes convinces me he's been saving the best for last. That he's found something we can act on, beyond the certainty that the man in the mask has been covering his tracks. "Fine," he says. "Let's do it," and we follow him back into the workshop.

My attorney insists that I take the chair this time, and I sink into it gratefully, my knees much weaker than I've been letting on. Weak not only from the residual fear of the man in the mask, but from anticipatory excitement.

Let this be something important. Let this be a way to find my son.

Shane produces a smaller cassette—not the VHS format—and fits it into a different machine.

"Okay, a little background," he begins. "Over the last few years the city has installed several thousand wide-angle cameras at busy intersections. Part of the Homeland Security precautions, with federal funds attached. So far they haven't caught a terrorist on camera, but the cameras been very useful in a number of criminal investigations. Needless to say, the department discourages publicity about the 'spy cams,' if only to discourage vandalism."

We're looking at an image of the intersection on the same block as the parking garage. I can make out a line of vehicles waiting for the light to turn, and the ghostlike images of pedestrians.

"Takes a little getting used to," Shane explains. "The spy cams run at sixty frames per minute. One frame per second. That's so they can store seven days' worth of images on each cassette. I synced to the time log of the primary tape. That's Bruce, exiting the garage."

It's hard to make out on the small screen, but sure enough, a silver Ford Explorer is nosing out the parking garage, waiting to merge into traffic on Queens Boulevard.

"The windows are tinted," I point out. "Just like I said."

"Excellent point," Shane says, as if proud of my powers of observation. "Which means we won't get a look at his face through the windshield. But we do have something that might be even better than a grainy head shot."

He clicks through several more frames, until the SUV is almost at the intersection, and therefore at the bottom of the image captured by the spy cam. "Two things of interest," he says. "First is the license plate. New York tags, which may or may not mean anything, since the vehicle was almost certainly stolen. Second, and this could be our big break, he has the driver's-side window down. And we have you to thank for that, Mrs. Bickford. If you hadn't seen him, alerted him to your presence, I very much doubt he'd have the window down."

"The window down? So what, if we can't see his face?"

"That pale spot against the window opening?" Shane says. "That's his elbow."

His elbow? That's what all the excitement is about? I feel like the air has been let out of my balloon, but before an involuntary groan of disappointment escapes my lips, Shane clicks to the next frame, and I begin to get a glimmer of what has so excited him.

"There, you see that? Looks like a discoloration on his left forearm, a couple of inches above the wrist? That, ladies and gentlemen—excuse me, ladies and ladies—that is a tattoo. Known in the lingo as a 'distinguishing characteristic.'"

Standing just behind me, Savalo snorts her approval. "Randall, you are amazing. Had me going there. Thought you were going to ID the guy by the shape of his elbow and really blow me away."

I'm holding my breath, not quite certain how important it can be—lots of guys have tattoos, lots of women, too, for that matter—but Savalo and Shane both seem so upbeat it fuels me with hope.

"That's why he's always wearing long sleeves, even in short-sleeve weather," Shane explains. "Kate described her attacker as wearing long sleeves, remember? He knows the tattoo is a giveaway. But after his encounter with Kate, he rolls up his sleeves and cocks his arm out the window. Probably wants to feel the wind on his face, remind him he's all powerful, able to terrify women and children."

"Is that enough to identify him? A blurry tattoo?"

Shane next produces a CD from his shirt pocket, slips it into a slot in one of the computer towers. "I made a deal with the homicide boys. They loan me the raw data—the spy-cam download—and I'd do the enhancement work free of charge. It helped that I developed the original tat-recognition software for the FBI."

"I thought you were into fingerprints," I say, puzzled.

"Fingerprints, too," he says. "Anything to do with distinguishing characteristics, as it pertains to the skin. Long story short, this particular tat tells us a lot we didn't know about Bruce."

The enhanced, blown-up image on the screen looks, to my uneducated eyes, like a winged angel standing on some sort of pedestal.

"You're partly right," Shane corrects me. "Those are, indeed, wings. But the dark area in the center of the wings isn't an angel, it's a dagger. An unsheathed dagger. The banner under the dagger reads: *Sine Pari.*

"I'm a little rusty on my Latin," Savalo complains.

"'Without Equal,'" Shane translates. "Bruce is or was a member of the Army Special Operation Forces. Very elite. Can't be more than a few hundred men in the greater New York area who have that insignia burned into their skin. Probably fewer who fit his particular age group."

"So this means you can narrow it down?" I ask. "We can find him?"

"Yes," says Shane. "I believe we can."

bing-bing **28**

Captain Cutter exits the enclosure with a smile on his face. He's snapping the padlock on the outer door when Wald, feigning casualness, asks, "So? Everything okay?"

"Everything is just dandy, Wald."

"You're not pissed?"

"Me? No. But in the future the boy is not to be harmed in any way," Cutter says, adopting a stern tone. "No puppy slaps. No matter how much you think he might deserve it. Are we clear on that?"

"Yes, sir. Clear."

"Hinks? Can you breathe?"

Hinks, cloth to his face, grimaces but nods his head. "I'm breeving froo my mouf."

"Good," says Cutter. "We're about to start the next phase and I need you fully functional. You and Wald can stop at the E.R. on the way to your assignment."

Wald jerks into his alert-posture mode. He's an action junkie, in need of a regular influx of adrenaline, and guard duty at the boat shed just doesn't cut it. "This about the hump you call Stanley?" he wants to know.

"It's about the mission," Cutter says somewhat evasively. He's patting his pockets, looking for the key to the old, gray metal office desk where he keeps some of his personal effects. "Change out of the overalls, I want you in civilian dress."

Hinks and Wald are stepping out of their blood-spattered overalls when Cutter removes a custom-silenced Sig-Sauer from the desk drawer and shoots both men in the chest. *Bing-bing, bing-bing.* He doesn't much like silenced weapons because the muzzle velocity is always compromised, no matter how good the muffling device, but in this case it doesn't make much difference, because the targets are less than ten feet from the desk. Can't-miss range. All four shots penetrate, and from the *pinking!* rattle, one or more bullets have exited and are bouncing around the boat shed.

Both men are down with mortal wounds, but neither is dead. Small-caliber bullets rarely kill instantly because the human heart continues to beat for a few minutes, no matter how devastating the damage, as Cutter knows from experience. So he's obliged to dispatch his unreliable employees with head shots, the classic coup de grâce to the cranium as he stands over their quivering bodies. Distasteful, but necessary. He's seen targets with truly awesome chest-cavity wounds get up and run around like bleeding zombies, effectively dead but still functioning on some level. Sever the brain stem, however, and the human body becomes a bag of cooling meat.

Bing-bing, it's over.

After returning the Sig to the drawer and locking it, Cutter goes to the sink, where he carefully soaps and washes his hands. Removing the smell of gunpowder. He deeply regrets having to kill Hinks and Wald. It wasn't part of his master plan, and he takes no pleasure from the executions. He'd known both men for several years, liked them on some level. But in there with the boy, it had suddenly become crystal clear that neither man was capable of carrying out even the simplest of assignments. Shocking, really. Both had been adequate soldiers in the field, performing dangerous and complex missions. To be fair, he'd known all along that Wald in particular had trouble controlling his impulsive behavior. Didn't matter when the unplanned victim was an Iraqi suspected of terrorist activities, or an Iraqi who looked threatening or mouthed off or whatever. But the boy had to be kept in pristine physical condition or he was no use to the mission.

The mission. The project. Cutter knew he had to remain focused. The next few days were crucial. Not having a guard team in the boat shed meant he would have to leave the boy untended for hours at a time. Which in turn meant he would have to reinspect the enclosure, make sure it was escape-proof for a very clever and determined eleven-year-old. The only other alternative was to keep him heavily sedated, and that wasn't a good idea, considering what the boy would have to do when the time came. When Cutter had everything lined up and ready for the final play. The big move that was going to return his own precious son to a normal family environment. Or as normal as it could be, assuming Lyla bounced back into something like sanity, as she had done several times in the past. At some point, after Jesse was back home, it would be safe to get her the medical attention she required.

Someday soon, but not now.

Before returning to the enclosure with a first-aid kit and a bowl of hot water, Cutter spreads a blue plastic tarp over the men he'd executed. Just in case an unexpected visitor somehow managed to get through the locked fence and the locked door. Unlikely, but you can't be too careful. Later he will decide the best way to dispose of the bodies. There are a few empty resin barrels in the shed that might suffice, assuming the barrels can be sealed. A problem to be solved. Or maybe there's something in the old Chris Craft that will work—can two muscular men be fitted into a two-hundred-gallon fuel tank? Can it be sealed and then the boat itself sunk in deep water? Or is that too complicated, a scenario where too many things can go wrong?

Have to give it some thought, once he's attended to the boy.

He'd never had to dispose of cadavers before. That was the nice thing about fatalities in a war zone—somebody else came along and cleaned up the mess.

As it happens, I was right the first time about the pizza. Randall Shane may not litter the floor with empty boxes, but the delivery guy treats him like an old friend, and seems interested that he's ordered more than the usual solo pizza.

"Ain't by any chance your birthday, is it, Mr. Shane?" he wants to know, leaning in the door to clock us. "Bet it's somebody's birthday, huh?"

"Nope," says Shane, moving to block his view. "Just having a few friends over. Thank you, Marty, keep the change."

I had offered to cook, thinking that the act of food preparation might be soothing, but Shane really doesn't keep much in the house other than Ritz crackers, Campbell's soup and a frost-bitten chicken potpie scabbed to the inside of the freezer.

So that's how we end up around the dining-room table, eating slices and discussing how to go about identifying the man who abducted my son.

"This is a back-channel kind of operation," Shane explains as he passes out paper napkins. "It's not like you can just call up 'Special

Ops' and ask for a list of guys who might have insignia tattoos. All information about personnel is classified, and it takes more than a court order to pry it out of the army."

"So who do we ask?" I want to know.

"A guy who knows a guy. In this case, a woman who knows a guy. Or to be even more specific, an FBI special agent who has a brother assigned to the Pentagon. The brother happens to be an officer and a lawyer, which is different from being an officer and a gentleman, apparently."

Maria Savalo makes a face. "Randall, can I ask you a favor? Give me a break on the lawyer jokes for a while. I'm feeling, you know, vulnerable and all that crap."

Even with a smudge of tomato sauce on her chin, the last thing Savalo looks is vulnerable. Petite, feisty, blazing with self-confidence, she's everything that vulnerable is not.

"Okay, fine," agrees Shane. "So this, ah, lawyer and gentleman is a high-ranking dude, works for the Pentagon equivalent of Internal Affairs. Which means he pretty much has unlimited access to a truly amazing amount of data. He's been a willing source for years. At the agency, the feeling is his superiors are aware he's a conduit to the FBI, and that he's aware they're aware, and that he's allowed and maybe even encouraged to pass on certain types of information to another branch of the federal government."

"Very cloak and dagger," says Savalo, staring at him with her large and radiant eyes. The comment is not intended as a joke, she means it sincerely.

Shane shrugs—it's all part of how he works, what he does. "It's how things are done when you have to work your way around an enormous bureaucracy. For this source, at his level, a list of SOF personnel, active and discharged, is no big deal. Much easier than, say, requesting medical records for the same men."

"Medical records?" I ask. "Why would you ask for medical records? Oh, wait, of course. The tattoo."

"Correct," Shane says approvingly. "Tattoos are noted in medical records for a variety of reasons, not the least of which is possible transmission of blood-borne disease. But they also like to have it on the jacket as a means of quick identification, which may or may not prove useful if every man in the unit has the same marking. What I'm going to do is wait for the first batch of names, cull through it, eliminating by age and height, race and so on, and then go back for medical records for the likely candidates."

"How long will that take?" I ask.

One of the many things I like about this man is that he takes all of my questions seriously. No matter how obvious they may be to him, or even how silly or inappropriate. So he thinks about it before responding. "As long as forty-eight hours for the turnaround. That's max. Could be much quicker if a name and location pops out. A Special Forces guy who lives in your town and banks at your bank, for instance. Or happened to be in a position to come into previous contact with your son. Could be a few steps removed from that and still have a connection."

"The six-degrees thing," Savalo offers.

"Yes," says Shane. "Exactly. Once we know how this man chose you and Tomas, we'll know who he is, where he is and where to find your son."

"What if there's no connection?" I ask. "What if he flew in from Idaho?"

Again, Shane takes his time considering the question. "I suppose there's a remote possibility that Bruce responded to an ad in *Soldier of Fortune,* or the Internet equivalent. If that's the case, then we're not only looking for him, we're looking for whoever hired him. But that still leaves us with a very specific connection to you, Mrs. Bickford. Why you? Why your son?"

"I've been asking myself that question ever since it happened. Maybe because I had money in the bank? He knew all about my bank accounts, down to the penny," I remind them both.

Shane nods, then pauses to pat his mouth with a napkin before proceeding. "No doubt money was a factor," he begins. "It may be possible that Bruce or one of his associates is a hacker and was trolling bank data, looking for a likely prospect, and happened to find you. But if I were planning a crime like that, I'd keep the child right in the home while I sent the mark—you—to withdraw or transfer the funds. That's how it's usually done."

"You've seen cases like this before?"

"Not exactly like this one," he says. "Every case is different. I wasn't directly involved with the bank robbery unit at the Bureau, but they worked ten or twelve crimes a year that involved taking a bank manager's family hostage in their own home, scaring the hell out of everybody, and then sending mom or dad off to get the dough and then hand it off to an accomplice. More than half the time the ploy was successful—nobody even knew what was going on until it was over. But if that's all it is, a way to extract money from you, why go to the trouble of filing phony paternity papers? Why kill the local police chief and try to implicate you in the crime? Why keep Tommy? No, this isn't just about the money. Bruce has an agenda."

"What is it?" I ask. "What's his agenda?"

Shane smiles grimly. "That's the big question. A lot of what he's done seems to be a diversion tactic. Trying to make sure the federal authorities aren't involved, at least not right way. It's as if he has a mission to accomplish. Something he needs to do that involves your son."

What that might be remains unspoken. It's simply too terrible to contemplate. Of course my mind has been wrestling with the possibilities, and when I start to settle on one—sick porno, for instance—it blares inside my head like a car alarm that won't shut off. I think Shane knows what I must be thinking, what I have to be worried to a point of madness about, and has decided not to name the possibilities. Until we manage to find something concrete it's all speculation, and anyhow, the only thing that matters is getting Tommy back.

Whatever has happened to him, whatever he's been exposed to, he and I will deal with it when the time comes. When he's back home in his mother's arms, safe from the evil things in the world.

"I've got to boogie," Ms. Savalo announces, glancing at her wristwatch. "I'll take you back to the motel, Kate."

"When can I go back to my own house?" I ask plaintively. "When can I go back home?"

Savalo sighs. "Your home is still a crime scene. The state police detectives want it for a few more days. And even then, there's that bottle blonde from Channel 6. She'll be parked on your doorstep."

Tears spill from my eyes. I hate this. I hate weeping like a weak sister when I need to be strong, but the urge to be home, to sit on Tommy's bed and inhale the smell of him, is almost more than I can bear.

Shane clears his throat. "Here's an idea. Stay here for a day or two. Use the guest room. We'll cab over and pick up the rental car in the morning."

"I'm not sure that's a good idea," says Savalo, her face betraying no expression whatsoever.

"Why not?" Shane asks.

Savalo shrugs. "It's up to Kate."

And so it's decided. The great relief of not having to return to the fetid, lonesome motel room almost makes me cry again. Almost, but not quite.

The bed in the guest room is freshly made, which makes me think that Shane's invitation wasn't as spur of the moment as it sounded back there in the dining room. But who's complaining, when a man changes the linen and takes the trouble to tuck in the corners? Maybe they teach that at the FBI, under self-sufficiency. Ted never made a bed in his life—what's the point, he'd say, when we're just going to mess it up all over again?—and Tommy thinks the idea is ridiculous, and worse, effeminate. Making beds and keeping your room tidy is something girls do. Starting short-stops are definitely exempted.

As to sleep, well, that's going to be difficult with my mind jangling with images of Bruce and his special tattoo, and all the unspoken stuff about what my son may be going through, and the possibility of arrest hanging over my head. My attorney, borrowing a strategy from Shane, seems reluctant to get specific about what will happen if I'm charged with murder. Not wanting to add to my burden, apparently. Is bail possible, or will I be held awaiting trial? I can't stand the thought of being shut up while Tommy is still missing. Strange how that's the only part of a possible arrest that really bothers me; my standing in the community, my business, what my friends will think, what Fred Corso's poor wife must think, none of it matters. Just not being there when my son comes home. That's unthinkable.

With sleep out of the question, I prowl the guest room, looking for clues about my host. Unlike the rest of the house, this room seems untouched by his personality. A couple of lighter spots on the wall indicate that pictures may once have hung there, but no more. Nothing in the closet—just a few empty hangers. No books, no knickknacks, no indications that the room has ever been occupied. But the place has a scrubbed feel, as if someone worked hard to eradicate any trace of human habitation.

The fact is, I'm a terrible snoop. Let me in your house and I'll seek out the secret you. I won't open a diary, but almost everything else is fair game. I'll check out your books, your refrigerator, your medicine cabinet. Shameful habit, but I can't help it. As it happens, the cabinet in the attached bathroom is as empty as the closet. There's an unopened bottle of generic shampoo in the shower stall, and a bar of soap still in the wrapper.

Back in the bedroom area, I slide open the top drawer of a pine chest and notice neatly folded linens, pillowcases and sheets with the factory creases still intact. And then, under the linens, I find what has been hidden. A framed photograph facedown against the bare wood. No doubt it will match one of the lighter spots on the unadorned wall.

In a way, the picture itself is shocking. A somewhat younger and much more relaxed Randall Shane grins at the camera. One arm around a willowy blonde with gorgeous eyes and a shy smile, the other resting on the shoulders of a girl who looks a lot like her mother. Nine or ten years old, with the clear eyes and the serious expression of a deep thinker. A little beauty who's going to be serious trouble as an adolescent, testing all the rules, you can just feel it.

So my knight in slightly dented armor was married, once upon a time. Married and the father of a brilliant little girl. One of those kids, like Tommy, whose personality is fully formed at a young age. Suddenly the family photo seems icy cold in my hands and I hastily return it to the bottom of the drawer, feeling deeply ashamed. How dare I intrude in the man's private life, simply to satisfy my curiosity? It's a violation of his generosity, of his trust.

Still, I can't help wondering. Divorced, or something worse? Something he does not share with strangers or clients. Most divorced men would have mentioned having a child by now. Shown off a well-thumbed snapshot. Alluded to the fact that they, being parents, had some idea of what I was going through. And yet Shane had done nothing of the sort. Never alluded to anything but his previous career and his present vocation. Is this loss—for it has to be a loss, one way or another—is this emptiness in his life somehow connected to his sleep disorder? And if so, how exactly?

Leave it alone, I urge myself. *None of your beeswax. And never dare mention this, or he'll know you for a snoop and never trust you again.*

And I depend on his trust. Shane is my hope. Despite my current reliance on the big man, and my interest in what makes him tick, there's no twinge of physical attraction between us, no prospect of romance. My heart is too full of Tommy for anything like that. Not to mention Ted, who still guides me in memory. But it makes me wonder what Ted would think of Shane. Would they be friends or rivals? Friends, I think. Buddies, even. He's exactly the kind of self-contained, self-deprecating guy my Ted gravitated to. For sure he's the type of adult male Tommy likes to be around. A true-blue father figure without any of that macho bluster that confuses boys—or girls, for that matter.

Determined to avoid another onslaught of tears—crying hurts when your tear ducts are empty—I strip off my clothes, shower, towel dry and slip into the neatly made bed. Not allowing myself to think about who this bed might have belonged to, back in the day.

Counting sheep, counting Bruce, counting my own heartbeats, I eventually drift off into a light, troubled sleep, and find myself floating down empty corridors, searching for my son.

Then out of nowhere I'm sitting bolt upright in the bed, wide-awake and shivering with fear. Because of the noise.

A dull *thump!* that seems to shake the floor. And then, very clear, a man shouting. Muffled, can't make out the word.

Wham!

Right outside my door. Sounds like two men fighting for advantage, bouncing off the walls.

Shane cries out in pain: "No! God, no!"

I'm out of the bed in a flash, grabbing a sheet to cover myself. Scared to leave the bed, but even more sacred of doing nothing. Fear drives me to the door, into the hallway. A flickering light from the living room shows me the way to the source of the shouting and thumping.

Shane lies on the floor, writhing and groaning. He's wedged between the sofa and the coffee table, face pressed into the rug.

The TV is on, with the sound off. One of the shopping channels, hawking jewelry.

As Shane's long arms flail, the coffee table staggers away, bumps up against my shins. "Gah!" he groans. "No, no!"

The man who doesn't sleep is having a nightmare.

I kneel by his head. At the touch of my outstretched hand his body goes still.

"Jean?" he says, his mouth muffled by the rug.

"It's Kate," I tell him. "Kate Bickford."

"Gah!" he says, spitting rug.

"It's okay," I say, and give his bristly head a pat.

"Oh, God." He rolls over, breathing heavily.

"You were dreaming."

"Not dreaming," he says thickly. "Hallucinating."

He glances at me in the sheet, then quickly looks away.

"Sounded like you were fighting," I tell him. "I thought the man in the mask was here. In the house."

Shane leans against the sofa, knees drawn up, still breathing heavily. Face slick with night sweats and his eyelids twitching. Careful not to look at me in the sheet, although I'm perfectly decent. Underwear, a full sheet, what could he see? But covers his face with his trembling hands, groans softly and says, "I'm really sorry, Kate. For scaring you."

"Don't be."

"Really sorry," he repeats, sounding mournful if not humiliated. "Look, I'm okay. Go back to bed, you need your sleep."

"This is what I'm going to do," I say, rising from the floor and adjusting the sheet. Very togalike, really. Almost formal. "I'm going to get dressed and then I'm going to make us breakfast."

"Okay," he says.

And that's what happens.

baking bread | **30**

Cramming a body into a steel drum is hard work, Cutter discovers. If the victims had happened to be small or slight of build, no problem, but Hinks and Wald are both solid men. Not giants, by any means, but well muscled, heavy of sinew and bone, and they seem to resist going into the barrels. It's like pushing huge lumps of stiffening taffy back into a tube. Grunt work of the worst kind. Digging shallow graves would, in hindsight, have been much less effort, but he's already committed to the barrels.

At one point Cutter has to take a break and get his breath back, toweling the slick of sweat from his hands and face. He had the foresight to cover their heads with plastic garbage bags, so as not to make eye contact with the dead, but the whole process is exhausting, both physically and mentally.

Putting the paunchy police chief into the home freezer in Mrs. Bickford's basement was a piece of cake compared to this. And the chief's death had been accidental, almost, a case of wrong place, wrong time.

Until quite recently, Cutter had never considered himself to be a killer. Certainly not capable of cold-blooded murder. He'd been a sol-

dier doing his duty, and that meant killing the enemy when necessary. But for the last three weeks or so he's been taking the lives of civilians, American civilians, and the toll is starting to add up. One in
Rhode Island, one in New York, and now a total of three in good
old suburban Connecticut, with at least two more to go before the
mission is completed. Could be even more, if Mrs. Bickford's rangy
investigator sticks his nose in the wrong crack.

The dead have gathered in a pile in the dark corner of Cutter's brain
and at some point they will, he assumes, demand a reckoning. Scratch-
ing like frantic bird claws against the windowpane of his soul. Hard
to take, even for a trained assassin. Maybe he'll let slip his sanity and
join Lyla in her twilight world. But no, he can't allow that to happen,
not if the plan works, not if he manages to get his own son back home.
He'll have to find another way to deal with it, another way to silence
his victims.

Start by not thinking of them as victims. Think of them as unfor-
tunate casualties. Collateral damage.

"Hear that, Hinks? You're collateral damage."

Talking to a dead guy stuffed in a barrel. Pretty funny really. It gets
him laughing so hard he has to shove a hand in his mouth to make it
stop.

Much to my surprise there's an unexpired packet of yeast hiding
in a dry corner of Shane's refrigerator, behind the butter dish. The
yeast, along with a tablespoon of sugar, a teaspoon of salt, a little melted
butter and a few cups of King Arthur flour is all that's needed to make
a simple loaf of bread. Making good on my impulse to shed flour on
the counters, and also provide us with something fresh and whole-
some for breakfast.

It's been a while since I've kneaded dough entirely by hand, without the help of commercial kitchen equipment, and I find it com-
forting. The world can't be entirely crazy, or completely evil, if you

can make bread with your own hands, and fill a kitchen with that wonderful smell.

"I could go out for doughnuts," Shane offers, watching me sift the flour through my fingers.

"Don't you dare."

"Just seems like a lot of trouble," he says, indicating the mixing bowl, the flour dust.

I suspect the idea of a woman baking in his kitchen makes him a little nervous. "Don't worry, I promise not to move in," I assure him, keeping it light.

The very idea makes him blush. "No, no," he protests. "It'll be great. I love bread right out of the oven. It's been years."

"I could thaw out the chicken potpie if you prefer."

"Might be dangerous by now," he admits. "That's just for emergencies."

"Like nuclear attack. Relax, Randall. I enjoy doing this."

"Right," he says. "The catering business."

"I loved cooking and baking long before I went into business," I say, setting the pan in the preheated oven. "What time is it getting to be?"

"Five in the morning."

"The sun is up," I notice. "Time to milk the chickens."

Shane ignores the lame joke. "Look, Kate, I wanted to apologize. You say it's not necessary, but I think it is. You've got enough on your plate without having to deal with my demons."

"Oh," I say, trying to keep it light. "Are they really demons?"

"Sort of."

"You don't have to tell me. Not unless you want to."

He's obviously been thinking of little else since I found him flailing about on the floor. "Better if you know," he says with some reluctance. "Not that it's a big secret. Maria knows. Anybody who knew me at the time, they know." He forces himself to meet my eyes and says, "I had a family. Wife and daughter. Both killed in an accident."

That explains the photograph in the drawer, the blank spaces on the wall, and, quite possibly, his obsession with finding lost children.

"I'm very sorry," I tell him. "It must have been awful. Must still be awful."

Lame words, but they come from experience. I'd lost a husband and faced losing a child. So I knew something of what he'd gone through, was still going through each day.

"We were driving up from Washington," he explains, sounding somewhat detached. Finding the necessary distance. "Amy had a project for her world-studies class, I figured it was our chance to show her the Smithsonian. Fabulous museum. We had a great time, stayed longer on the last day than we intended, and then it was time to come home."

I'd like to know if home was here, in this very house, but don't want to interrupt him. And figure he'll make it clear at some point.

"It's night, heavy traffic," he says. "We're on the New Jersey Turnpike when my eyelids start getting heavy. So I pull into a rest area and let Jean take over driving. She's wide-awake and raring to go. Amy's in the back, sound asleep. Next thing I know, I'm waking up in a wreck and I'm the only survivor. While I was asleep, Jean got sideswiped by a tractor-trailer and dragged under his rear wheels. Totally his fault." He pauses, studies the backs of his hands before looking up, eyes incandescent with remembering. "So that's my story. And yes, the sleep-disorder thing happened afterward. I'm fully aware it has to be related to the accident, to losing my family, but awareness doesn't make it better."

My impulse is to give the big guy a hug, but my instincts are picking up a vibe that says a hug is the last thing in the world he wants. It won't change anything, and it can't possibly ease the pain. So I let it go and continue to fuss around, cleaning up after myself, making the place tidy again.

"Okay," I finally say. "You make coffee while we wait on the bread."

Later, after scoffing down two slices of warm, honey-drenched warm bread, Shane grins at me. "This was a good idea. Thank you."

"You're welcome. Figure we've got a busy day ahead of us, right?"

"Absolutely," he says.

"Care to share?"

He shrugs, takes another slug of strong coffee. "Got several irons in the fire. Waiting for an ID on the vehicle Bruce was driving. Waiting on a list of suspects from my Pentagon source. Waiting on whatever Jared Nichols is cooking up for the state of Connecticut. So while we're waiting, I'll try calling around Pawtucket."

Pawtucket. That stumps me for a moment. And then I remember why Pawtucket, Rhode Island, is important. "The adoption agency," I say. "Where we got Tommy."

Shane nods. "I tried phoning them yesterday. They're no longer in business, so we need to check with the city and possibly the state or county, see where the adoption records are being stored. We might have to run up there, I won't know until I call."

Eleven years have passed, but the thought of what happened that fine and glorious evening gives me a heart-size pang. Ted drove, of course, while I chewed my nails. He'd tell me nothing, not even the gender of the baby, in case it fell through, like so many of the other attempts had fallen through. And I knew better than to ask, though I longed to know. Which made for a long, near-silent ride. The only reason I could stand it without freaking out was because Ted had seemed so confident, so certain that our long ordeal was over. Confident not in words but in posture, in the way he gripped the wheel, the way he glanced at me and smiled. And I remember thinking, in the midst of a near anxiety attack, that whatever happened I'd always have Ted, and that even if we never got a baby it would be fine, we'd have each other.

Ignorance was a kind of nervous bliss, on that fine day. In the end we hadn't gone to Pawtucket, where Family Finders was located, but to the airport in Providence. And there in Arrivals we'd been introduced to baby Tomas, scrawled our names on a few sheets of paper and walked out to the parking lot as parents. Ted had hidden a car seat in the trunk, but I insisted on holding the baby. Sitting in the back, in the so-called safe seat, cooing at the beautiful baby and crying and giggling and talking a mile a minute while Ted drove us home. Both of us knowing we'd never be the same, that two had become three. Never imagining that three would become two again. Or that two might, in some terrible way, become one.

"You okay?" Shane wants to know.

"I'm fine."

Shane checks his watch. "Should be answering the phones at the town offices in another hour or so. We'll just have to hold tight until then."

Long before the hour is up, a car pulls into Shane's driveway. Looking through the drapes, I see Maria Savalo open the door to her BMW, stick out her bare feet and put on her heels. As she takes her briefcase from the seat and makes for Shane's front door, I'm thinking she doesn't look happy, but maybe she's not a morning person.

Wrong.

"Bad news," she tells me. "You're going to be arrested."

3

THE GOOD HEART

Cutter knew what his line was going to be long before the door opened.

"Dr. Munk, I presume?"

Of course, he'd had to flash the NYPD shield at the peephole, also as planned. The badge was a cheap fake, but looked mighty impressive through a fish-eye lens.

He could have written Dr. Munk's lines, too, because he knew exactly what he was going to say. Peering through the crack in the door with one nervous, twitching eye as he keeps the chain on the lock. "There must be some mistake," the good doctor manages to say. Sounds like he swallowed a hockey puck, has trouble getting the words out. "My name is, uh, Barnes. Luther Barnes."

Cutter lifts his coat jacket, revealing a holstered handgun. "Your name is going to be 'dead body in room 512' if you don't take the chain off the hook right now."

Only two ways it can go from here. Munk will either do as ordered, or he will make a move to slam the door, run to the bathroom and attempt to call the front desk, reporting an intruder. Cutter sees it in his eyes—maybe some doubt about the dime-store shield—and he kicks through the chain before Munk can react.

The guy ends up on his butt, looking astonished as Cutter closes and locks the door and tosses him the broken chain. "Stanley Joseph Munk, M.D.," he says. "Looking good, Doc. Tell you what, scoot back and you can lean against the wall, make yourself comfortable."

Munk glances nervously at the laptop computer open on the desk, LCD screen glowing. Catches himself and pretends he wasn't looking. "Who the hell are you?" he demands without much force. "You're not a cop. What do you want?"

Munk is an imposing-looking man in his late forties, with curly, salt-and-pepper hair shaped by a stylist to the stars. Strong chin, highly intelligent gray eyes, and the long, elegant hands of a classical pianist. In fact, he does play quite competently, although not professionally. Even on his butt, with his back against the wall, he has a commanding presence. Type A personality, used to getting his own way, and confident that he's one of the meritocracy, the self-invented masters of the universe. Not as easy to dominate as, say, your average enemy combatant, or your average suburban housewife. Definitely a challenge.

"I don't believe this," Munk mutters, shifting on his haunches. Obviously considering his options for some sort of escape mechanism that has not, as yet, presented itself.

Cutter drags over a chair, takes a seat, gives the doc his best stone-cold-killer smile. An evildoer grin that he's practiced in the mirror until he damn near scared himself. Killer grin that got him through Iraq without a scratch, physically at least. Dr. Munk blanches. The man is shit-scared, but even so he's desperate enough to be thinking about launching himself at Cutter, wrestling him for the gun.

He's at a disadvantage, is Stanley, but he's not without balls.

"Don't even think about it," Cutter advises him. "Thing is, even if you manage to take the gun from me—very unlikely—you'll still have to shoot me. Won't look good, 'Famous Surgeon Murders Federal Agent.'"

As intended, his target is confused by the retort. "You said you were a cop," Munk protests. "A city cop."

"I lied," Cutter responds cheerfully. "That was just to get through the door. Here's my real badge."

Cutter tosses him the absolutely genuine Federal Bureau of Investigation, Special Agent shield, along with the matching photo ID that helps seal the deal. Badge is real but the ID is fake—and a civilian will never be able to tell the difference.

"Take note of the name," he suggests. "Paul Allen Defield. After our conversation if you decide to file a complaint, they'll need a name."

Munk is handling the badge like it's radioactive. Cutter can almost see the wheels turning in the doc's big, fast-reactor brain. FBI masquerading as NYPD, what's the deal here, how bad is it? Can't be a good thing, that's for sure. Starting to grasp that the unexpected visit has to do with what's on the laptop, but not quite believing it. Letting himself hope it's something else entirely, and not quite believing that, either. Very expressive face, has Stanley, while under stress. Something of the boy showing through, under all those layers of sangfroid and studied confidence.

"Just try and relax, Dr. Munk," Cutter suggests amiably. "We don't need no stinking badges, do we? You want to know what this is all about? It's all about you. You the man, Stan." He lets that sink in before delivering the zinger. "You're the man with the sick kink for kiddy porn."

That does it, Munk's eyes dim just a little, like he's lost crucial amperage. And now he knows there's no hope that the sudden intrusion isn't connected to what he's got on the laptop, and what that forbidden connection means to his business, his career, his life.

"Funny thing about secrets," Cutter says, enjoying himself, taking strength from Munk's reaction. "Lots of fun when you control the se-cret, am I right? You've been getting a real kick out of your secret life for years. You put on your dress-down disguise, the baseball cap and jeans. Then you saunter over here with your laptop in the briefcase, and once the door is closed, you're in another world. A world where you and your special friends can openly discuss what, exactly, turns you on."

"You have no right," Munk protests weakly.

"In your case, what turns you on is girls between the ages of ten and twelve. Very age specific, your kink."

"How could you possibly know something like that?" Munk says, his face going even paler. Tiny droplets of cold sweat appear on his forehead, make his eyes blink rapidly.

"I know because it's all there," Cutter says, indicating the laptop. "Every sick conversation you've had online. Every photo you've downloaded, every film clip you viewed."

"That's not possible. You're bluffing."

"Am I? How about this—you like to joke about a 'perfect ten' being ten years old. Your pedophile pals find it very amusing. In fact one of your many screen names is P–10."

"Oh, God."

"God has nothing to do with it, Dr. Monk. Blame it on the Child Pornography Task Force. That's where I come in. I'm the agent-in-charge of the Child Pornography Task Force, New York. Which gives me access to all the hi-tech goodies, including some rather amazing spy-ware that's going to put your nuts in a blender."

"Spyware?" blusters Munk, who clearly understands the terminol-ogy and grasps what it implies. "But the firewalls—I thought…"

His voice trails off, unable to complete the sentence, as it all sinks in.

"You know the amazing thing?" Cutter says, training the pistol on Munk's jean-clad scrotum. "Sickos like you always manage to convince themselves that a thirty-nine-dollar piece of firewall software can protect them. What a joke. It's like using a piece of cheap cardboard to stop a speeding bullet. Our task force uses a spyware program developed by the NSA, on loan to Treasury. You know what the program is called? Creepster. Because it finds creeps like you, Dr. Munk. It finds you and lives in your computer and every time you go on the Internet, Creepster reports directly to me, and makes a record of everything you've done and said, everywhere you've gone on the Internet, every image you've looked at. Every keystroke, every downloaded file. I know your screen names, your passwords. I know every dirty, sick thing about you."

That isn't strictly true, about the NSA developing the program, but Cutter figures the doctor has heard of the National Security Agency, and that it will impress him. In actual fact, the spyware had been liberated from a counterterrorist intelligence unit assigned to Delta Force. Payment for the shaft job he'd gotten from the Army Special Operations Force, their ever-so-polite suggestion that he'd be more comfortable as a civilian. In that desperate hour he'd offered to take a drop in rank, or even return to the enlisted ranks, but the offer was declined "without prejudice." Meaning shut up about what you did and please go away. So he'd burned the very useful spyware program onto a CD and smuggled it out, with the intention of selling it on the black market. Good thing he hadn't, as it had made everything else possible. No spyware, no mission, simple as that. Spyware that had allowed him to explore every digitized aspect of Stanley Munk's complicated life and find a way to make him malleable.

The good doctor—and he's a very good doctor, as far as that goes—is the founder of one of the most exclusive and successful surgical clinics on the East Coast. The clinic rakes in millions in fees, enough to support himself and his five partners in high style—much, much more than any of them could have commanded in the public hospital sector.

Near as Cutter can determine, none of the medical partners is aware of or share in Munk's sexual proclivities. His trophy wife—third in a line of trim, tiny-breasted little blondes—has no clue. He's never been arrested, never been reported, never been caught, and when he seeks actual flesh-and-blood victims, he apparently ventures to safe foreign locales like Thailand and Bangkok and the Philippines, where his anonymity can be assured.

Sick bastard is careful but not, as it happens, careful enough.

"What do you want?" Munk asks, managing to sound both plaintive and angry. "Money?"

Cutter leans in, using his killer smile, and is gratified to see the good doctor wince, pressing himself against the wall. Nowhere to go, nowhere to hide.

"What I want," Cutter says, "is for you to understand what is at stake. I have in my possession, and duplicated on agency files, evidence that links you to possession and exchange of illegal child pornography. If this evidence is introduced into normal channels, you will certainly be arrested. If convicted, you may or may not serve time, depending on the deal your lawyer cuts, but you will be registered as a sex offender. No way to avoid it."

"Oh, my God," Munk blubbers. "Oh, my God." Panting like he's about to be physically ill, as if he can taste the gorge rising in his throat.

"Luckily, you have a rare skill. One that's going to make things right for both of us."

For the first time in the most terrifying five minutes of his life, Dr. Stanley Munk looks hopeful. "What do you want?" he asks.

"An exchange of value," Cutter says. "We're going to help each other."

"I'm listening," Munk says.

Cutter leans back in the chair, lets the man think about it for a crucial minute or so. Tenderizing his enormous ego, an ego that won't let him admit that despite being brilliant and successful, he's allowed his sick sexual deviance to put him in peril.

"I can make all of this evidence disappear," Cutter tells him, nodding at the laptop. "In exchange, you will arrange for the admission of a new patient at your clinic. You will schedule a certain procedure for the day after tomorrow, and then let your famous hands do their magic. That's it."

"New patient?" Munk's eyes light up, convinced he's figured it all out. "So that's what this is all about! You're the new patient."

Cutter smiles, shakes his head. "Not me," he says. "My son."

Tomas has been walking the wall edge for an hour. Or maybe for ten minutes. Without a watch or a clock or window or a television there's no good way to gauge the passage of time. He's tried counting his pulse, but doesn't know how fast his heart beats, so it tells him nothing useful. Not that knowing what time it is would make any difference to his present situation. Whatever time it is, time is running out.

He must find a way to escape or he will die. Of this, Tomas is certain. Steve is going to kill him, or do something that's even worse than death. Something so bad it can't be imagined. Not that Steve threatened to hurt him. The man promised to take care of him, to make sure he wasn't hurt again by the men he called the wild boys.

"No more wild boys," he had promised, holding Tomas so close against his chest that the boy could feel the thumping of his heart. "They've been taken care of, son. Fired, I mean."

The way he sometimes called Tomas "son" makes the boy shiver inside. Something is wrong with Steve, inside his head. At first he'd seemed better than the other two, who had cursed at him for wetting the bed. But when he'd taken off the black ski mask and made Tomas look at his face, the boy had sensed that something was terribly wrong with him. He had no experience with mental illness, so Tomas didn't know if the man who called himself Steve was insane or just so deeply unhappy about something that it had made him sick in the head. Whatever it was, he was all twisted up inside. It made him smell, too. A stink of bone-deep anger that frightened Tomas even more than the sneering violence of the wild boys who had broken his nose and promised to kill him.

The stinky smell made Tomas want to barf, it was that bad. Smell like that story in the book when he was little, about the Stinky Cheese Man. It was a funny story, really, but for a while it had been scary, just thinking about a stinky cheese man, a weird little guy with a round wheel of cheese for a head, and Tomas used to ask his mother to look under the bed and promise he wasn't there. Which she always did, and in a way that never made fun of his being scared of the dark.

Good old Mom. It was her voice he listened to now, in the white room. Telling him to get out.

Use your brain, young man. Use your brain and find a way out RIGHT NOW.

That's why he was walking the edge of the room, looking for a way to escape. Because she'd want him to, because she'd insist he not give up. More than anything, Mom hates quitters. Quitters and complainers. Tomas learned that early, and it was confirmed when his father died. Mom never complained about Dad dying, she just got to work and tried to make things better. Worked so hard all day, cooking and baking and on the phone, that sometimes she'd fall asleep at the dinner table, waiting for him to finish. When that happened he'd get his own special blanket from the bedroom and cover her. The blanket that kept him safe would keep her safe, too. That's what he'd believed at the time, because he was too little to know any better. Part of him still believed it. Part of him wanted his blanket right now. Wanted to curl up and be four years old and not have to worry about the real stinky cheese man, the one who was sick in the head and sometimes called him "son," as if he was confused, as if he didn't quite know who Tomas really was.

Has to be a way out, if only he can find it. He's discovered that the walls are made of heavy plywood—he can feel the grain of it under the white paint—and the floor is concrete. Probably the ceiling is plywood, too, but he can't tell for sure because he can't reach that high. The dresser is gone and even if he stands on top of the stupid potty-chair he can't touch the ceiling, can't touch the bare bulb that lights the room. The door is made of metal and, if anything, it feels more solid than the heavy plywood walls. Even if he finds a way to get through the door, he knows there's another door beyond it, equally heavy and impenetrable.

Has to be the walls. Once a couple years ago a squirrel got trapped in the attic because Tomas must have left a window open. Then Mom closed the window and that night the squirrel chewed right through the attic roof and escaped. Tomas had been amazed by the tooth marks, and by the frantic will of the squirrel, grinding through solid wood to get out. Like he'd read where wolves and coyotes sometimes chewed off their own feet to get out of a trap. Or that guy out in the wilderness who hacked off his leg to get out from under a boulder, and then crawled ten miles to the nearest town.

Tomas isn't ready to cut off his own limbs, but he feels like that mad squirrel, ready to chew through solid wood. Only, his teeth aren't sharp enough. If he had a jackknife he could whittle a hole and then make it bigger, but the only knife he owns is in his top drawer at home, along with his albums of baseball cards and the ball recovered after his first home run. He had three home runs so far, but had decided to keep only the first ball, because keeping all of them was like bragging about it, and Major Leaguers like A-Rod never bragged.

Unable to find a workable seam on the wall—nothing his fingernails can get at—he veers for the pile of food and water left by Stinky

Steve. Enough granola bars and breakfast cereal for more than a dozen meals, along with a half gallon of milk, a case of bottled water and a plastic Tupperware bowl for the cereal. There's no way to keep the milk cool and it's already going sour, so Tomas had tried eating Frosted Flakes with water instead of milk. That was disgusting, so he eats the cereal right out of the box, like Mom won't let him do at home.

A dozen meals was enough for at least four days, if he doesn't pig out. Does that mean Stinky Steve won't be back for four days? Maybe, maybe not. But Tomas figures this may be his only chance to escape, if he can only find a way.

Munching on a handful of Frosted Flakes, he returns to the room perimeter, looking for something, anything. And that's when he sees it, stuck where the plywood meets the concrete floor.

A dime.

Tomas gets down on his knees, puts his clotted-up nose to the floor and eyeballs the dime. Pries at it with his nubby fingers and almost dies when the dime starts to disappear under the bottom edge of the plywood, like a bug slinking out of sight.

Fighting tears, he stops what he's doing and thinks about it. Has to be a way to get the dime out. Can't push it. Needs something flat, like a knife blade, to pry it from the side. But if he had a knife he wouldn't need the dime, would he? Stupid. *Use your brain, dirtball. Think of a way to pry it out from under the plywood.*

What he does, he empties the sour milk into the potty-chair—truly disgusting—and tears the plastic jug with his teeth. Harder than he thought it would be, tearing the milk jug, but he finally gets it started and then the whole thing rips apart in his hands and he has a strip of flimsy plastic thin enough to fit under the bottom edge of the plywood.

A minute later, triumphant, he has a dime in his hands. Remaining on his knees, he uses the edge of the dime to scrape along the butted seams of the plywood wall. Finding the dimple of filler that hides a screw head.

He scrapes away the filler, exposing the screw head. Uses his fingernails to clean out the slots. Sets the edge of the dime into the slot and tries to turn the screw.

The dimes slips, falls from his hands. Rolls around. He tracks it with the same sharp eyes that can focus on a moving ground ball, and when the dime lies still he picks it up and tries again. Putting more weight into it this time, gripping the coin with all his might. The screw moves a quarter turn and stops and the dime jumps out of his hands again.

Takes forever to find the dime where it rolled up against the foam mattress. This time, before setting the dime into the slot, he studies the screw and realizes he's been turning it the wrong way, tightening the screw rather than loosening it.

Left to right tightens, right to left loosens. Good to know.

Fearful that the slots on the screw head are getting worn, he scrapes away the dimple of filler from another screw and tries that, remembering to turn the other way.

Three minutes later, his whole body shaking with excitement, he has removed the first screw from the wall.

Jackals with blue eyes. That's what Maria Savalo calls our friends in the media. Mostly local TV-news folks, with satellite trucks and boom antennas and big hair, but I recognize at least one print reporter from the *Fairfax Weekly*. Frankly, the poor woman looks a little frightened by the violent enthusiasm of her TV colleagues, who appear ready to stampede at a sudden noise or, as it happens, the sight of me emerging from the police station in handcuffs.

"KATE!" they roar. "KAAAAAATE!"

As if they know me. As if we're old friends. Lunging with microphones on poles. One of the padded microphones clobbers Deputy Sheriff Crebbins in the side of the head, and I'm not so secretly pleased to see him wince with surprise, if not pain. Back in the station the smug little man sounded so certain of my guilt. That self-satisfied glint in his eye as they took fingerprints, snapped mug shots. As if he, too, knows me intimately, has so deeply communed with my soul that he can discern the impulse to kill.

Mug shots. It won't take long for the tabloids to obtain copies of the very unflattering photographs of Mrs. Katherine Ann Bickford looking stunned as she is compelled to hold up a slate with her name and arrest numbers. Crebbin will probably be handing them out as party favors.

I never thought about how unfair mug shots are, how they make anyone look like a criminal. Put name and numbers under a harshly lit head shot and Mother Teresa herself would look like a felon. And I, obviously, am no Mother Teresa. I'm the killer mom who hid a body in the freezer with the frozen cookie dough and the lobster-stuffed ravioli, the she-devil who kidnapped her own son, the monster with the minivan.

A couple of Fairfax's finest deputies have me firmly by the arms, hands cuffed behind my back. They're leading me from the police station to the police van that will transport me to the county courthouse. All part of the elaborate arraignment dance choreographed by my attorney, after hurried negotiations with the state prosecutor. With me in the lead role, however reluctantly.

"You'll be fine!" Maria shouts beside me. My little cheerleader, all five feet of her almost disappearing beneath the surging crowd. "Everything will be okay!"

Maybe, maybe not. If all goes well, I will be booked, arraigned and released on bond. Out by noon, possibly. Fingers crossed. The prosecutor will not oppose bail, but as Maria reminds me, final determination will be up to the court. There's always the chance that an unsympathetic judge, or one who plays to the media, will deny bail and order me held over for trial. I've been informed that we will be appearing before Judge Irene "Good Night" Mendez, rated as moderate-to-conservative, so it could go either way.

The nickname comes from the song, apparently, and has nothing to do with putting the lights out on felons. Or so Maria wants me to believe. As if concerned about how I'll react. Wanting to avoid a client meltdown, especially in public.

How do I react? With numbness, shock, disbelief. Several days of being told an arrest is probably imminent failed to prepare me for the reality. For the humiliation of a felony-arrest booking, the full-bore assault by the media, the knee-knocking realization that mere innocence does not guarantee exoneration.

Shane is nowhere to be seen. Camera shy. Last thing I'd said to him, before leaving for the station was "Find my son."

He'd promised to do his best. I believe him, but will his best be good enough? I can't bear the thought of being locked up while Tommy is still out there, at the mercy of the man in the mask. But it's out of my hands. All I can do, all that lies within my limited power, is to trust my attorney.

Just before we arrive at the police van, a grinning, anorexic blonde with an outstretched microphone manages to worm her way to the front.

"Mrs. Bickford, were you having an affair with the victim?" she demands breathlessly.

Victim? For a moment I don't know who she's referring to. Probably because I feel like the victim here. But of course she means Fred Corso. Savalo has warned me not to answer any question. To keep, as she says, my lips firmly zipped. But I can't let that one stand. What would Fred's poor wife think if I refused to answer?

"No, of course not," I say. "He was a good friend."

"A good friend? Then why did you kill him?"

The cops pull me away before I can formulate an answer, and no doubt my startled expression—and my silence—will be featured on the local broadcasts.

Guilt all over me. I never harmed Fred Corso, but I feel guilty anyhow, and it shows.

Another few yards of struggle and I'm being pushed into the van, one of the officers keeping my head down, and then we're under way. Padded microphones bumping against the windows like malignant palm fronds, a fading roar of questions from my newfound friends.

Maria hands me a hankie, makes soothing noises. Can't remember when I started crying. Was I crying when they shoved the mic in my face? Is that what they'll see on the news tonight, killer mom in tears?

Jared Nichols, the handsome young prosecutor, looks like he just stepped out of the pages of *GQ*. Gorgeous suit, perfect hair and a smile that has to be artificially improved, because human beings don't come with teeth that white. A smile directed at my attorney, not at me.

"Maria," he says, offering his hand. "You'll be happy to know that Judge Mendez has barred the media from the arraignment. I see you made it through the gauntlet."

"Not quite," she says. "Broke my heel."

"Your heel?" He seems genuinely concerned.

"My shoe, Jared. My best Blahniks."

He turns a searching gaze at me, as if memorizing the face of an enemy combatant. "Bill it to your client," he tells Maria. "She can afford it."

"Jared," Maria responds sharply. "Be nice."

Because she doesn't dare appear before the court in bare feet, Maria grips the table so as not to wobble disrespectfully on her broken shoe when the judge enters.

"All rise," declaims a stentorian voice.

We're already standing. The judge enters, regal in her black robe, and I'm stunned by her youth. I'd been expecting someone with gray in her hair, peering over bifocals. Instead "Good Night" Mendez can't be a day older than me. Is that possible? Do people my age get to be judges? And what does it mean for my chances? I'd been hoping for grandmotherly concern and now find myself fearful that a contemporary may assume what the media assumes, that I was having a fling with the local police chief and killed him in the heat of passion, or to further my own agenda somehow.

Mendez glances at something on her desk, presumably the arraignment papers. "State of Connecticut versus Katherine Ann Bickford," reads the judge. "Mr. Nichols, you may begin," she adds, squinting slightly, as if prepared to be dazzled by his radiant smile.

The prosecutor reads from a paper held in his rock-steady hands. "The state charges Katherine Ann Bickford with the murder of Frederick Napoleon Corso, in the town of Fairfax, on or about June 21, in violation of General Statutes 53a–54a, that she did cause the death of Mr. Corso and did subsequently seek to hide her crime by secreting his body in her home..."

He drones on, but I'm having trouble following the legal jargon, or coping with the surprise of Fred's rather grand middle name. Napoleon? What was his mother thinking? I'm trying to see Fred as a little boy on the playground, defending the name, or hiding it. But then children wouldn't necessarily know who Napoleon was, would they? So maybe it was okay, no harm no foul, as Tommy likes to say.

Maria, aware of my faltering concentration, gently nudges me to sit up straight as Judge Mendez grills the prosecutor about the evidence supporting his charge.

"I assume the state has sufficient evidence to justify an arraignment for felony murder?"

"Yes, Your Honor."

"Do you intend to keep it a secret, Mr. Nichols?"

"No, Your Honor. Sorry. The victim's body was found in Mrs. Bickford's home freezer. There was a document on the body that the prosecution will show implicates Mrs. Bickford in the disappearance of her adopted son."

"How very convenient," says the judge. "Anything else?"

"Yes, Your Honor. A gun was found hidden in the same freezer, inside a bag of frozen peas. Ballistics has confirmed that this was the weapon used to kill Mr. Corso."

"In a bag of frozen peas?"

"Yes, Your Honor."

"I suppose the defendant's fingerprints were all over the gun?"

"Ah, no, Your Honor. The gun was wiped clean. But the prosecution would expect that, Your Honor."

"Expect what, Mr. Nichols? Would you care to be more specific?"

"That the perpetrator would remove fingerprint evidence."

"I see. You would expect the killer to remove fingerprints but not to remove the body or the weapon from her own basement? I'm not sure I follow the logic."

"Murder isn't always logical, Your Honor. And the victim weighed over two hundred pounds. The defendant would have had trouble moving the body on her own."

"But no trouble loading the body into the freezer?"

"We, ah, believe the defendant capable of, ah, leveraging the deceased into the freezer."

"Leverage?" says the judge. "As in 'give me a lever and I shall move the earth'?"

"Yes, Your Honor. But in this case the body of the victim, not the entire earth."

"Well, that's a relief, Mr. Nichols. Is there more?"

"Not at this time, Your Honor."

"Ms. Savalo?"

Maria stands, gripping the edge of the table. Beneath the table, I notice she's got the broken shoe partway off, and is poised on tiptoe, like a ballerina. "Your Honor," she begins, "my client is not guilty of this or any other crime. Her son was kidnapped, and she was subsequently drugged and threatened by one of the abductors, who forced her to transfer funds to an offshore account that is thus far untraceable. The bank will verify this. The fact that the money hasn't been traced is evidence of a professional criminal enterprise, which supports my client's version of the events. We believe lab results will eventually confirm that she was, indeed, drugged. My client has stated that she asked the police to check the basement because of a phone call she received from the kidnapper. Records confirm a call moments before the police entered Mrs. Bickford's domicile, and that the call was from an untraceable cell phone, a throwaway. Which also confirms Mrs. Bickford's statement."

"Mr. Nichols?"

"The defendant has an active imagination. It's 'the dog ate my homework' defense."

That results in a glare from Judge Mendez. "The victim is not a dog, Mr. Nichols, and murder is not homework."

"I apologize, Your Honor. Poor choice of words. But the fact remains that the state has sufficient evidence to proceed to trial."

Judge Mendez smiles faintly. "So you'd be ready for trial today, would you?"

"Excuse me, Your Honor?"

"It was a simple question, Mr. Nichols. If I scheduled this case for trial this very afternoon, would you be ready to proceed?"

"No, Your Honor."

"So you want to arrest Mrs. Bickford now and then develop further evidence before proceeding to trial?"

"I wouldn't put it quite that way, Your Honor. But the investigation is ongoing. We anticipate more evidence shortly."

"That's all you've got?"

"Yes, Your Honor."

"Thank you, Mr. Nichols. Ms. Savalo?"

"Your Honor, the defense has reached an understanding with the state. We will not appeal the arrest of my client on these charges at this time, if the state does not oppose my client being released on bond."

"I see. And why would you do that, Ms. Savalo, considering the entirely circumstantial evidence thus far presented by Mr. Nichols?"

There's a snapping noise as my attorney's pricey shoe heel completely lets go, and in that instant she has to grab me to keep herself from falling.

"Shit!"

"Ms. Savalo, are you okay?"

Maria kicks off both shoes, grimaces. "I'm very sorry, Your Honor. I broke a heel on the way into court."

"Are those Jimmy Choos, Ms. Savalo?"

"No, Your Honor. Blahniks."

"Ouch," says the judge. "My commiserations. And don't bother trying to hide your bare feet. We'll suspend proper dress rules just this once. Now, where were we?"

The court reporter reads back a few lines before the judge stops him. "Got it. Thanks. So I repeat, Ms. Savalo, why would you agree not to contest this charge, considering the entirely circumstantial evidence thus far presented by Mr. Nichols?"

Maria takes a deep breath before answering. "Because, Your Honor, it is absolutely critical that my client be able to continue searching for her missing son. Aside from anything else, he's the key to the whole conspiracy. To this end, we have engaged a private investigator skilled in abduction cases. Mrs. Bickford is working closely with him, and we have developed evidence crucial to the defense. Evidence that could have been developed by the state or local police, but was not, because they failed to pursue other leads."

"Mr. Nichols?"

"The investigation remains open, Your Honor. If evidence arises that justifies another line of investigations, then I'm confident it will be vigorously pursued."

The judge taps a pen on her desk, seems to be mulling something over. "If I may ask you another question, Mr. Nichols."

"Certainly, Your Honor. Ask away."

"Do I detect a certain lack of enthusiasm from the prosecution?"

For the first time, Jared Nichols looks slightly taken aback. "I'm not sure what you mean, Your Honor."

"From where I'm sitting, Mr. Nichols, it very much looks as if you've arraigned the defendant in response to pressure from the local police, or possibly from the news organizations, rather than from a sincere belief that you can win a conviction. Does that explain why you will not oppose bond?"

"Yes, Your Honor. I mean no, Your Honor. I mean we do not oppose because we don't believe Mrs. Bickford to be a flight risk, or a further danger to the community."

"Hmm. So that's your story and you're sticking to it?"

"Yes, Your Honor."

"Well, I'm not inclined to release the defendant on personal recognizance. Not for felony murder, however thin the evidence. Bond is therefore set at one hundred thousand dollars."

"Thank you, Your Honor."

Before standing up, the judge leans down from the bench with a word of advice. "Get busy," she urges me. "Find your son."

His fingers are bleeding but Tomas pays no heed. Wipes his hands on his shirt and concentrates on gripping his improvised screwdriver. He's learned the trick of carefully backing out the screws that hold the plywood and he's halfway done with the first sheet. The wood has warped away from the metal studs and he can see the pink of insulation stuffed behind it. He knows the pink stuff is itchy because once he made the mistake of lying down in a pile of it up in the attic. Thinking it looked soft, like cotton candy, and discovering that it itched like a thousand ant bites.

Mom put him in the shower, squirted shampoo all over him. What a goon. Himself, not Mom. She'd been concerned about his eyes, telling him the pink stuff was made of little bits of glass, and his eyes had stung, but that was from the shampoo.

No harm done, as it turned out. And right now he could care less about the itchy pink stuff. If it means he can get out, he'll gladly burrow through the insulation and worry about washing it off later.

Only trouble, he can't get all the way up the plywood, to release the last few screws at the top. If he had a board or something, maybe he could pry it loose. But he doesn't have a board, or anything to produce leverage. All he has is his own body. His bleeding hands, his skinny arms. His feet.

Feet.

Tomas lies down, back against the floor, and works his Nike into the gap where the plywood warps. It pinches his toes—hurts—but he ignores the pain and pushes harder, worming his foot farther into the gap. He can feel another board on the other side of the metal studs—a discouraging discovery—but decides not to think about how he'll get through that. Enough to concentrate on his immediate task, using his legs to push the plywood away from the studs. Legs are way stronger than arms, that's what Coach Corso says. It's legs that make the swing, legs that enable a pitcher to throw a fastball. Legs that are going to help him escape.

When he's halfway up to his hips, his foot encounters another metal stud. No surprise, he's already backed out the screw, knows it had to be there. Turning sideways so he's facing the wall, Tomas pushes with all his might. Using his hands to push against the wall and straightening his leg at the same time. Like doing a push-up, only sideways.

He can feel the plywood moving, bending away from the wall.

Harder. Push harder. Stinky Man is coming back. Stinky Man is going to get you.

Tomas groans, sweat popping out on his forehead, tears coming to his eyes. *Stupid plywood!* And then, suddenly, no pressure, and the plywood is moving, the upper screws pulling through, and he's able to push with both knees. Aware of a great bend in the plywood, his arms shaking with the effort, until finally the whole sheet of plywood pops free of the studs, teeters on end and crashes to the floor behind him.

If he'd hit a home run, Tomas would have whooped and pumped his fist in the air. This is way better than a home run, but he knows he's running out of time. So instead of celebrating he gets on his knees and uses both hands to burrow into the pink insulation, sending chunks of it flying over his head. Exposing the gray backing paper of the Sheetrock that forms the outer wall of his prison.

Not plywood, but Sheetrock. He recognizes it as the same stuff from the inside of his closet at home. It looks hard, but it's not as strong as plywood, and he knows that, too.

Tomas starts clawing at the Sheetrock with his bleeding nails.

Dr. Stanley Munk is striding through the gleaming halls of his exclusive clinic when the cell phone in his Canali trouser pocket starts to vibrate. He considers not answering. He considers throwing the damn phone to the floor and crushing it underfoot. Instead, he ducks into his office, locks the door and flips open the phone.

"Yes."

"Good afternoon, Doctor. How's every little thing?"

Munk recognizes the voice of his oppressor. The fake cop or phony FBI agent or whatever he is. Paul Defield, if you can believe it. Man with the gun, and with the power to shatter his world. Also the man who can make everything better.

"Fuck you," says Munk.

"I see you've recovered your sense of well-being. That's good. I want you at the top of your game."

Munk has been awaiting the call. Dreading it ever since Defield pressed the phone into his hands. "What you ask is impossible," he says, repeating what he's been rehearsing in his own mind for hours. "Can't be done on short notice."

"Oh, you can make it happen, Doctor," the voice says, sounding oddly cheerful. "I checked the schedules for your surgical team."

"How could you possibly—?" Munk stops himself. Of course, the spyware. The bastard not only knows about the laptop, about the perfect tens, he knows everything that happens in the clinic, and when. It makes Munk feel unclean, violated, and his burst of anger morphs into a cold, lingering fear. He has to find a way to get this man out of his life. Tells himself he'd cheerfully kill the son of a bitch, but Dr. Munk has never killed anyone. Not intentionally.

"The new patient will be delivered to you in Scarsdale tomorrow morning at 0600 hours," says the cool, confident voice. "Six o'clock sharp, at the rear entrance. You will meet the ambulance yourself. You will not delegate the task, do you understand?"

"Listen to me," Munk says, whispering fiercely as his eyes flick to the locked door. "What you ask can't be done! It takes days to prep a patient for surgery like that. Dammit, we don't even know the blood type."

"Blood type is A negative," responds the voice.

"It's more than blood type. You don't know what you're asking."

"Here's what I know about your clinic, Dr. Munk, and what you can do on short notice, given the proper motivation. Two years ago you performed a similar procedure on a certain Arab gentleman, a member of the Saudi royal family. Do you recall the gentleman?"

"Yes," Munk admits. "But that was different."

"Not so different," insists the voice. "His private air ambulance landed at JFK at 5:00 a.m. and was whisked through customs. By nine he was in surgery. It's all in the files."

Munk sinks into his custom-built ergonomic chair. Eight grand and it feels like a chunk of lumpy ice under his buttocks. Cold sweat runs from under his arms, soaking his shirt. He feels like puking, and forces himself to swallow the gorge rising. He remembers the Saudi prince vividly, and the enormous fee paid by his grateful family.

"A million bucks," says the voice. "Not bad for a day's work. I don't blame you for not declaring a nice tidy sum like that, or keeping most of it secret from your partners. They have any idea what a deceptive bastard you are? Any idea what you're doing when you go to Thailand twice a year?"

The doctor feels his stomach slip away, as if he's just gone over the top of a particularly steep roller coaster. A roller coaster with no bottom, no end in sight.

"You still there?" the voice wants to know. "Cat got your tongue?"

"Who are you?" Munk asks. "Who are you, really? And how do you know these things?"

"My sources are not your concern. Your only concern is the surgery you'll be performing tomorrow."

"We had full medical records on the prince," Munk protests. "We knew exactly what to expect. This is different."

"My son comes with full medical records, too," says the voice. "You'll have them tomorrow morning. The driver will hand you a file. It's all there. Everything you require."

"You're insane."

The voice chuckles, very intimate, as if he's right there in the room with Munk. "Maybe I am," he says. "That doesn't change what will happen if you don't do exactly as I say. We have a deal, Dr. Munk. A deal that keeps you out of jail. A deal that keeps your ugly little secret. As soon as we conclude this discussion, you will put your surgical team on alert. Tell them it's another celebrity. The son of a politician or a movie star. Another Saudi prince, if you like. Very hush-hush. Use your imagination."

"They'll never believe me."

"Of course they will," says the voice. "You're a really good liar, Dr. Munk. World-class. Make them believe."

when the dark lightning strikes | **35**

Our first big break comes at five after two in the afternoon. Connie has helped me raise the ten grand for the bail bondsman and now we're back at my dingy motel to pick up the rental. Shane looks almost as discouraged as I feel. The inquiry into the adoption records has been a bust and he's about to tell me how bad it is when his cell phone chirps.

He glances at the incoming number. "I have to take this call in private," he explains, somber-faced.

I offer to leave the room, but he waves me off, and a moment later he's outside. I can see him through the window, holding the phone to his ear with one hand while he extracts pen and notebook from his shirt pocket. The fact that he's avoiding eye contact is more than a little disturbing. Is this more bad news on the way, is that why he doesn't want me to overhear the conversation?

Maybe the worst has happened. Maybe the state police have found a body. Maria would surely contact him first, let him break the bad news.

It's a fairly mild day for late June, but the room suddenly feels claustrophobic and it's all I can do not to open the door and bolt.

Please, God, don't let this be when the black lightning strikes.

When Shane finally slips back into the room my heart is pounding so hard it makes my ribs hurt. But his eyes are crinkled up in a slow smile, so it can't be the news I've been dreading. Something else has happened, and he's quick to let me know, sensing my anxiety.

"My contact at the Pentagon came through," he announces, holding up his notebook. "We've got a list of Army Special Operation Forces personnel in the area, active and inactive, and several of them fit the general description."

I'd forgotten to breathe, and take a deep, shuddering lungful. The air burns, but it feels oh so good.

Reading from his notes, Shane begins to go into detail.

"There are five men within the thirty-five-to-forty age group who would be likely to wear the unsheathed-dagger tattoo," he says. "No specific confirms on the tats, unfortunately. Not yet anyhow. But get this, one of the guys has a ten-year-old son. An adopted son with medical problems. We'll start with him."

One minute later we're back on the road, heading north.

Cutter is starting to think that following Mrs. Bickford is a waste of time. Time that's rapidly expiring, and that is starting to feel like small bubbles in his blood, spurring him on. Fortunately they're all heading in the same direction—north on 95—and since Cutter doesn't want to exceed the speed limit in his stolen Cadillac, he might as well remain behind his quarry, keeping an interval of five or six vehicles between them, for at least another few exits.

He assumes they're heading to Pawtucket, to check out the adoption records. Which will prove to be another dead end for Supermom and her faithful sidekick.

So far as Cutter has been able to determine, all the bases had been covered. Assuming he hasn't left behind any DNA or prints—and he's one hundred percent certain he has not—there's no way a solo investigator will be able to identify him as the culprit. Planning and execution have been meticulous. He's used all of his skills, his training, his battlefield-honed instincts, and now he's less than twenty-four hours from completion.

Between now and then he'll do whatever has to be done to keep the enterprise on track. Kill, maim and terrorize as necessary. As he sees it, the primary challenge is managing the surgeon, Stanley Munk. At this point, control of Munk is strictly a psychological operation, and psych-ops are always dicey and unpredictable. At present Munk is cooperating, but that could change, and if it does, Cutter has to be ready. If threatening to expose the good doctor isn't enough, he'll find another way. Take Munk's latest trophy wife hostage, if necessary. But abductions are inherently risky, requiring complicated logistics and timing and he hopes it won't come to that.

Cutter doesn't think of himself as a kidnapper. In his mind kidnappers are vile monsters, damaging children for money or depraved physical pleasures. His appropriation of Tomas is completely different, and necessary. The choice had been clear. He had to take Mrs. Bickford's son so that his own son might live. And if that means his soul is damned to hell, so be it.

His foot knows something is wrong before he does. Why has he jammed on the brakes? Because five cars ahead, Mrs. Bickford has done the unthinkable. She's supposed to be going to Pawtucket—he'd been absolutely certain that's where she was heading—but instead she's put her blinker on and is edging into the right-hand lane for the exit to Route 9, just south of New London.

The fact explodes like shrapnel in his hyperactive mind. Something is wrong, and for the first time in weeks, he has no idea what it means.

Our first stop is in Sussex, and as we wend our way up Route 9, Shane is explaining what happened to the adoption records.

"According to the Rhode Island attorney general's office, Family

Finders was a shady outfit, licensed but not always compliant with state laws on the adoption process," he begins.

"We had no idea," I tell him. "Ted would have told me if there was something wrong."

"He couldn't have known. It was a very slick operation. Their fees were anywhere from ten to fifty grand, depending on the client. They squeezed out as much as they could, apparently, after checking the financial statements that adoptive parents have to file. They were in the baby-selling business, plain and simple."

Shane speaks in a just-the-facts-ma'am voice, but each word pounds into my head like an ice-cold spike.

"Are you saying Tommy's birth mother might really be alive?"

He studies me with concern. "It's possible. My best guess is that Bruce has his own agenda, but there could be birth parents involved. We might never know for sure because the records were destroyed in a fire six weeks ago."

"What happened?"

"After Family Finders went out of business, the files were in file boxes in the basement at the county records office. Six weeks ago somebody doused the files with lighter fluid. That's as much as the arson squad was able to determine. And the one employee at Family Finders who might know died at about the same time. Fell from a ladder, supposedly."

"It was him," I say. "Had to be Bruce."

Shane agrees. "He found something, doesn't want anybody else to know what it is."

"I'm not sure it really matters now," I say. "Not when we show up at his front door."

He's not the one. That's obvious to me the moment he opens the door. Too big, not the right age, and he doesn't move like the man who abducted my son. And if there was any doubt, his voice confirms it. He's not Bruce, not even close.

We're in Sussex, which bills itself as "The Nicest Small Town In America." No argument from me. It's the sort of place I think of as Old Connecticut, far removed both in miles and mind-set from the towns and cities within commuting distance of New York. A quiet little riverfront village with a mix of lovingly restored colonial-era homes and a few quirky-looking buildings that had been patched together over the centuries, without help or guidance from *Architectural Digest*. That's not to say that developers haven't had their way here and there, among the slightly precious shops and inns, but I can't imagine upscale destinations like Greenwich or Fairfax allowing a giant plastic groundhog to be featured in the main square. The locals apparently have great affection for Sussex Sam, and parade him around on Groundhog Day. It's late in the month of June and Sussex Sam is still there in the square, wearing his jaunty plastic top hat and searching for his shadow.

A few crucial blocks from the waterfront, and thus far free from renovation, there stands a row of wooden, three-story tenement buildings, sheathed in dented aluminum siding. We've located Lieutenant Michael Vernon, U.S. Army (Ret.) on the third floor of the middle building, where he lives with his wife and son in a four-room apartment that smells of sour milk and boiled potatoes.

According to the information from Shane's source at the Pentagon, Lieutenant Michael Vernon is forty-one years of age, but he looks ten years older, and his broad-shouldered, linebacker's physique has sagged a bit over the years. Thinning red hair, close-cropped, and the kind of freckled skin that eventually shows serious sun damage. A big brawl of a man with forearms like Popeye. He's not entirely clear on why we've sought him out, but seems glad to have company on a summer evening, and makes us welcome.

"Family Finders, huh? Yeah, I knew they went bankrupt or whatever. One time when things were bad Cathy and I talked to a lawyer about suing the bastards. Pardon me, miss. But you know what I mean. Anyhow, it was too late. Nobody left to sue."

Shane and I have been offered seats on the plush green sofa, which is relatively new, unlike anything else in the apartment.

"Gift from my mother-in-law," Lieutenant Vernon explains. "Couple months ago she plops down and a broken spring bites her in the butt. Next day a delivery truck pulls up. Hell, if I knew that's all it took I'd have bitten her in the ass myself. Pardon me, miss. No offense intended."

"None taken," I respond.

His wife, Cathy, is a special-needs teacher at the local middle school, so he stays home to look after Mike Junior. "Not my idea to name him after me," he says. "That was Cathy. You guys want some iced tea? 'Scuse my saying so, but it's hot as a bitch in here."

Iced tea would be great. There's no air-conditioning and the windows are screwed shut because this is the third floor and Mike Junior has a habit of lurching out of open windows.

"He's not really trying to jump," Lieutenant Vernon explains. "He just sort of rocks forward, you know, like they do, and if he loses his balance, out he goes."

The black-haired, olive-skinned boy has been relegated to his bedroom while Daddy talks with the nice man and woman. The handsome little boy went willingly enough—it's obvious he enjoys pleasing his father—but every minute or so he makes a high-pitched shriek that startles all of us, even his father, who knows to expect it.

"He's just playing. That's the voice he uses when he's playing with his toys. Tea okay? Good. Now, how can I help you?"

Shane explains that my son has been abducted, and that the kidnapping may have had something to do with Family Finders.

"Your kid got snatched? No shit. Sorry, Mrs.—what is it again? Brickyard?"

"Call me Kate," I tell him. "Don't worry about swearwords, Mr. Vernon. I'm not offended by salty language."

That makes him chuckle. "Salty language? That's the marines. I was army, we just plain cuss. Anyhow, Kate, you please call me Mike, okay? Around here they call me Big Mike so as not to confuse me with the boy, but just plain Mike is fine."

"You were Special Forces?" Shane asks.

"Yeah. How'd you know?"

"The tattoo."

"Oh, yeah." Big Mike glances at his massive forearm, as if he'd forgotten the image of the unsheathed dagger inked into his skin. "Ancient history now. I got out five years ago on a hardship, because of Mike Junior. Had him in a special-needs school for a while, but really it doesn't work for him, having all those other kids around. With

Little Mikey, you got to control his environment, make him feel safe and secure. Then he's fine. Really, he's a great kid."

From the bedroom, the boy shrieks. I've begun to recognize that the shrieks do indeed have a playful quality. And I've decided that Big Mike Vernon is a thoroughly decent man for staying home with the boy, and for speaking about him with such obvious patience and affection.

"Maybe we could start at the beginning," Shane suggests. "How did you establish contact with Family Finders?"

Big Mike shrugs. "Cathy wanted a baby, that's how it started. We'd been hitched for what, five years, and no luck. Something about her plumbing. 'Scuse me, Kate. Woman troubles. Anyhow, I was fine with that, but she wasn't. Really wanted to have a baby, it was all she thought about, raising a kid. Army isn't real big on fertility therapy because it's so costly, but what they had we tried. Didn't work. We talked about adopting and that seemed like a good idea, so we put ourselves on the list with our church organization, you know? Only there aren't a lot of babies up for free adoption. Couple years went by. Then I'm on this temporary assignment and there's a guy in the unit, a captain, he's a pretty good guy and it turns out we both married Connecticut girls, so we had that general connection. Turns out and he and his wife have just adopted the cutest little baby boy you ever saw. So I ask him how he did it and he told me about Family Finders, up there in Pawtucket. Said all it took was cold hard cash. Not a lot of paperwork and no long waiting lists, if you didn't mind adopting a brown-skinned baby."

"What did they tell you about your son's background?" I ask. "Anything about his birth parents?"

"Nah, not really. That's supposed to be a secret, unless the birth mother wants to make contact. Which they assured me she wouldn't do. And it's not like we wanted the mother coming in a month later, taking him back."

"No," I agree. "Of course not."

"Just between us chickens, I formed the impression the mother might have been a prostitute. Cathy didn't pick that up—didn't want to think about it—but I been stationed in places not a whole lot different than San Juan. Young women, girls, they get roped into the life because they're poor, it don't mean they're bad people. Anyhow, the main thing you worry about with a baby from a situation like that is if the mother passes on a disease. Syphilis or HIV or whatever. But Mikey was clean. Whatever's wrong, it's not something they can find in his blood. Not that it would have mattered, long run."

"Why is that?" Shane wants to know.

"You adopt a kid, he's yours, for better or worse. You don't give him back because he's not perfect."

"No."

"I'm not saying we didn't freak out when we realized something was wrong with Mikey. But by then he was part of the family. So you deal with it. You do whatever is necessary."

"Of course. Did this fellow officer, did his son have problems, too?"

Big Mike slowly shakes his head. "Nope. They lucked out. Kid was perfect, far as I know. Smart and healthy and, you know, a normal kind of kid. 'Course, I haven't seen them in years, not since I left active service."

"But the child was adopted through the same agency?"

"Yep. That's how we got onto it. Cathy had ten grand from her dead aunt, and that's exactly how much they charged. The captain, I think he paid a little more."

"Could you tell us how to get in touch with the captain, if we have any further questions?"

"I can tell you his name," Big Mike says. "Cutter. Captain Stephen Cutter. 'Course, he might have been promoted since then. Maybe he made colonel. Guy was smart, a real brain."

Shane flips open his notebook, grunts, and uses his thumb to indicate one of the names he'd scrawled down. *Captain S. Cutter, 23 Crestview, New London.*

"The captain have a tattoo?" Shane wants to know.

Big Mike has to think about it. "Good possibility. Most of the officers got 'em, in those units. Unit cohesion and all that good stuff."

"He built like you?" Shane asks.

Mike grins. "Nah. Not many are. No real advantage to being a big guy in Special Ops. Harder to be stealthy, sneak up on the enemy. The cap, he's about average size. And like I say, a real smart guy, too, which I guess is why he made captain."

"Thank you, Lieutenant Vernon. You've been a big help."

"Can't see why. How's this all connected to Family Finders, anyhow?"

"We're not sure," says Shane.

"But you think it was an army guy grabbed him, huh? That's why the question about the tattoo?"

"We're not sure. Just running down leads."

"'Cause the cap, he's not the type to be stealing kids, my opinion. Very stable guy, devoted to his family and all. His wife now, that's another matter."

Shane instantly perks up, as do I.

"How so?"

Mike taps his big, freckled forehead. "Poor woman is a little off. The cap was always very protective of her, but you pick up on things like that."

"You think she has mental problems?"

He shrugs. "Just off, someways. Real nervous and flighty in this dreamy sort of way. Never let the kid out of her sight, I'll tell you that, like maybe he'd vanish if she couldn't see him for even a minute." He notes my crestfallen expression and adds, "Sorry, miss. No offense."

At the door he says, "I'd walk you down, but Mikey, he gets upset if you leave him alone. Likes to know there's someone in the house."

"We'll be fine."

He hesitates, looks worried. "You know what? Probably I shouldn't have mentioned about the wife being a little off. Everybody's got their own problems. So if you see the cap, you just tell him Big Mike says hello, okay?"

By the time we get downstairs the sky has clouded over, looks like thunderstorms rolling in from the west.

"Next stop New London?" I ask Shane.

"Absolutely. We'll cruise by, see if anybody's home," he says. "Interesting, that part about the wife. This could be the one."

"I'll know him when I see him up close, when I hear his voice. I realize that now."

"Good," he says. "I've got a strong feeling that things are starting to break our way, Kate."

"You know what? Me, too. For the first time in days I really feel good about this. We're going to find Tommy."

Shane takes my hand, gives it a reassuring squeeze. "The next few hours are going to be crucial. I want you to be very, very careful. This man, whoever he turns out to be, he won't hesitate to kill."

"I'll be careful. You be careful, too."

"Always," he says with a grin. "That's my motto."

I'm thinking that I've known Randall Shane for less than a week, but already we're so comfortable in each other's company that it's like we're old friends. Is it because we've been thrown together under incredible stress and pressure, or is there something else going on?

A voice hails us from the doorway to the apartment building. Big Mike Vernon stands on the steps with his son, who clings to his hand. "Mikey decided he wanted to say goodbye to the nice lady," he explains.

The boy shrieks gleefully, then buries his face in his father's ample midriff, as if hiding from the world.

We wave and turn away. Spatters of cool rain hit my face, and thunder rumbles in the distance.

"God is bowling," I say. "Tenpins in heaven."

"What?"

"My mother used to say that."

"Uh-huh. We need the rain, I guess."

We're crossing the street when a car pulls out from the curb. I'm not really paying attention, other than to note that it's silver or gray, and looks like a new model. Shane, however, is alert, and that's the only reason I'm alive, because when the car suddenly accelerates with a screech of rubber, he scoops me up in his long, strong arms, and flings me out of the way.

I land on my back and get the wind knocked out of me, and sense the *whoosh* of the tires just missing my head. But there's a horrible sound of flesh on metal, and then Shane is flying over the hood, spinning through the air, and he comes to earth with a sickening crunch, head-first.

Behind me, Mike is shouting, but I'm not really paying attention. All I can think about is Randall Shane, and the blood, and the way he lies as still as death.

Four miles from the scene of the hit-and-run, with sirens keening in the distance, Cutter pulls into the breakdown lane, opens the door and pukes his guts out, spattering the pavement. Not because he's revolted by what he's done—assault with a motor vehicle is a whole lot less visceral than slitting an enemy's throat—but because he lost control of the situation. Because he allowed himself to react without thinking.

He'd been parked there at the curb, engine quietly ticking over, debating whether or not to be on his way. So far as he was aware, no one in Sussex had any connection to him. Whoever Supermom was visiting up there, it was not likely to be anyone who could point her in the right direction. She and her hired hand were spinning their wheels. Maybe the tall, lanky dude was intentionally running up the bill, taking her on wild-goose chases for billable hours. Wouldn't be the first time that lawyers and private dicks conspired to strip a client of assets.

Almost made him feel sorry for the lady.

And then, incredibly, just as Mrs. Bickford and company were about to leave, a familiar figure had appeared in the entrance of the tenement building. It took precisely one heartbeat for Cutter to recognize Big Mike Vernon—hadn't seen the guy in eight years—and to understand with sickening finality that all his elegant survival plans had just been blown sky high.

If they knew enough to seek out and question Mike, then they were already onto him, or soon would be.

In that moment he simply reacted, pedal to the metal. He'd felt the collision, seen the investigator airborne, flying over the fender, but was less certain about the woman. Maybe he'd hit her, maybe not. Didn't dare turn around and attempt to finish the job, not with Big Mike present and screaming for the cops. The guy looked huge and slow, but the glacial appearance was deceptive. When he had to move, Mike was more than capable. Best to flee the scene before the cavalry arrived.

Not that killing Mrs. Bickford would put the cork back in the bottle anyhow. The knowledge was out there, no doubt already passed on to lawyers and prosecutors and various law enforcement agencies. He had to face the fact that for all his elaborate precautions, he'd somehow been identified, that cops would be looking for him in the next few hours. So, a major alteration in the plans. The surgery would proceed, of course—there was no turning back from that—but he had to stop entertaining the notion that he'd be able to return to his life as a devoted father, that they'd all live happily ever after, he and Lyla and Jesse.

Wasn't going to happen. The ever-after was already here.

You're a dead man, he tells himself. *Deal with it.*

After rinsing out his mouth with a bottle of warm springwater, Cutter takes a deep breath and carefully maneuvers the Caddy back into traffic. Have to ditch the vehicle at the first opportunity. But not before he returns to the boatyard. Not before he prepares Mrs. Bickford's boy for what must come.

Sad but true. The boy has to be sacrificed. Tomas will be sedated—Cutter doesn't wish to cause him any discomfort—and then at the appropriate moment an ice pick will render him brain dead, and he will begin the short journey to the end of his life.

When Ted passed away I was sitting in the hospital cafeteria, sipping a cup of coffee, munching on a chocolate-chip cookie and mindlessly watching CNN. Talking heads jabbering about politics or crime or maybe something inane, who knew, since the volume was blessedly down. And I was having trouble holding a coherent thought in my head, not having slept in more than twenty-four hours. Ted had been through about four crash codes in that time period, but when I'd left him he'd been resting peacefully, and it was my intention to return to his bedside and stay with him for however long it took, days or weeks, it didn't matter. That's what I tried to tell myself. The truth is that knowing he was dying didn't mean I was ready for it to actually happen. Just as I hadn't been willing to accept that his form of lymphoma was a death sentence.

At first I'd wanted him home, made comfortable with hospice care, so it would happen in familiar surroundings, but he'd said no. Afraid of spooking Tommy by letting death into house. If the boy were older and could comprehend what was going on, maybe, but how would a child react at four? Why risk inflicting more trauma than necessary? Ted wanted Tommy to remember him alive and happy, not in pain and dying. Best to stay under medical supervision, where they knew what to do, how to cope with the terminal cases.

Trouble was, *I* didn't know how to cope. And to this day I'm convinced that Ted chose his moment, sending me away for coffee and a cookie while he prepared to leave his poor, ruined body.

Randall Shane is different, but somehow the same. Not a husband or a lover, but most definitely a friend. And here I am, keeping vigil, at least for a few precious minutes.

"Mrs. Brickyard?"

It feels silly and a bit stupid answering to the wrong name—must have been Mike Vernon's doing, as they loaded Shane into the ambulance—but I can't bring myself to correct the E.R. doctor, just in case he's been tuned in to the local news.

The man in the white coat looks a bit like Doogie Howser, M.D., but he's all business, with none of Doogie's sympathetic bedside manner. Only on TV, I guess. Impossible to say what he's about to impart, as his expression gives nothing away.

"I'm Dr. Vance," he announces, then checks his notes before continuing. "Mr. Shane is badly concussed, as we assumed."

"He's alive?"

"The patient hasn't regained consciousness, but vital signs are stable for the moment. Head injuries, these first few hours, are crucial. We'll be monitoring his condition, ready to intervene if his brain swells."

"The way he hit, I thought sure he broke his neck."

"X-rays showed no serious damage to the spinal column," the doctor says, ticking off the injury list. "Most of his ribs are broken. Various scrapes and cuts. Let me see…his kidneys may be bruised. He sustained a hairline skull fracture that may eventually require surgery. We'll make that decision later. Are you next of kin, by any chance?" he asks, indicating his medical notes.

"There are no next of kin, as far as know." I fumble in my purse for Mario Savalo's business card and give him her number, which he dutifully writes down.

"And Ms. Savalo would be?"

"His employer. May I see him?"

"If you like. I must warn you, Mr. Shane is nonresponsive. What we'd expect at this juncture, with a severe blow to the cranium. Oh. The police are on the way. They'll want to interview you about the accident. I understand it was a hit-and-run."

"Yes, it was. I'll be in the ICU if anybody needs me. Thank you, Dr. Vance."

He nods, walks away, on to the next patient.

Shane is barely recognizable. Every aspect of his face is swollen and misshapen, including his ears, scrapped raw on the pavement and now tinted with green antiseptic. I'd been expecting to see his poor head swaddled in bandages, but the ICU nurse explains that it's best to leave the scalp stitches exposed for the time being. The hair has been shaved away around the scalp wound, making it look even more vulnerable.

"He's breathing on his own," I observe.

"Mr. Shane is getting oxygen," the nurse says. "That little tube in his nose."

"But no respirator."

"Not unless he needs it."

"That's a good sign, no respirator."

"Very good," agrees the nurse.

I slip my hand into his, give it a squeeze, hoping for some sort of instinctive response. His hand is cool, dry, and does not respond.

"That doesn't mean anything one way or the other," the nurse says, trying to be helpful. "Think of him as being deeply asleep."

"He'd like that," I say.

"Excuse me?"

"Never mind. His belongings?"

"In the plastic bag, hanging from the bed."

Shane's notes are spattered with blood but legible.

"I'll give these to the police," I explain. "It may help."

Then I kiss his swollen lips and leave.

I'm lying about the police. My son is still out there. I can't risk being detained. I can't even wait to see if Randall Shane is going to live, but as I hurry from the hospital I know one thing for sure. He'd understand.

already dead | **38**

Cutter pulls the stolen Cadillac into a slot behind the boat shed, where it can't be seen from the access road. Not much traffic in this part of the waterfront, but with his ID out there in the wind, he needs to be ultracautious for the next twelve hours. After that it won't matter.

Not that he intends to let himself be arrested. When the moment comes, he'll do a Houdini, or maybe check out permanently, he hasn't decided. No rush, he's good at making instant life-or-death decisions under pressure, and right now he has to concentrate on getting the job done. Not for the first time he regrets having to terminate Hinks and Wald, not only because he rather enjoyed their moronic banter, but because it makes the execution of his plan more complicated.

No use crying over split blood, he tells himself. Have to play the hand that's dealt. Living happily ever after had been, he now realizes, a fantasy, a way to keep focused. The odds of getting away undetected had always been low, on the order of drawing to an inside straight flush. *Let it go, Cap, get on with the show.*

Next move, prepare the boy.

Inside the shed, Cutter carefully snugs the padlock to the inner hasp.

Insuring there will be no surprises from an inquisitive landlord, not that the old man was likely to drop by unannounced. Still, you can't be too careful.

Turning from the padlocked entrance, he senses that something is wrong. Can't put his finger on what exactly. A noise or sound? Possibly.

Cutter stops breathing, listens. Notes the transformer hum of the idling air compressor. A barely audible metallic ticking that could be steel drums expanding in the heat—the interior of the shed has gotten quite warm—and from outside the faint cry of a wheeling gull. Nothing out of the ordinary.

He wonders if the contents of the fifty-five-gallon drums are spooking him. Yesterday it seemed vitally important to dispose of the drums and the bodies they contained. Today, much less crucial. It's just dead meat. Nothing human about it, not anymore. But he's keenly aware of Hinks and Wald, their telltale hearts beating in the back of his mind. The look in their eyes as they died.

Stop it.

Cutter smacks his palm against his forehead, hard. Grunts and grimaces and forces the kinks out of his mind. The kinks and the hinks and the hinks and the kinks. *Stop it. Take a deep breath, hold until your mind clears. Focus on the mission. Focus on saving Jesse, on returning your son to his grieving mother, on making things right in her world, if not your own. You have no life to lose. You're a dead man, and dead men feel no pain. Dead men do not suffer from guilt or regret. Dead men do as they please.*

The boy. Concentrate on the boy in the white room. He's waiting. He knows what must be done because he saw it in your lying eyes. You think Hinks can haunt you? You ain't seen nothing yet, amigo. The boy will send your soul to hell like a rocket-propelled grenade, exploding into eternity.

Stop, stop, stop.

Cutter shudders, a full-body writhing, like a snake speed-shedding it's vile skin. He vomits hot, foul-smelling air. And then he's clean again and ready for what he must do. Quick-marching to the enclo-sure, he keys the outer padlock, remembers to lock it behind him. Clever boy, he'll be plotting an escape. Four strides and he's at the inner door of the enclosure, noting the blood spatter left by the late Walter Hinks, furious because the clever boy had broken his nose. Hinks complaining, *I'm breeving froo my mouf,* totally unaware of the comic implications, or that he'd made himself redundant, expendable.

In the white room, chaos.

Cutter instantly notes the missing plywood wall panel, the stink of the upended potty-chair. Sees the ragged hole clawed through the Sheet-rock of the outer wall. A hole just big enough for a boy to pass through.

Gone.

The loss brings a banshee howl from his throat. A broken scream of grief, because if the boy is gone, if he's found a way out of the boat shed, then all the killing was for nothing.

Cutter lets instinct take over. Instinct shaped by years of training. With-out even thinking about it, he crashes through the damaged Sheetrock, finds himself standing in the back of the boat shed, with the dilapidated stern of the ancient Chris Craft rising above him.

He searches for a breach in the outer walls. Walls and roof con-structed of galvanized steel, fastened from the outside. One of the fea-tures that had attracted him to the building in the first place. The boy unscrewed the plywood inner wall somehow—how did he manage that without tools?—but galvanized sheathing is another matter. Needs a drill and a hacksaw, at the very least, or better yet a cutting torch. No torch on the premises, but there's got to be a hacksaw lying around somewhere. Did he find it? Did clever Tomas cut his way to freedom?

Cutter forces himself to complete a circumnavigation of the outer walls. Smacking on the sheathing as he goes, looking for weak points. With great relief, he ascertains that the outer barrier remains intact, se-curely fastened to the steel frames of the building.

The boy is inside the shed. Inside and hiding.

"Tomas?" Cutter hardly recognizes his own voice. "It's Steve. Guess what, you passed the test."

Making it up as he goes along, as he so often did while interrogating prisoners and suspects and civilian troublemakers. Breaking them with his mind, molding them to his will. Creating stories and scenarios that seemed so plausible that they were soon dying to cooperate.

"This whole thing was a test, Tomas! An elaborate test! We had to know if you were strong enough, clever enough to find a way out of the white room. You passed the test with flying colors. Congratulations!"

Cutter prowls the boat shed, eyes scanning every dark corner, searching for movement, for the quivering of a frightened boy.

"This is part of a top-secret government project, Tomas," he says, riffing. "You've been chosen. We need a boy of your size and your cunning to complete a very important mission. Your mom knows all about it. She gave us her permission."

Cutter finds the ladder on the floor, under the boat. That's what his brain noted when he first came into the shed. Not a noise, but a visual clue: the old wooden ladder was missing from the side of the Chris Craft.

He sets the ladder against the hull, climbs up into the cockpit. The engine hatch is open, tools strewn about. All staged, part of making it look good as if the landlord came by to check on progress. *Yup, we're tearing apart that old Chrysler engine, make it purr like an eight-cylinder pussycat.*

He crouches. Gets a visual line from the back of the engine compartment into the ruined cabin. Interior panel laminations peeling away, the floor all funky with dry rot. There's a V-berth forward, a small galley, lazarette lockers under the seats, cupboards and a small enclosed toilet. Plenty of places for a determined eleven-year-old to hide.

Inside the cabin, Cutter sniffs. Amazing how strong and detecta-ble the stink of fear, if you let your brain sort out the various odors. He detects motor oil, rust, mildew, rotting carpet, his own rank odor. Can't detect the boy, but he must be here. Hiding in a locker, under the V-berth, somewhere very close.

Time to reach out and touch someone.

"Tomas? I've got a cell phone in my pocket. Your mother really wants to talk to you. She wants to explain what's been going on these last few days. I know you won't believe me—why should you?—but you'll listen to your mother."

Using the toe of his boot, Cutter lifts the lid on the lazarette, ex-posing bundles of rotted rope, rusted anchor chains.

"Come on out, Tomas. You passed the test."

Cutter moves to the V-berth, all the way forward. He's about to lift up the ruined cushions and look under the berth when the door to the enclosed toilet creaks open and the boy streaks out.

Clever kid waited until he had a clear shot at the cabin hatchway, must have been clocking him through the keyhole. Doesn't matter be-cause Cutter is fast and ready and his arms are long. His right hand locks on the boy's ankle as he tries to scamper up the hatchway.

The boy kicking to no avail.

As Cutter yanks him back inside the cabin, the boy turns, wield-ing a hacksaw blade in his fist. Cutter doesn't dare let go of the flail-ing boy, who is able to rake the saw blade across Cutter's cheek, laying him open to the bone.

Blood everywhere. Amazing how much flows from a facial wound. Makes things slippery and difficult, but Cutter is a pro and he man-ages to subdue the struggling boy. Holding him tight, jabbing him with a loaded syringe, hanging on until the powerful anesthetic takes effect and the boy goes limp in his arms.

"Good night, son," Cutter whispers, and then he allows himself to weep. Weeping for lost boys and sick boys and mothers who yearn for their missing children. Weeping for the already dead and the soon-to-be dead and for a man he used to know.

When the tear ducts finally empty, the dead man gently puts the unconscious boy on the deck and prepares to attend to the wound on his own face. Nothing fancy, just a rudimentary repair that will get him through the next few hours. He sets a shaving mirror on the galley table and lights a wax candle for illumination. Using a sailmaker's needle and waxed-cotton thread, he stitches himself together. He has in his possession an extensive kit of pharmaceutical drugs, including various anesthetics, but chooses not to numb the wound or dull the pain.

It hurts, and he deserves it.

Back in the day, this was the American dream house. A tidy clapboard Cape-style home with a green patch of lawn and a white picket fence. Friendly neighbors leaning over the fence, trading recipes, resuming conversations that lasted a lifetime. Now the dream is more likely to be a gated community and a million-dollar ski retreat in Vail, and a waterfront condo in South Beach, and enough luxury cars to fill all three garages.

Expectations have changed, but the Cutter family home still looks like a Norman Rockwell postcard. Driving to New London, to an address scrawled in Shane's hurried hand, I'd been terrified of what I might find. Imagining a dark dungeon where children are tortured, or a crime boss's fortress, all razor wire and seething menace. The last thing I expected was a cheerful, if somewhat smaller, version of my own home.

Back in our walk-up-apartment days, Ted and I would have killed for a perfect little house like this. Bad choice of words, but my every thought is shaped by morbid anxiety. The rational, analytical part of me knows that my son might well be dead—that's what kidnappers do, all too often—but if I'm to get through this day, I have to believe that Tommy is alive. That's the only way I can function, and what gives me the courage to proceed on my own. That, and the feeling, odd as it may seem, that Randall Shane still guides me.

Shane with his head smashed. Shane unconscious, fighting for his own life. And yet somehow he's along for the ride, long legs folded into the passenger seat, making his little self-deprecating jokes, quietly urging me not to give up hope. What would he think of the white picket fence? Probably remind me that criminals sometimes live in houses just like this. Scratch that rare suburban dad and find a monster. God knows the cable channels are full of them. Moms who drown their children and blame it on a black bogeyman. Dads who set fire to their families to collect enough insurance to buy jewelry for a trophy mistress. We've all heard the stories, watched them play out on TV. Getting some sort of vicarious thrill, I suppose, in the certainty that our own lives will never be touched by evil, no matter how familiar the shape it assumes.

But for all that, first impressions count, and I'm almost certain the owner of this house will be another dead end. Stephen Cutter will turn out to be a regular guy, want to know about his old army buddy Big Mike Vernon. He'll introduce me to his wife and his adopted son and we can commiserate about the sleazy way Family Finders took advantage. But maybe, just maybe, he'll know something useful, point me in the right direction.

I promise myself that I won't waste time, that as soon as the Cutters are eliminated as suspects, I'll move on to the next name on Shane's list.

The thunderstorm has swept on by for the moment, leaving the black street glistening in the moonlight. Amazing how night rain makes everything look shiny and new. There's no car in the driveway. Maybe the Cutter family keeps their minivan in the garage, out of the weather. I've already decided they drive a car a lot like mine. In any case there are lights on inside, glowing like yellow cat eyes, so I know someone is home. Probably watching TV and munching popcorn. It's ten o'clock, will their son be in bed by now? Not if he's anything like Tommy, who has to be herded to his room, no matter how exhausted.

The civilized thing would be to locate their phone number and give them a call, rather than ring the bell at this hour. No time for the social niceties, however. I'm on a mission that won't end until I've cleared every name on Shane's list.

The gate creaks shut behind me as I move up the walk to the breezeway. Making no effort to be stealthy. Look out, folks, crazy woman on the warpath, come to disturb your peaceful evening.

It occurs to me, approaching the door, that despite the benign look of the place, the Cutters may be paranoid types. New London is not without crime, and home invaders sometimes ring the bell. So there's always the possibility that Mr. Cutter, a military man, don't forget, will come to the door armed. Who will he see through the peephole, a desperate woman or a killer mom? A lot depends on whether or not they watch the local news and have an eye for faces.

In this case, I'm hoping that darkness will be my friend.

I'm unable to locate a doorbell button, so I raise my fist and knock. At first there is no responding sound from within. If they're watching TV, the sound is too low to be detected from the breezeway, so my knock should be audible.

Footsteps. Light footsteps approaching, those of a woman or perhaps a child. I step back and wait for the door to open.

Nothing. I can feel a presence on the other side of the door, but nothing happens, so I knock again, louder.

"Mr. Cutter? Mrs. Cutter? Can I have a word, it's very important."

My voice sounds strange and threatening even to me. The footsteps retreat. I pound my fist on the door, rattling the frame. "Please! I just want a word!"

The shadows shift, as if a light somewhere in the house has been

switched off. Time to go for broke, let it all out and hope for a connection.

"Mr. Cutter! My name is Kate Bickford, I need your help! Please give
me a minute of your time! It's about my son, my missing son!"

Silence.

Cold anger rises. The Cutters must know by now that I'm not a
home invader, not a gang of drug addicts come to rip them off. Probably in there dialing 911, reporting an intruder. And although I'm legally released on bond, I've no doubt the cops will want to hold me
for questioning in the assault on Randall Shane. I can't let that happen.

Out of the breezeway I go, around the corner into the backyard.
Bang my knee on the leg of a swing set obscured by the shadows. Parts
of the backyard bright in the moonlight. Ignoring the thump of pain
in my knee, I head for the back windows. Note the curtains tightly
drawn, but not so tight as to completely obscure light from what I assume to be the kitchen.

I'm banging my fists against the kitchen window and crying, "Help
me! Help me, please! It's about my son! It's about my boy!" when a
white figure emerges from the ground, a white lady in the moonlight, floating toward me.

A thin, terrified voice asks, "Is this about Jesse? Have you come
about Jesse?"

"Mrs. Cutter?"

"You said a boy. A missing boy."

As the shock of her sudden appearance subsides, I realize that she's
come up out of a basement bulkhead, and that of the two of us, she's
by far the most frightened.

"Can we go inside?" I suggest. "It's kind of spooky out here."

Really I'm more concerned about alerting the neighbors, getting
called in for disturbing the peace or whatever. And I'm worried that
this thin, ethereal wisp of a woman could vanish into the night. A

woman who approaches me with great caution, reaching out a slender hand to tentatively touch me, as if to make certain I'm real. Dressed in a thin white robe and fluffy house slippers, she has the glistening brown eyes of a frightened doe.

"Can you keep a secret?" she asks with little-girl shyness.

"I can try."

"Stephen locks the doors," she confides in a husky voice that barely carries above a whisper. "He thinks I can't get out. Promise not to tell?"

"I promise."

She takes my hand and leads me into the dark basement.

I'm no psychiatrist, but I've always assumed there's a fine line between mental disturbance and full-blown insanity. Equating the former with neurotic behavior or compulsive disorders, and the latter with a disconnection from reality. My impression is that Lyla Cutter lives somewhere in between, in a netherworld where reality comes and goes. The way she keeps studying me, as if waiting for my image to dissolve into hallucination. The nervous things she does with her elegant hands, and a peculiar, affected way she has of clearing her throat. Some of the physical manifestations could be from medication, I suppose, but the important thing is that she's taken me into her home, into her world—and she wants to talk.

"You came about Jesse," she says in her whispery voice.

"Not exactly."

We're sitting in her living room. Lyla perched on the very edge of a beige divan, so frail she looks like she could be shattered by a loud noise. Her big, nervous eyes imploring me—for what exactly, I can't quite fathom. She has lovely, waist-length hair. Dark blond streaked with silver, carefully combed—a hundred loving strokes before bed, no doubt. The premature graying is incongruous, because her elfin face is that of a child, unlined and porcelain pale. A woman-child from a nineteenth century melodrama, waiting for Heathcliff to return from the barren moors.

"I'm searching for my son," I tell her. "Tommy Bickford. He's been abducted."

She nods knowingly. "You turn around and they're gone."

"Is that what happened to your Jesse?"

She shrugs and makes a vague gesture, as if wafting away invisible smoke. "My beautiful son."

"I believe your son and mine were both adopted from the same agency," I tell her. "Family Finders."

"Stephen would know."

"Is your husband here, Mrs. Cutter?"

Rather than answer, she leads me to the mantel of a small brick fireplace. "There he is," she says, indicating a framed photograph of a solidly built but otherwise nondescript man in a military uniform. On closer examination he's almost but not quite handsome. Could be Bruce, or not, it's impossible to say. "Stephen was an English teacher, did you know that?" she asks.

"I thought he was a soldier."

"Before the army he taught at the University of Rhode Island for a year. They let him go, that's when he decided on an army career like his father. He'd done so well in ROTC, scored off the charts. He's very, very smart, Stephen. Too smart."

"Why do you say that?"

"What good does it do, being smart? Thinking he's oh so clever. He must think I'm stupid, locking all the doors but forgetting about the basement."

"Yes," I say, just to be agreeable.

"Thinks I'm stupid about Jesse, too. Telling me lies. That's what put holes in my brain. Dirty lies. Lies turn into little worms, once they get inside your head. They eat your thoughts."

"What does your husband lie about, Mrs. Cutter?"

"Oh, just everything," she responds airily.

"What happened to your son?" I ask. "What happened to Jesse?"

"Shh," she cautions, holding a pale finger to her lips. "You'll wake him."

With that she links her hand in mine and guides me to the stairway. A braided rug on each tread, warm light spilling from the upstairs.

"Your son is here?" I whisper. "Asleep in his room?"

Lyla smiles but does not answer. Her eyes shine with an unbearable, incandescent joy, or madness, or both. Clutching my hand, as if we are little girls about to visit the best dollhouse in the world, she leads me up the stairs and down the hall to her son's room.

A boy's room, no question. The posters, toys and carelessly stacked video games could have belonged to my own son. More than that I can't quite make out, because Lyla doesn't switch on the light, and the only illumination comes from a wall-socket night-light. A plastic Goofy, glowing in the dark.

Tommy's night-light is Mickey Mouse.

"Where is he?" I ask, keeping my voice low. "Where's Jesse?"

Lyla points at the bed. If her eyes get any bigger they're going to fall out of her head.

"There's nobody in the bed, Mrs. Cutter."

I reach out, flip on the light.

Lyla covers her eyes with her pale hands and moans. In other circumstances, my instinct would be to comfort the poor woman, maybe even play along with her delusions. But my cold heart has only one concern and it is not, for the moment, the state of Lyla Cutter's mental health. I need answers and the empty bedroom makes me think that I will find them here, if only I can get this frail creature to tell me what really happened to her son.

She does not resist as I gently pry her hands away from her eyes and turn her to face the empty bed.

"I'm begging you," I say. "Please help me. My son was taken from me. I think your son was taken from you. What happened, Mrs. Cutter? What happened to the boys?"

Tears well in her eyes, but she seems to be focusing on me, which is encouraging. "Jesse wasn't taken," she explains. "He wasn't kidnapped. Jesse got sick, is what happened."

"Sick?" I ask, taken aback.

"It was just a cold, like kids get, you know? That's what we thought. His head hurt, so I gave him a children's aspirin. Just one. You know how dangerous aspirin can be with children. But the headache wouldn't go away, so Stephen took him to the E.R."

Lyla's eyes flutter and her focus dissolves. She begins to hum a little tune I can't quite recognize. Could be the theme to a kids' show, maybe *Sesame Street*. Wherever she's going, I can't follow.

In the movies a slap to the face always returns the mad to sanity, if only for a moment. But I'm convinced that any violence or threat will send her further into whatever place she presently occupies. So all I can do is implore her to continue.

"Your husband took your son to the hospital. What happened then? What happened to Jesse? Did your son die, Mrs. Cutter, is that what happened?"

She shakes her head forcefully. "A virus," she mutters. "It was a virus. Like a cold but worse, much worse. It made him sick, very sick, but he didn't die. They wouldn't let him die, not my Jesse. Not my beautiful boy."

She's drifting away again, head moving to music only she can hear, and I decide desperate measures are in order. I open my purse, take out the photograph I've been carrying like a talisman. And then, God forgive me, I force her to look at the photograph. Shove it in her face like an accusation. "You see this, Lyla? I'm searching for this boy. He means everything to me. He's my life. Have you seen him? Did your husband steal my son?"

She grows utterly still, staring at the picture. Tommy in his Little League uniform.

"You're trying to trick me," she says, looking away. "You're a liar. A liar just like Stephen."

"Look at the picture, Lyla."

She folds her slim arms across her chest, as stubborn and unrelenting as a child. "You want me to think that's a picture of Jesse, but I know it's not. A mother knows. Besides, that's not even the right uniform."

"This boy looks like your son?"

"Who are you?" she asks me. Then her expression gets canny. "You're Stephen's girlfriend, aren't you? He sent you here to punish me. To put worms in my head."

"Lyla, do you have a picture of Jesse?"

"I don't blame him for having a girlfriend," she says wistfully. "You're very pretty. Prettier than me."

"Mrs. Cutter, I'm not your husband's girlfriend. I'm a mother looking for her son. Please, this is very important, could you show me a picture of Jesse?"

Something in my desperate tone touches her. She goes to a bureau in the boy's room, slides open the top drawer and hands me a framed photograph.

A boy posing in his Little League uniform, sporting a smart-aleck, mischievous grin that floors me.

"Oh, my God."

"You tried to trick me," Lyla says. "That's not right."

"I didn't try to trick you," I say, showing her the two photographs side by side. "Your son and my son are twins. Identical twins."

A glance at Lyla reveals that she isn't buying it, that she thinks I'm still trying to deceive her. "Did your son get sick, too?" she asks. "Did he go in the hospital and not come home?"

"No. Tommy is as healthy as a horse."

"Then they're not identical, are they?" she says tauntingly.

"They're brothers, Mrs. Cutter. Look at the pictures. My God. See how they stand the same? Smile is almost the same, too."

She shakes her head, denying. "Liar, liar, pants on fire. Did you take your pants off for Stephen? I bet you did."

"Please, Mrs. Cutter. Look at the pictures. They're brothers. Family Finders must have thought they'd get more money selling them separately."

"Ask Stephen. He knows everything. He's a know-it-all."

"What exactly happened to Jesse in the hospital, Mrs. Cutter? What did the virus do?"

Her hands float up to her heart and she hugs herself. And then with her eyes closed, in a singsong lullaby, she tells me what I need to know. "The virus went to his heart, his heart. The virus went to my little boy's heart."

It hits me like a body blow. Then with an abrupt sensation of sick-making vertigo, I'm falling down an endless elevator shaft, free-falling to the end of my world. Because I remember what the man in the mask said to me, that first day when he invaded my home. When he told me what the consequences would be if I didn't cooperate.

I'll cut out Tommy's heart, he said. *I'll cut out his heart and give it to you in a plastic bag.*

That's what he wants. What he's wanted all along. My son's good heart.

Prominently displayed on the reception desk at the Health East Medical Complex, a glass jar of Hershey chocolate kisses. Taped to the jar, a hand-lettered sign advising me that Chocolate Is Good For Your Heart and the admonition to Help Yourself To Health. Under normal circumstances I'd be tempted, but the world has tilted off normal and I'm a madwoman pretending sanity. Holding myself together with psychic duct tape while the elderly volunteer, a woman with orange hair so thin her freckled scalp shows through, searches the register for Jesse Cutter, a long-term-care patient. It's all I can do not to leap over the counter and search the photocopied lists myself.

"Cutter, Cutter," the woman mumbles. "Should be in the Cs, right?"

Why is it that so many people work as unpaid volunteers for for-profit medical chains? Maybe because they got in the habit when hospitals were nonprofit, owned and run by communities. Or because making themselves useful gives them a purpose, a reason to get up in the morning, or in this case late in the day for a midnight shift.

Whatever, the volunteer is trying her best and I have to refrain from screaming out that my son has been designated as an involuntary organ donor. As it is I've got one eye on the TV bolted to the wall. The sound is off but the local news broadcast is filling the screen with images of burning homes and grisly automotive accidents. Matter of time before they get to me, I assume.

"Here he is," says the volunteer, looking up with a brightly dentured smile. "Room 212, Wing C." Then with a puzzled look she adds, "No, wait, that's wrong. The patient has just been discharged."

"When?"

"Today. An hour ago, as a matter of fact."

"Where has he been taken?"

"I'm sorry, Mrs. Cutter, but the desk doesn't have that information. Just that he was, um, discharged into the care of his father, Stephen Cutter."

"Dammit!"

The volunteer has that uneasy look people get when they're about to be involved in someone else's domestic dispute. "Perhaps you should talk to one of the security staff, Mrs. Cutter. Are you the boy's mother? You can explain the situation to security. If you could show me some identification, I'll see about getting you a pass."

My eyes are riveted on the TV screen, where my own face seems to be staring right at me. That horrible mug shot from my arrest and booking. The running caption reads: *Katherine Bickford, Wanted for questioning*. Next, a video of Jared Nichols being interviewed by a reporter who looks suitably appalled by what he has to say about the suspect killer mom. *We're asking Mrs. Bickford to surrender to authorities, and undergo further inquiries about the hit-and-run of a local investigator.*

Thanks, Jared. Perfect timing.

"Mrs. Cutter?"

"Sorry. What?"

"Your driver's license, please."

Clutching my purse, I tell her, "Be right back. I have to, um, call my husband."

And then I'm fleeing the reception area before hospital security can be alerted.

Slumped down in my rental car, I make several hurried cell-phone calls. The first to Maria Savalo. Naturally I get her voice mail, and leave her a barely coherent message detailing the events of the last few hours. Trying not to sound hysterical when mentioning what Cutter intends to do to my son.

"For God's sake, Maria, tell the FBI we've identified the kidnapper. Stephen Cutter of New London. He was a Special Ops guy in the army. He and his wife adopted Tommy's identical twin. That's the connection. That's why he grabbed Tommy, because his own son needs a transplant and Tommy's the perfect match. Somebody has to do something. The FBI, the cops, the state police, I don't care. Somebody! The guy has just taken his son out of the hospital—Health East in New Haven—so whatever it is he's got planned, it's going down tonight or early tomorrow morning. Do you understand what that means? If Tommy's alive, he won't be for long. While you're at it you can tell that bastard Jared Nichols I'll turn myself in when they get off their asses and rescue my son. They can keep me for a million years, I don't care, but they have to DO SOMETHING TONIGHT, okay?"

Next call to Connie Pendergast. I'm assuming she's at home in bed at this hour, but she's set her home number to ring at the warehouse, and that's where she answers. Hearing her cheerful voice announce, "Katherine Bickford Catering, how may we help?" sets off a convulsion of sobbing. Weeping so inconsolably that I'm afraid my tears will short out the cell phone.

"Kate? What's happened?"

There's an underlying element of panic in her query that for some reason calms me down. She's thinking the worst, that I've found Tommy's body and fallen apart. Have to set her straight, let her know what's actually happened, and what's likely to happen if I don't find Tommy soon.

After blowing my nose, I give her a rundown of what has transpired in the last few hours, my voice steadier than hers, as it turns out.

"Oh, my God, Kate, I don't know how you're still functioning. I'd be a puddle."

"I am a puddle," I admit. "But I can't quit now, not when we're this close. Connie, what are you doing at the warehouse at this hour?"

"Wedding tomorrow in Westport. Two hundred hungry guests expecting the usual Kate Bickford romance with food. Sherona just finished up the pastry order, I'm giving her a hand. Everything's ready for the catering crew, they'll be here at the crack of dawn. So where are you, exactly?"

"Hospital parking lot. I thought the security guards might come after me, but so far nobody seems to care about a woman alone in a car, crying in the middle of the night. I suppose it happens all the time."

"How can we help? Sherona's right here, says she wants to kick some butt."

"I can't go back into the hospital," I tell her. "They'll grab me for sure and I haven't got time to sort this out with the cops. But I need to find out where Cutter took his son, and that information has to be somewhere in the hospital. Somebody has to know."

"We're on our way," Connie announces. "Traffic will be minimal this time of night, so figure what, twenty minutes?"

What transpires is the longest half hour of my life. During that endless interval I check my watch two or three thousand times, tune in to several radio stations in a fruitless search for breaking news, and call for an update on Shane's condition. It takes a couple of tries, but finally they patch me through to the attending nurse, who tells me that Mr. Shane remains stable.

"Is he still unconscious?" I want to know.

The RN hedges, but admits that Mr. Shane has been what she calls "responsive."

"That's good, right?"

"That's very good. Better than it looked a few hours ago. Is this Mrs. Bickford? Because the police have been here. They want to interview Mr. Shane and they want to talk to you, too."

"Yeah. Listen, you sound like a really nice person," I tell her. "Can you do me a favor?"

"Depends," says the RN, sounding very guarded. "I won't do anything illegal."

"This isn't illegal. If Randall wakes up, give him a kiss. Not on the lips, I wouldn't ask that, a kiss on the forehead, okay? Tell him the kiss is from me and I'm sorry and I'm grateful and I wish I could be there, but I can't. He'll understand. I'm going to hang up before you can say no, so please think about it, okay? Please?"

Then I'm alone with the disconnected phone and the useless radio and I'm weeping again, weeping for Tommy and Shane and for all the sick kids in the world and for desperate parents crazed with fear, trying to make things right. Weeping for myself, too, I guess, wondering if the situation was reversed and it was Tommy sick and needing a new heart, how far would I go? Takes less than a millisecond for my gut to tell me that never, never would I endanger another child, no matter how much grief it caused me. There are some things that simply aren't allowed, no matter how much you want your own child to live. The man in the mask, he may be a parent, no doubt he loves his boy, but he's also a monster, a man who does not hesitate to kill. Killed the lawyer, tried to kill Shane, just missed killing me. And he intends to kill Tommy, that's certain, that's been his plan all along.

I feel certain that if Shane were here he'd already have the information about where Cutter has taken his ailing son. Shane has that air of authority, folks respond to it, they want to please him by cooperating. Whereas I can't seem to summon that sort of gravitas, all I can do is keep searching for information that will bring me closer to Tommy. Making it up as I go along, trying not to fall apart. People keep telling me I'm strong, but that's not how I feel. Far from it. Makes me wonder if those who act courageously under fire are actually so terrified that they simply function on instinct. Too scared to act scared. Does that make sense? Or is fear making me as wigged out as Lyla Cutter?

My cell rings. Connie announcing that she's here, in the hospital parking lot. There's more than one lot, so it takes a few minutes to make physical contact, but when I finally spot her Beetle it feels like witnessing a miracle. The sight of that happy little car cruising out of the shadows floods me with warmth.

This I know for sure: Whatever happens in the next few hours, I'm really, really going to need a friend.

Connie, as promised, is accompanied by Sherona, as well as her Pekingese, Mr. Yap.

"Sorry about that," she says, embracing me. "I couldn't leave him at the warehouse. He's totally unreliable when it comes to food."

"The dog is fine. Thanks, Connie. Thanks, guys. You didn't have to do this."

"Ain't done nothing yet," the master pastry chef responds.

"Sherona's got a plan," Connie explains. "I'm going to target the administrator's office and she's going after the staff."

"What I'm going after is the colored people," Sherona says, her ample chin jutting out. "They see me coming, they're gonna give it up. We'll find your boy, Mrs. Bickford. You hang in there, honey."

Fortunately, Connie has brought along a box of tissues, because my eyes are leaking and it's not the slight allergic reaction I have to the excitable Pekingese. It's watching these two unlikely warriors march into combat, both of them looking resolute and determined, and risking God-knows-what on my behalf.

I'm waiting in Connie's Beetle, feeding milk bones to Mr. Yap, when Maria Savalo rings me back. "Don't tell me where you are," is the first phrase out of her mouth. "If I knew that, I'd be obliged to inform the authorities."

"Fine. I'm in Nome, Alaska, selling ice to Eskimos."

"My God, you're joking! One o'clock in the morning and you made a joke, after all you've been through?"

"What can I say, I'm in a very weird mood. You know when people say they don't know whether to laugh or cry? I'm doing both."

"That's good, I guess."

"I'll let you know."

"You actually went to the kidnapper's house and talked to his wife? That's amazing. And truly dangerous. What if he'd been there?"

"He wasn't. I knew he wasn't there."

"How did you know?"

"A feeling. I can't explain it. Is the FBI going to do something?"

Maria sighs. "Maybe yes and maybe no. I got hold of the local bureau chief in New Haven. Apparently he goes to bed early, but he returned my call and said he would 'take appropriate action.' I asked him what that means, exactly, and he said I'd have to wait and find out. So either they're all over it or they're not."

"Great. Wonderful. My tax dollars at work."

"The thing is, they have agents on the night shift, I assume, but I really don't know if anything will happen until tomorrow morning, when the boss comes in."

"Tomorrow morning will be too late. What about the state police? Can they help?"

"We'll see. I gave them the information, identifying the alleged kidnapper and urging them to respond immediately. They sounded very interested, but the thing is, I'm a defense attorney and they don't want to let me know what they're doing, or not doing."

"So it all boils down to, there could be a dozen FBI agents and a hundred troopers swarming around, searching for the man who took Tommy," I say. "Or maybe nothing is happening yet. Or somewhere in between."

"I'd guess in between."

"Thanks, Maria. I can hear car noises, where are you?"

"On my way to see Randall."

"He saved my life, you know."

"That's what he does."

"Got the name of the kidnapper, too."

"And that's what he lives for," says my lawyer. "Is there any point urging you to be careful?"

"No," I tell her quite honestly. "Gotta go."

My pastry chef is tapping on the window, and I can tell by the look in her eyes that she has important news.

In a wooded cul-de-sac a half mile from the highway, Stephen Cutter stands under a drooping willow tree and takes his pulse. The night sky is so overcast, and so dark, that he can see only the illuminated dial of his watch. The rest of him, indeed, the rest of the world, might as well be invisible.

A few yards away, the boxy ambulance blends into the darkness, leaving only a faint ghost image, a shadow of a shadow.

According to the timer, his pulse races at ninety-four beats a minute. Impossible. His resting heart normally clocks about fifty beats. Been that way for years. A runner's heart, a soldier's heart, sustaining him through trauma and combat and the slow torture of grief and disappointment. He's never been an excitable boy, even under circumstances that would turn a civilian's cardiovascular system into a frizzle of sparking nerves and quivering muscles.

Ninety-four? An overdose of caffeine, perhaps. Or a low-grade infection from where his face got opened by the hacksaw blade. Whatever, it can't be fear making his heart race, because life itself has become such a complicated struggle that he almost welcomes the looming prospect of his own demise. *Hello, death. Come on in, take a seat, I'll be right with you.* "Lights out, eternal peace." What did the old boy say? *"For in the sleep of death, what dreams may come?"* No dreams, Cutter hopes, most fervently, *"for the worm of conscience still begnaws the soul."* Fucking Shakespeare, how did he know these things? What could an itinerant actor know about killing, about murder? Did playing a role somehow impart the grim, pulse-pounding reality? Must have, because there it is, *"begnaws the soul"* is exactly right, conjures up an image of rats nibbling exposed organs, and that's how it feels when a man begs for his life and you kill him with your bare hands, his life passing through your fingers like a cool breath.

Up until about three minutes ago the EMT was a nice young guy, trying his best to be to be supportive and cheerful. Snuffing out his lights wasn't like terminating Hinks and Wald, professional killers, or Rico Vargas, a professional scumbag, or even that empty suit from Family Finders—killing him had been like stepping on a cockroach. But the boy driving the ambulance, he'd been one of the good guys. Right up until the moment his hands closed around the young man's neck, Cutter had been trying to think of a way to spare his life. Dope him, tie him up, whatever. And then his hands had made the decision. Squeeze and kill. Keep it simple. Do not be dissuaded from your mission by pity or sympathy or the illusion of human connection.

Cutter is keenly aware that his killing chores are far from over. There will be several more retractions from the world of the living, culminating in the boy Tomas. Tomas who lies drugged and unconscious in the ambulance. No more than a foot from the twin brother he has never known, and never will know, except in the most fundamental physical sense, by providing the heart that will return Jesse to the world of normal boys. Boys who run and play and tease their mothers for worrying about them. Boys who smile in their sleep and dream their big-league dreams. Boys whose very existence gives mean-

ing to the lives of hopelessly flawed fathers, fathers willing to sacrifice their souls so their sons might live.

Get a grip, Cutter tells himself. *You're a soldier, not some limp-wristed
drama queen quoting the Bard. Suck it up and do your duty, if not for God
and country, then for your son. For the boy who loves you without reservation.
For Jesse.*

You chose this road. No turning back.

Cutter steels himself for the task of stripping the still-warm body
of his latest victim. The EMT uniform will soon enough prove useful. As to the racing heart, he knows the reason, knew it all along.
Not caffeine, or the simple act of murder. Something much more pro-
found is at work, splashing adrenaline into his system. Something way
beyond fear.

In this dark night of his soul, his dead are forming rank.

ask dr. google | **42**

Sherona looks like a very plump and very serious cat who has suc-
ceeded in swallowing a somewhat difficult canary.

"They all know the boy," she announces moments after sliding into
the passenger seat, displacing an aggrieved Mr. Yap. "Nurses, janitors,
everybody. He's a sweet boy and they love him."

"How sick is he?"

"Sick as they get," she says. "Been in a vegetative state for six
weeks. Feeding him through a tube, like they do."

"Vegetative state?"

"He's there and he's not there. Nurses say he'll look right at you and
smile, but it's just a reflex. Some habit of the muscles and brain. He can
breathe on his own, but that's about it. Mostly likely, he'll never improve."

"Oh, my God."

Dead but not dead, I'm thinking. The ultimate nightmare.

"He's on a heart pump," Sherona continues. "I asked about a new
heart for the poor boy, the nurses look all hurtful and say he's not a candidate for transplant. They think his daddy's taking him home to die."

"That's the destination he gave? New London?"

Sherona nods. "You think that's where he's at?" she asks doubtfully.

"No chance," I say. "The guy is a technical whiz, but he's not a heart surgeon. He's got a plan, a destination."

At that moment Connie returns and I have to get out and move into the back seat with the nervous Pekingese.

"Hope you did better than me," she says to Sherona, sounding sheepish. Looking into the rearview mirror to make eye contact, she adds, "Sorry, Kate, the records are in the business office and the office is locked and this security guy threatened to have me arrested if I didn't quit messing with the doors."

"Tommy's brother is in a coma," I tell her. "He's dying."

"It sounds so strange, that Tomas has a brother," she says almost wistfully. "I can't get used to the idea. Coma, huh?"

"You want to know where the ambulance took the boy, right?" Sherona interrupts, no patience for chitchat or lame excuses.

"More than anything," I tell her.

"Best get back on the road," she suggests firmly. "Ambulance service has a dispatcher. Let's see what he says."

She directs us to a chain-fenced parking facility several miles from the hospital. A district of freight warehouses and trucking firms. We park in the street, but even before we get out, the dogs are barking. Attack dogs inside the perimeter of the chain-link fence that encloses a number of boxy, orange-and-white-striped medical transport vehicles. The dogs are showing a lot of teeth. Not what you'd call a friendly location. As we approach the main gate—Sherona in the lead, all business—motion detectors set off bright lights and an armed security guard emerges from a metal shack, yawning.

As it happens, the guard is Caucasian, but ethnicity is no immunity to Sherona's persuasive charms. Within three minutes he's apologizing for the barking dogs—he does not control the animals—and explaining that the heavy security is necessary because, as he puts it, "the junkies think an ambulance is a drugstore on wheels."

"We never leave narcotics in the unattended vehicles, but that don't stop 'em from breaking in," he adds. "Now, what can I do you ladies for?"

Out of politeness he's addressing all three of us, but it's Sherona who has his undivided attention. I'd been aware of our pastry chef's impressive skills in the kitchen, but this is my first experience watching her mind-meld with males. It's uncanny, and Connie and I look at each other and shake our heads. Not so much a sexual allure on Sherona's part, more a way of presenting herself that makes men want to please and protect her. This from a woman almost as wide as she is tall. Makes me realize that her shyness around me on the job, and with Connie, as well, apparently has more to do with the racial divide and class distinctions than any lack of confidence on her part. Out here in the big bad, black-and-white world, Sherona is Oprah and Dr. Phil all rolled into one, and I'm fortunate to have her on my side.

Sherona gives the guard an abbreviated version of what's going on, and asks may she please confer with the dispatcher. It's three in the morning, but the guard affects to find this reasonable and makes a phone call from the shack.

"Hank's waiting for you," he says, and seems more than a little disappointed that our charismatic colleague will be passing out of his orbit.

The building that contains the dispatching center for Hale Medical Response is directly across the street, behind an iron-barred door. Sherona lets it be known that it might be better if she approached the dispatcher on her own.

"That's fine," I say. "That's great." And refrain from adding, "You go, girl," only because I don't want to come across like some sort of wannabe to the sisterhood.

Connie and I wait in the car, fretting while Sherona does her thing.

"Who knew?" Connie says. "Is this the same woman who spent six months in a shelter for the abused?"

"Amazing, huh? I wish Shane could see her in action—he'd probably offer her a job. If we're still in business after this is over, she gets a raise. You, too."

"Oh, we'll be in business," Connie says confidently, reaching over to pat my hand.

Mr. Yap, no doubt jealous, climbs into her lap and nuzzles at her chin. Connie coos at him softly, eyes keen for the door to the dispatcher's office.

Fifteen minutes pass. More than enough time for the strange fit of giddiness to be displaced by another heavy dose of dread. My very blood feels heavy, turgid. It's true that tremendous progress has been made in the last eight or nine hours. The man in the mask has been identified and his motive revealed. But he's still out there in the wind, heading for an unknown rendezvous where, I am absolutely convinced, my son will die. It's all happening now, today, in the dog hours of the night, and every minute we idle here, our quarry is another minute farther on down the road. Another minute closer to taking Tommy's life.

My mind supplies the next phrase—*if he hasn't already done so*—but I force that terrible possibility out of my thoughts. No room for doubt. Doubt is fatal. Watching Tommy's teammates taught me that, if nothing else did. The kids who doubted they could hit the ball never made contact. At best they closed their eyes and swung just to get it over with. Whereas the better players like my son never doubted they'd make contact, never stepped into the batter's box anticipating failure. Each swing was a stroke of confidence, even if the result was a whiff or a pop-up.

Connie and I both inhale sharply as Sherona exits the barred door and strides purposefully to the car. Her strong arms pumping like a majorette leading a parade. The determined expression on her face letting us know that something is up, facts have been learned.

"All kinda things going on," she announces, panting just a little as she settles into the passenger seat. "Best get you back on the highway. Go south."

She doesn't have to tell Connie twice. As we glide through the deserted streets of the freight district, Sherona fills us in. "Silly kind of man," she says. "Keep sayin' how I'd make a good wife for somebody like him, when he means *exactly* like him. But he knows about the missing ride, that's what counts, right?"

"Missing ride?"

"That's what they call the vehicle, the ambulance. Call it a 'ride.' Four rides on the street, six more in the lot on standby. Upstairs, above where the dispatcher works? They've got a bunk room, like for fire-fighters. I ask do they slide down a pole, he says no. Never mind about that. The ride that picks up the Cutter boy, he's a driver name of Tim. Tim's real reliable, always calls in, keeps in touch, like they do. Only he doesn't keep in touch. I ask can the radio break, he tells me sure, the radio can break but they also got the cell phone."

"So they think the ambulance has been hijacked?"

"Something like that. When Tim doesn't call, Beavis checks him out on the locator."

"Beavis?"

Sherona looks slightly embarrassed. "The dispatcher. Beavis isn't his real name, his real name is J.D. or some kind of initial name, but I'm callin' him Beavis cause he's a butt head. Okay?"

"Okay."

"Beavis, he's got this satellite thing going. Look on the computer screen, all his rides are showing. Knows exactly where they are at all times. Driver stops to pee, Beavis knows about it."

A GPS locator. It makes sense an ambulance service would use the latest technology to monitor its fleet of vehicles. It's all I can do not to rub my hands with glee. We've got him.

"Beavis sees Tim driving south on the highway instead of north to New London, he tries to get him on the squawk. That what the fool calls his radio, a squawk. Minute later the ride stops at the Route 90 exit, at a rest area, and the locator stops working. Ride disappears from the screen."

My spirit plummets. What was I thinking? The man in the mask—

Cutter, Kate, his name is Cutter—he knows about GPS locators. He used one on my minivan, the day I transferred the money. The query from the dispatcher confirmed that the diverted ambulance had a locator, and Cutter silenced it.

"Beavis, he calls the cops, reports a stolen ride. Say they'll get right on it. Beavis say, 'Don't hold your breath.'"

"But the last known location was 287. Heading into Westchester."

"From 287 you can go south, hook into the Sawmill, get you into the city," Sherona points out.

"Or go north, up along the Hudson, all the way to the Tappan Zee," Connie adds. "Face it, 287 could be just one road on the way to anywhere."

"What do we know?" I ask them. "We know he has his comatose son in a stolen ambulance. We know the boy needs a heart transplant. How many places can do that, in Westchester, or in the metropolitan area? A few, a dozen?"

"No idea," says Connie. "But I can find out."

"How?" I ask eagerly. "You know a heart surgeon we can call up at this hour?"

"Sort of," Connie says, grinning at me in the rearview mirror. "We'll make a pit stop at my place and ask Dr. Google."

While Connie boots up her home computer, I make another call to Maria Savalo, expecting the usual dump to voice mail. Amazingly enough, the real deal answers, bright and chipper at four in the morning.

"Once again, don't give me your location," is her first admonition.

"I'm in the company of friends," I tell her. "What's the word on the FBI? Any positive response?"

The cell connection isn't that great, but good enough to transmit her sigh. "Had to call in a favor and get home listings for a couple of the special agents who work out of the New Haven bureau, because, of course, the office won't officially reopen until 8:00 a.m. Figured I'd try some of the working stiffs in addition to the agent in charge. Kind of stir things up."

"How'd that go?"

"Not well. Threatened to prosecute me for harassment. Apparently there's an obscure statute forbidding the transmission of an agent's home number."

"So they're not going to do anything?"

"I didn't say that," Maria says. "As a matter of fact, I get the distinct impression they've opened an active investigation. But these are guys who keep their lips zipped for a living. They'll never admit to anything, even when they're doing the right thing."

Exasperated, I say, "Got a pen? I'm going to give you the tag numbers for the ambulance Stephen Cutter hijacked. My guess is he's swapped the plates already, disguised the vehicle somehow, but it's all we've got to go on. Last located on 287, heading west. Route 90 exit. Give the highway patrol a heads-up."

"I'll be darned," Maria says with a chuckle. "You sound like Randall Shane."

Ignoring that, I continue, "Hale Medical Response has already notified state police in the tristate area. What they'll do about it is anybody's guess. They may assume it's just another hijacking for drugs."

"I'll make a few calls, see what I can find out."

"Have you spoken to Jared Nichols?"

"I got him out of bed," Maria admits.

"So you've got his home phone number. Is that a violation of the law, too?" I add caustically.

My lawyer mumbles something. I ask her to repeat.

"Didn't have to use the phone," she says. "Jared and I are engaged. We've, um, been living together for the last six months."

The mind boggles—my lawyer and the prosecutor in bed, literally. "Isn't that a conflict of interest or something?" I ask lamely.

"We're pretty careful about that," Maria says somewhat defensively. "If anything, it's to my client's advantage. I never tell Jared about a case, not one word, but I sort of know what he's up to, depending on who he's scheduled a meeting with on any given day."

"Whatever." The fact is, there's no room in my fevered brain for worrying about my lawyer's domestic and professional entanglements. "We're checking hospitals and transplant centers and so on," I tell her. "Seeing if we can determine a likely destination. I'll let you know."

"Kate, if you find the guy, call the locals, okay? Let the cops handle it."

I feel my face growing hot. "Like they've handled it so far? My son is going to die in the next few hours if I don't find him. So far the cops haven't done anything but screw this up. Last I heard, they didn't even believe there *was* a kidnapper."

"I'm sure that's changed, thanks to you and Shane."

"Maybe. I hope so. But I have to assume nothing has changed, that I'm the only one searching for Tommy. If they prove me wrong, great. But I'm not stopping until I have that little boy in my arms, do you understand?"

"Perfectly."

I end the call just before the tears start flowing again. How much can a body take before overdosing on adrenaline and anxiety? Guess I'm about to find out.

Connie and Sherona are huddled in front of her monitor.

"What have you got?" I want to know.

"So far so good," Connie says, working her mouse as she clicks through Web sites. "There are nine transplant centers in the metropolitan area. All associated with major hospitals or medical schools. Locations in Manhattan, Brooklyn, Long Island, a couple in New Jersey."

My heart sinks. "So many? I thought two or three, max."

"Sorry, no. There are about a 150 centers nationwide, and a fair number of them are in the northeast. Says here there are about 2,300 heart transplants a year. That's a lot of surgeons, a lot of hospitals."

"Any obvious military connections?"

"Not that I can find. If there are any military facilities for cardiac transplants in the area, they're not popping up."

Weary but agitated, I plop into a seat, tent my hands over my tired eyes. "Let's think about this. I want to get my son a new heart, where do I go? Remember, the nurses told Sherona that Jesse Cutter wasn't a candidate for a transplant. If he was, none of this would be happening. The man in the mask—Cutter—he's trying an end run, outside the usual channels. Outside the system somehow. He can't just show up at an E.R. and demand surgery, right?"

"I wouldn't think so."

"Therefore he must have a place that's willing to handle an illegal procedure. Or if not exactly illegal, then outside the rules. Does that make sense?"

"Unfortunately, yes," says Connie.

"See what Google comes up with when you put in 'transplant surgery' and 'lawsuit.'"

Connie keys it in, clicks on the button. "Ten thousand hits," she says, sounding frustrated.

"Try searching results with 'New York' and 'controversial.' Cutter has to find a way in. Maybe he researched it on the Internet, just like us. We're looking for something edgy. A flaw he can exploit."

"Down to five hundred," Connie announces.

"Search results with 'unethical,'" I suggest. "See if we can find a back-alley transplant surgeon."

Sherona grimaces. "This ain't an abortion, honey. Can't do it in a back alley or a storefront."

"Fine," I say, unable to mask my irritation. "The high-end version. A hospital that cuts corners, breaks the rules, whatever."

"Hmm," says Connie, her prominent, elegant nose almost touching the screen. "This is interesting. Didn't pop up with the other trans-plant centers for some reason."

"Hospital? Medical school?"

"Nope. Better. A private clinic with a clientele of celebrities and the superwealthy."

The hair tingles on the back of my neck. A private clinic for the wealthy. Which means the place is all about money. And the man in the mask didn't just take my son, he took all of our money, too.

"Go on," I urge her.

Connie's grinning—obviously she's found something. "According to the *New York Times,* they've been sued for ignoring the federal guide-lines for organ donation, specifically the waiting list for liver trans-plants. Seems they obtained a liver for a famous rock musician who ruined his own liver shooting drugs. Quote—'one-stop organ shop-ping, with an all-star transplant team ready to deliver, provided the price is right.'"

"What about heart transplants?"

"It's not the thrust of this particular article, but there is a reference to a heart-lung transplant for a Saudi prince. Once again, the prince wasn't on the approved list, but the clinic got around that somehow. Reporter says it's not like there are federal regulators hanging around the operating rooms. Quote—'It's basically an honor system. The major medical centers follow the guidelines, but private clinics can make their own rules.'"

"Where is this place?"

"Scarsdale," she says, grinning like a kid who knows that teacher is about to award a big fat gold star. "That's what they call themselves. The Scarsdale Transplant Clinic. And it's right off 287."

D~r.~ Stanley J. Munk paces the loading dock, puffing on an unfil-
tered Lucky Strike cigarette. Another personal vice unknown to his
wife. The occasional stench of smoke on his clothing he always blames
on others—patients, partners, one of the surgical nurses, whoever. Fact
is, he only smokes while under stress. Stress, in his life, is not defined
as surgery. He loves to cut, loves being in control of an anesthetized
life. Stress he reserves for financial, professional or marital difficulties.
He's not sure where this particular situation fits into the scheme of
things, but if it goes wrong it could encompass all three areas.

One thing he's surmised, the man who calls himself Paul Defield
is not only dangerous, he's quite possibly becoming psychotic. Over
the last few hours Munk, awakened at three in the morning, has received half a dozen cell-phone calls from the man, and he sounds not
only aggressive but increasingly disorganized. Not at all the icy control freak who claimed to be a special agent for the FBI masquerading as a cop. A claim Munk now doubts. But if not a government
agent, what is he? How did he get access to electronic and computer
surveillance so sophisticated that Munk, something of techie himself,
has never even heard of it?

Whatever his sources or methods, the man managed to crawl inside Stanley Munk's skin, shared his secret life for a time. That alone makes him hideously dangerous. As for the proposed surgery, Munk remains confident that if things blow up legally he can successfully argue that he cooperated under duress. Which happens to be true. Other than whatever medical records Defield may or may not provide, he has no actual knowledge of the prospective patient or the prospective donor. It's not as if he's personally gone out on the black market to illegally obtain an organ, which if discovered would likely cause the revocation of his license to practice medicine and therefore endanger the partnership. From the beginning, Munk and his partners have been exquisitely careful about that particular distinction. Patients or the families or associates of patients have always obtained the necessary organs, at whatever the going rate. Thus providing plausible deniability, and legal cover, if not ethical purity.

Munk glances at his Rolex. Almost six in the morning. The days are so long this time of year that the sun has been up for more than an hour. Looks like a beautiful day on the way. Clear blue skies, perfect temperatures. A day to play hooky if ever there was one. Savoring his images, his trophies from the last junket.

Best not to think about that now.

His role in the transplant surgery will require something less than six hours, barring complications. Assuming that all goes well, and he's able to remove Mr. Defield from his life, Munk has decided that he will reward himself with a spur-of-the-moment trip to Bangkok, or possibly Manila.

Definitely Manila. He's due for a change, for something new. He can feel the anticipation building like a small, refreshing wave. In his mind, Dr. Munk is entering a certain room, wondering what, exactly, he will find beyond the beaded curtains, when the ambulance backs into the loading dock.

New Jersey plates, he notices. Is that where Defield hails from, some sweaty little suburb in the Garbage State?

The EMT gets out, advances to the dock. Light behind putting him in silhouette.

"Morning, Doctor."

In the warmth of a summer morning, Munk shivers. He recognizes the voice.

"Everything groovy?" the man who calls himself Defield wants to know as he comes up the steps. "Team assembled, ready to go?"

"No problem," says Munk. Chill is over and now he's sweating. "Strictly routine."

"What did you tell them? Son of a rock star?"

Munk shrugs, attempting to embody a casualness he does not feel. "State Department connection," he says. "Child of an important diplomat."

"The ambassador's boy. I like that. Very classy."

"Rock-star connection, somebody might tip off the press."

In the blink of an eye, Defield is on him, rushing him backward until they both slam into the painted cinder-block wall at the rear of the loading dock.

"Are you playing me?" Defield hisses, pressing a gun into the soft flesh of Munk's neck. "Tip off the press? What the fuck are you thinking?"

Physical fear of the gun makes Munk's throat constrict, but he manages to say, "No press, that's the point."

"Who'd tip them off?"

"Nobody. Happened once with a nurse, she, um, leaked the story to a tabloid. Johnny Beemer gets a new liver. We fired her."

"Johnny Beemer?" The gun is slowly lowered. Defield's eyes are so bright they might be illuminated by inner lasers. "Oh yeah, I read about that. The punk rocker with the smack habit. What first put me on to you guys, as a matter of fact. Your high ethical standards."

Munk wonders if the man is on something, or if the madness in his blood comes naturally. At the same time admonishing himself to keep his own mouth shut, no chitchat about the many celebrity connections to the clinic. No telling what will set Defield off or how he'll react.

"Who have you told?" Defield wants to know.

"About you? Nobody."

"About the transplant."

"Just my partners. They had to know we'd be cutting this morning."

"Cutting? That's what you call it?"

"Surgery. We'll be in surgery. There are six people on the team, you know that."

"To fix the ambassador's son."

"Exactly," says Munk. "What I told them. All they need to know. Strictly routine."

Suddenly the man who calls himself Defield changes. Like watching a cloud-shadow rapidly pass over a landscape. He visibly relaxes, and the lack of tension alters his expression. "Okay, good," he says with a tight smile, and a kind of dreamy look in his eyes. "Time to meet my sons, Dr. Munk. Time to meet my beautiful boys."

"Sons?" Munk asks, confused. "Boys?"

Defield opens the rear door of the vehicle, revealing two slender, unconscious bodies strapped to a pair of matching gurneys. One fitted with a respirator, the other breathing on his own.

"My God," says Munk. "Identical twins."

Suddenly, it all makes sense. And he knows why Defield is so confident of a tissue match. A glance tells him that the twins are not Defield's progeny, not his children by birth, but there's no doubt about the man's paternal connection. Munk doubts the man's sanity, but not his bond as a father, which informs and explains everything he has done so far. All that he has risked, and all he is about to sacrifice.

"Welcome to my tragedy," says Defield. "I've had to choose. Who lives, who dies. You know what that means? Do you? Can you imagine?"

The surgeon shakes his head.

"Means I go to hell," the man who calls himself Defield says quite affably. "Maybe I'll see you there."

As Munk helps unload the first gurney, he can't help thinking that when the man smiles, he looks like a grinning skull.

Rush hour starts early on the 287, and by the time we get to the Scarsdale exit it's almost six-thirty. Fortunately Mr. Yap has been left at home, or else he'd be going nuts, because I've been playing backseat driver and Connie's been pushing the Beetle for all its worth. Weaving in and out of traffic, using the breakdown lane, scooting through traffic lights with a blaring horn at my urging.

Should I be concerned about risking lives other than my own? Yes, but I'm not that good a person. All I can think about is Tommy, and what might be happening to him. What might already have happened. How every fiber of me wants to be with him right now, this instant, but I can't. All because every truck in the world has decided to converge on this particular highway, at this godforsaken hour of the morning.

"What do we do when we get there?" Sherona wants to know. "You got a plan?"

"I don't know," I tell her. "Rush in the place and shout the medical equivalent of 'stop the presses,' I guess. If we even have the right place."

"I feel good about it," says Connie, trying to keep my spirits up as she hunches over the wheel like a NASCAR driver. "The ambulance was on 287, the clinic is just off 287, where else could he be going?"

"Could be heading to the Sawmill," I fret. "From there he could go anywhere."

"We'll get there, check it out," Connie promises. "One more light, and then we turn left on Fennimore, then the second right."

After what seems an eternity—I'm debating whether to get out and run—at last we're on a boulevard that isn't clotted with commuters. Professional offices and plazas, all beautifully landscaped.

"It's here somewhere," Connie says as I crane my neck, searching.

Sherona spots the sign before I do, and Connie screeches into the tree-shaded parking lot of the Scarsdale Transplant Clinic, an ultramodern ground-level concrete structure with darkly tinted windows, the whole structure painted in shades of pastel that fail to make it welcoming. In the center of the wide swath of perfectly manicured lawn, a heliport pad with a shiny gold MedEvac helicopter strapped down with what look like silver bungee cords.

At this hour there are only a few vehicles in the lot—a matched pair of Mercedes coupes and a Lexus sedan—taking up the slots assigned to staff. The place is utterly quiet, no sign of life. Except for the telltale doctor cars, it doesn't even look open for business.

"What now?" Connie asks, sounding much less confident than she did while fighting us through traffic.

"Sherona, how about you try the front desk," I suggest. "Use your powers of persuasion. Tell 'em what we know, see if it does any good. Connie and I will circle around the back, see if we can find a back way in."

"'Powers of persuasion,'" says the big woman as she eases her weight out of the tiny Beetle. "I like that."

She struts away like a drill sergeant looking for troops to rally.

Around the back we find a hospital loading dock with an ambulance in the slot.

My heart slams and my mouth goes dry.

"Jersey plates," says Connie, sounding thoroughly discouraged.

"Doesn't mean anything," I tell her. "Plates can be swapped. You notice the doors?"

"What about them?"

"See where it says Beacon Medical Transport? Those are magnetic signs."

I vault out of the car, approach the ambulance. It's a big, boxy vehicle with orange-and-white stripes that look very familiar. A quick inspection reveals that the magnetic stick-on signs cover the logo for Hale Medical Response.

We've found it. Against all odds, we managed to track the monster to this very place.

My heart lifts. At the same time my anxiety level spikes so high it feels like my head is about to explode. And my knees, well, they seem to have dissolved, leaving me with legs like limp spaghetti.

This is it. Somewhere inside this building, my son is waiting. Alive or dead, I'm going to find him in the next few minutes.

"Where are you going?" Connie wants to know, hurrying to catch up.

"He's here," I say.

"We should call," Connie suggests. "Alert the cops."

My hands shake as I hand her the cell phone.

The loading doors, I soon discover, are bolted from the inside. Pounding with my fists produces nothing but a dull thump. Running around the corner of the building, I'm confronted by mirror-tinted plate-glass windows that extend from the roofline to the ground. Crazy with fear, I search the ground for a rock. Wanting to smash the hateful glass. Finding nothing but grass and imbedded paving stones.

What would Shane do?

"Connie! Your keys!"

Without a word, Connie hands me the keys to the Beetle.

"Stand back," I tell her, and run to the car.

The engine starts instantly, but the little car has a standard transmission, and the first time the clutch is popped the engine stalls. Grinding the starter, begging it to go. The engine chugs to life and I ease it into first gear and run up over the curb, onto the pristine lawn. Gathering speed across the lawn, I'm in third gear by the time the building looms. Somewhere in my peripheral vision, Connie is raising her arms, her mouth as round as that Munch painting of *The Scream,* either cheering me on or shouting for me to stop, or maybe both.

What I'm thinking, as the little car crashes through the plate glass, is that my friend Connie will be mad at me, and then the rear wheels catch and I'm thrown hard into the steering wheel.

Then nothing, blackness.

When I come to, bells inside the building are ringing like a giant alarm clock. The windshield has been reduced to diamonds that litter the dash. I can feel them in my hair, particles of shattered glass, and my face is hot and wet. The front air bags have deployed, pinning me to the back of the seat, which is now in the rear of the vehicle. Can't move. Can barely breathe, a great pressure on my chest and lungs.

And then Connie is there, frantically reaching through the broken side window and trying to pull the air bags away from me.

"The door is jammed," she informs me in a strangely calm voice. "You'll have to scrunch through the window."

Somehow she gets her hands under my arms, pulling and guiding me, and I'm popping out through the shattered window and both of us fall to the floor with a great *woof!* of expelled air.

"You're bleeding," she says, panting as she touches my forehead.

"Sorry," I say. "Your poor car."

"Can you stand up? Anything broken?"

My ribs hurt like hell, but a wobbly version of my legs seem to be functioning. Looking around, my vision is blurred but I can make out that we're in some sort of conference room. Smashed chairs and tables, a lectern gone vertical, a torn projection screen hanging like a sparkly white rag. And the alarms making the insistent all-hands-to-battle-stations *ring...ring...ring* as if somewhere a nuclear-reactor engine is about to melt down.

Then, bursting into the room, a young security guard who can scarcely believe what he's seeing.

"My God, what happened?"

With Connie holding my arm to steady me, I'm crunching through the glass fragments, heading for the guard.

"The police are on the way," he tells us. "What happened? Did the accelerator stick?"

He thinks it was an accident, and I see no reason to disabuse him of the notion, particularly since he's got a holster on his belt and, presumably, a gun.

"My son," I tell him. "Surgery."

Since he still seems befuddled by the shock of having his building invaded by a Volkswagen Beetle and a couple of suburban females, I hurry past him, out into a brightly lit hallway with slick, shiny floors. Behind me I hear Connie talking urgently to the guard and I'm thinking, *Isn't that nice, she's taking care of business, good old Connie.*

Floating into the hallway. Somewhere from the back of my mind, or maybe the inner ear, comes a single, high-pitched musical note. A dreamy violin with only one thing to say. Very odd, but sort of pleasant.

"Tommy," I want to say, but my mouth doesn't seem to be functioning for the moment.

From somewhere in the building, a flat popping noise. Somebody lighting firecrackers? Don't they know it's not yet the Fourth of July? Or is it? Have I missed the Fourth?

Trying to recall what day it is, exactly, when a man in green surgical scrubs hurries toward me, gowned and masked. There may be spatters of blood across his chest, I can't be sure. My vision is still off, as if some internal part of me remains tilted inside the wreckage of the car.

"Are you a doctor?" I demand, trying to keep him in focus. Good, mouth working again.

He shakes his head, eyes on the ruined room behind me. "Nurse," he mutters, and keeps on going.

Probably thinks they're being invaded by an outraged patient, a transplant failure gone postal.

Then I'm jogging along the hallway, having trouble keeping upright. Something wrong with my sense of balance. The alarm bells have ceased, and in the distance I hear the *whoop-whoop* of a siren. Strangely, it sounds like it's going away, but all of my senses are distorted, and for all I know the siren is actually inside the building.

That's when I notice how hard it is to breathe. Something wrong inside? Can't tell. Maybe the air is too thin. Very rarefied brand of air they have here in Scarsdale. Lurching around a corner, it feels like I'm attempting to manipulate a very difficult marionette, one whose limbs do not correspond to the strings.

Ignore it. Find Tommy.

"Tom-eee-eee-eee…"

Is the echo in the hallway or inside my head?

The wall steps out and slams me. *Whoa. Keep it vertical, girl. Miles to go before you sleep. Somewhere in these tilting funhouse hallways your boy is waiting. You can almost see him sitting up in his hospital bed, a big grin on his beautiful face, saying, "Hey, Mom, what's the haps?"*

Did Tommy say that? Did I hear him? Must be close. Just a little farther on down the road.

Somewhere nearby, or a million miles away, a pair of doors beckon. The double doors to an operating room. On *E.R.* the O.R.'s always have double doors. Try saying that three times quick. Unless I'm seeing double, which is entirely within the realm of possibility. Or triple, is there such a thing as triple doors? Glass walls, lightly tinted, make me feel like I'm floating outside a space station, looking in. Carts of surgical equipment lurking in the tinted shadows behind the glass. Some of the shadows moving—no, those are people, not shadows. What are they doing? Why are they hiding behind the glass?

In the center of the glass-walled room, a pool of light. And there, stepping into the light, another figure wrapped into a green surgical gown, weird magnifying glasses that make him look really dorky, and in his gloved hands, a glint of light.

"Scalpel, please."

No, no, no.

Must get through the doors. Must grab the hands of the man in the silly green gown, make him stop whatever it is he's intent on doing.

Yell at him, Kate. Make yourself heard.

"Gahhh!" and then I slam through the doors and spin into the glass-walled operating room and the spin part gets out of control and the floor comes up and kicks me in the butt.

Looking up into lights so bright they make my head hurt. Can't breathe. I try to say something but all I can do is gurgle like a baby, isn't that odd? Isn't that strange?

Then some icky green rubberized fingers are inserting themselves into my mouth and I'm no longer even trying to breathe—too much trouble—and a small, insistent voice in the dimmest part of my brain is telling me to stop struggling because I'm already dead, dead, dead.

Shane is waiting to greet me on the other side. "Hi, Kate," he says in a husky voice. "Welcome back."

How strange is this? I'm thinking. If anybody's waiting to greet me it should be Ted. I've only known Randall Shane for a few days and it's not like I've fallen in love with him, right? Not possible, too many important things on my mind, although I can't seem to recall what, exactly. So what's Shane doing here—wherever "here" is? And then I feel the gurney under me and background noise of life in tumult and the first word out of my mouth is *Tommy*.

"You should rest," Shane advises, patting my hand. "You had a collapsed lung."

"What about Tommy?"

The world slowly comes into focus. Doctors and cops rushing around, and a couple of suits that could be state police detectives or FBI agents, all of whom seem to be studiously ignoring me. So what's new? Waiting at the end of the gurney, Connie and Sherona are giving me little encouraging waves. Deferring to Shane, apparently.

"It's amazing what medical science can do," Shane tells me, ignoring my question. "They put a tube down your throat and inflated your lung like a balloon. They tell me collapsed lungs are common in front-end collisions."

Shane, with a huge chunk of white gauze taped to his head and two black eyes that make him look like a mournful raccoon.

"He's dead, isn't he?" I say. "We were too late. Tommy's already dead."

Shane grimaces and keeps patting my hand, as if not sure what to do, or how to respond. He glances at Connie, who bursts into tears and then throws herself on me.

"Hey!" Shane exclaims, backing away. "Careful!"

"Terrible," Connie mumbles, embracing me. "Just terrible."

"I want to see him," I say, forcing myself up from the gurney. Woozy but able to breathe, more or less. No tears. I feel frozen emotionally, unable to react. "Take me to Tommy."

As the world reorients itself around me, it becomes obvious that I've been lying on a gurney outside the clinic O.R. Apparently I stumbled through the doors just before passing out, and the attending surgeon quickly determined what was wrong and fixed it. Whether or not he saved my life is questionable, as a single collapsed lung is not usually fatal, at least in the short run. Everybody keeps assuring me I'll be fine.

"Where is he?" I demand.

Shane thinks I mean Cutter, the man in the mask. "He got away. We don't know how, exactly, with all these cops and agents converging on the place. They're conducting a thorough search of the building and grounds, but he's gone."

The figure in the green surgical scrubs.

"I saw him in the hallway," I tell them as it all comes flooding back. "Said he was a nurse. It was him. I couldn't focus, but it had to be him. He took the ambulance. That was the siren."

"You have to tell the agents about this," Shane advises.

"After I see my son."

Frankly, it no longer matters to me, what happens to the man in the mask. Arresting him won't bring Tommy back. I simply don't care about him, one way or another.

Shane and Sherona are guiding me down the hall, shielding me from the harried cops, who look grim and impatient and much too busy to bother with the emotional needs of mere civilians. Connie hovers fretfully, tears freely streaming down her narrow face, dripping from her chin.

"Did they do it?" I want to know. "Did they save the other boy?"

"You stopped 'em," Sherona says. "Hit the building, all the bells went off, they stopped whatever it is they were doing. Right after is when he started shooting."

"Shooting?" I vaguely recall thinking about fireworks.

"One of the doctors, he's been gut shot. Guess what happened, he tried to stop the man from running away."

It's all too complicated. My entire being is focused upon one simple goal. See Tommy, hold him in my arms, tell him how sorry I am that I wasn't able to save him.

After that, I couldn't care less.

They're guiding me into a small recovery room when Shane says, "Kate? There's something you need to know before you go in there." He hesitates, looks helpless. "Something that needs to be clear."

I'm in no mood for this, for trying to shield my feelings. I haven't got any feelings so there's nothing to protect. "Just tell me, Randall. Quickly."

"Your son is brain dead."

"Of course he's brain dead," I say angrily. "They took his heart."

"No," says Shane, holding me back from the room. "No, no, his heart is still beating. He's breathing on his own, too. But the nurses just gave him a brain scan. There has been terrible damage, quite recent. Nothing anybody can do to bring him back. He's gone, Kate, I'm so sorry."

I wrench my arms away from Shane and run into the room. Smells faintly of disinfectant. Stark lights glinting off tile floor and walls. In the center of my vision, a gurney. And lying on the gurney, a small figure with his head carefully balanced on a special supportive pillow. Not moving, not reacting. Not dead, exactly, but not fully alive, either.

I fall to the floor, weeping. Ashamed of myself.

Connie hugs me from behind. "Oh, Kate. I'm so sorry."

"You don't understand," I bleat.

"I know, I know."

"That's not Tommy," I explain, dragging myself to my feet, and Connie with me.

Shame on me, but I'm crying tears of joy.

"I don't understand," says Dr. DeMillo, looking perplexed.

A vain-looking man with a very expensive hair weave and beautifully capped teeth, DeMillo is one of the clinic partners. A surgical specialist in diseases of the liver and kidneys, he had been preparing to assist Dr. Munk with the hastily scheduled heart transplant, and apparently still believes the recipient was somehow related to a Very Important Person in the State Department. Whatever that might mean. I'm having trouble keeping all the partners straight—there are five at the clinic—but I'm aware that a Dr. Stanley Munk was the one who was shot, and who evidently had some sort of prior relationship with Stephen Cutter. The fact that Munk is expected to survive is apparently due entirely to DeMillo, who performed emergency surgery to repair an artery torn by a bullet fragment.

"Stan said one boy was breathing on his own and the other was on the respirator. That they had run a preliminary scan and one had recently suffered irreversible brain damage. Gone from vegetative to brain dead. I naturally assumed it was the donor. Neither patient had been prepped. The nurse accompanying the brain-dead boy was very upset. It's been so confusing. We just assumed that—"

"Doesn't matter," I interrupt, waving him off. "Let me guess, the donor, the boy on the respirator, he was still in the ambulance?"

DeMillo looks started. "As a matter of fact, yes. We were on our way to bring him into the building for evaluation when the explosion happened. I mean the car crash. I thought it was an explosion. Sorry, I guess that was you."

Ignoring DeMillo, I turn to Shane and give his arm a squeeze. "Get it?" I ask. "Do you see what happened?"

"Yes," he says. "Cutter still has Tommy."

"I let him walk right by me. And before, when Connie and I first got here, I was standing right next to the ambulance while Tommy was inside."

Can't believe I was so stupid. Why hadn't I thought to look in the ambulance? Why had I assumed Tommy was already in the building?

"Where are you going?" Shane asks, hurrying to catch up.

"I think I know where he's headed," I tell him. "How long was I out?"

"Not sure exactly," he says, consulting his watch. Squints as if he's having trouble seeing with his trauma-blackened eyes. "I got here almost exactly when the crap hit the fan. Or rather when you hit the building. You were unconscious for an hour or so, is my best guess. They had to sedate you to get the tube down your throat."

"Sherona! Do me a favor?"

"If I can."

"Find out if there's anyone here who can fly that helicopter. Be nice, and if that doesn't work, threaten to sue. Got it?"

Sherona grins. "Yes, ma'am," she says. "Get you a flyboy."

My idea of transportation involves wheels on the road, or the rails. To my way of thinking, flying is about as glamorous as falling. Both involve speed, fear and the uncertainty of a sudden stop. When Ted surprised me with a three-day getaway for our first anniversary he learned the hard way that "small aircraft" and "Kate Bickford" should never appear in the same sentence. The flight down to Fort Lauderdale was okay—I was determined to make it okay—mostly because if you try really hard, you can pretend that a 757 is a big fat train compartment in the sky. It's important never to look out the window, and if the ride gets bumpy, think of frost-heaves on the road. Plus, I was deliriously pleased that my handsome husband hadn't forgotten after all, that his baffled looks in the preceding days were feigned. At the time we were basically broke, paying off school loans and a car payment, so our destination wasn't exactly a five-star resort, but it was in the Caribbean, so who cared? Palm trees, steel drums, reggae in the moonlight—until Ted gently informed me that steel drums and reggae were Jamaica and we were heading for the Bahamas, a scant fifty miles off the coast of Florida.

I didn't care where we were going as long as we were going there together, and I was so impressed with his ability to surprise me that at first I thought the little airplane in Fort Lauderdale was part of the joke. You're kidding, right? That's not the real thing, it's a model airplane! Ha, ha, ha. *No, it's a six-seater Cessna, honey, and the flight takes less than thirty minutes. As soon as we take off you'll be able to see our destination. It'll be fun, all part of the adventure.*

Flying in the clinic's helicopter—a Bell 407 EMS, whatever that is—makes the Bahamas flight seem like a bike ride to the end of the block. My first helicopter experience and, I hope, my last. Can't get airsick because to be sick you have to have a stomach and mine has been left somewhere far below. We're crossing a swath of Connecticut at a hundred and fifty miles per hour and the roar of the Rolls-Royce turbine is so loud you have to wear shielded headphones.

Shane is in the jump seat behind me. I hate that they call it a jump seat, but his voice in the headphones is totally calm.

"The local police have been dispatched," he tells me. "The SWAT team won't deploy until the situation is accessed. They've been informed that the suspect has your son, and that any police presence may set him off."

"What does it mean 'until the situation is accessed'?"

"Means they'll keep out of sight until told otherwise. Nobody wants a hostage situation, Kate. That much is clear."

At the moment I've lost all faith in the ability of the authorities to deal with the man in the mask. I know he's got a real name, but I can't seem to lock onto it—he's still the man in the mask to me. Ski masks, surgical masks, whatever it takes, he's got a way of making himself invisible when necessary. He managed to slip away from about fifty cops and agents converging on the clinic, all because nobody thought to stop an ambulance with emergency lights flashing. So the idea of a SWAT team doesn't exactly thrill me. Anxious snipers, a gun battle, hostages down, it all adds up to a nightmare.

Sherona and Connie have been left behind in Scarsdale, not required on this part of the mission, and to be truthful neither seemed all that thrilled about a helicopter flight anyhow. Maria Savalo has promised to rendezvous with us on the ground as soon as she can get there, to handle any legal problems that may arise. My indictment will surely be dropped as they develop new evidence with a new suspect, but I'm not out of the woods yet. Apparently an understanding of what actually happened will take a while to seep into the various bureaucracies, from the Fairfax P.D. to the state prosecutor's office. I'm no longer killer mom but remain a "person of interest," whatever that means.

Considering the time of day, we'd be at least two hours away by car, crawling in morning traffic around the urban centers. As the crow flies—or rather as the Bell 407 flies—we're less than forty minutes from our destination. A rough calculation means there's a chance we'll arrive before he does, even though he had a ninety-minute head start. That's what I'm praying for, to be there when he arrives, before he has a chance to set up whatever sick scenario he has in mind.

The state cops are on the lookout for the stolen ambulance, but my own feeling is, he'll have new wheels. Something faster, more maneuverable. Van or a pickup. Maybe a station wagon with tinted windows. Whatever he needs to blend in while transporting Tommy to the scene of the standoff. Because that's where all of this is heading, now that his cover has been blown, his identity shared with every law enforcement agency in the Northeast. As a military man he'll understand about snipers, he'll have made preparations. Spider-holes, tunnels, who the hell knows what has taken shape in his sick and desperate imagination?

One thing I know for sure: A man willing to steal a heart from a living boy is capable of anything.

As for Randall Shane, he worries me. The man should be in a hospital bed, under observation, but he insisted on signing himself out, and now he insists on accompanying me. Says he's fine, no problem, but his eyes have a funny way of going out of focus, and when he walks he looks like a deep-sea diver maneuvering in lead boots.

In my headphones his husky voice says, "You're convinced he'll go home. Was it something he said?"

"No. His wife. He left her locked up in the house—or that's what he thinks. Besides, where else can he go?"

The question is rhetorical, of course. There's no correct answer, just a gut feeling, and obviously my gut feelings are far from infallible.

As we approach New London, Shane begins to confer with the pilot about strategies for approach. The navigational equipment can direct us to a street address, but it's not like he can land the thing on a rooftop. Maybe in the movies. In reality there are radio towers and poles and power lines and crosswinds to be taken into account—a wide-open space is required. Plus, if we land too close, the sound of the helicopter will give us away.

"How about there?" Shane asks, pointing. "Would that work?"

"Baseball field," the pilot says. "Perfect."

And then the bottom drops out and we're plummeting. Feels like we must be crashing but the pilot seems calm, so I stifle the shriek in my throat and concentrate on not throwing up. At the last moment we slow down, rising slightly—my stomach suddenly finds me—and then, with a slight bump, we're down.

Shaking like a leaf, I unbuckle the harness, take Shane's outstretched hand, and find myself standing in the outfield grass. The ground seems to be moving and Shane has to grab hold to keep me from falling down.

"Take it easy!" Shane shouts as the turbo winds down.

He's a little rocky himself, and in the end we hold each other up while the pilot grins and shakes his head—amateurs.

"This is a Little League field," I tell Shane. "I bet he played here."

"Who?"

"The other boy. Tommy's brother."

Spooks me out, thinking about it, so I shove it out of my mind and concentrate on the mission at hand. The authorities are under the impression that I'll be standing by in case there are hostage negotiations, but that's not what I have in mind. I intend to be waiting in Lyla's kitchen when her husband comes marching home. Knowing I can't be dissuaded, Shane wants to be there, too.

"Which way?" I ask a bit too loudly, my ears still ringing from the helicopter noise.

"Three blocks east." Shane takes my arm, supposedly to guide me but really to steady himself.

If I knew the Vulcan nerve pinch I'd render him unconscious, leave him sleeping safe and peaceful on the outfield grass. Then again, he's probably thinking the same about me, although to my way of thinking a collapsed lung isn't half as serious as a concussion. The cracked ribs hurt like hell, but it's only physical pain. Nothing compared to the yawning emptiness I've been fighting ever since learning that I'd been within a few feet of my son—right there in the ambulance, you fool!—and that I might have blown my last good chance.

Please be alive. That's my three-word prayer, my mantra, the faint chorus of hope that keeps me going.

We're on an ordinary sidewalk, the kind with cracks that will break your mother's back, but the concrete feels spongy under my feet. Shane isn't faring much better—no words of complaint, but every move is a wince of pain. An observer might suppose we're an elderly couple shuffling along on our morning walk, holding each other up. The holding-each-other-up part is true enough, and our progress seems agonizingly slow. I suppose we're moving at a more or less normal rate, but to me it feels like we're struggling every step of the way. Running in slow motion through deep sand with a tidal wave poised to crash over us.

Three blocks, but it feels like a journey to the end of the earth. At last the trim little house with the white picket fence comes into view. No vehicle in the street or driveway. Looks like we're going to make it before Papa Bear comes home.

"Don't turn your head," Shane cautions. "Can you see that hedge?"

He means the hedge at the other end of the block. I squint, and bring into focus the figure of a man in a blue flak jacket, crouching behind the hedge.

"They're covering the house from both sides," Shane says.

When we're about a hundred feet from the house, the commander of the local SWAT unit steps out from behind a tree and tries to wave us off.

"Do they know who I am?" I ask Shane.

"Not sure," he says. "They might. Or they might think we're from the neighborhood."

"Will they shoot us?"

He shrugs. "I seriously doubt it."

"Good enough for me," I say, and steer him around the picket fence, into the yard.

All the curtains are drawn. The house looks sleepy somehow, as if waiting for something, or someone, to wake it up.

"What's your plan?" he wants to know, keeping his voice low.

"Get in the house."

"Yeah, but how?"

"Around the back," I say. "There's a bulkhead door."

Behind the adjacent home, barely in our line of sight, men in camouflage gear have assembled, sniper rifles at the ready. More furious arms wave, trying to warn us off. We studiously ignore them and proceed to the bulkhead. It's not fair to these brave and dutiful men, but I can't help thinking about the SWAT unit at Columbine, waiting until all the killing had been done before they send a man into the school. Following procedure, even if it means a courageous teacher bleeds to death while they "access the situation."

Shane wraps both big hands around the bulkhead handle and attempts to ease it open. "Locked," he whispers.

I lead him around to the breezeway. When in doubt, ring the doorbell. Before pressing the button, I try the knob and much to my surprise, find the door unlocked.

"Let me go first," Shane whispers.

Shaking him off—not hard, considering his condition—I ease the door open and step into Lyla Cutter's kitchen.

Pancakes. The kitchen is rich with the smell of frying pancakes. And I can scarcely believe my eyes. Lyla stands at the stove, wearing a frilly white apron, a spatula raised in her hand, as if conducting a symphony only she can hear. Slumped at the table, looking wan and sleepy and confused, is an eleven-year-old boy. Tall and lanky for his age, dark hair matted to his head, as if he's been deeply asleep for an eternity and just been awakened by the smell of breakfast.

Tommy.

Every fiber of my being wants to rush to the table, but there's an impressive rack of knives on the counter, within easy reach of Lyla's pale, nervous hands, so I approach cautiously.

"Good morning," says Lyla with manic brightness. "Is everybody hungry?"

My son is alive. That's blinking in my brain like a giant neon sign. But if Tommy is here, so is the man in the mask. Is he waiting, watching? Tormenting me one last time before he brings the hammer down, pulls the trigger, whatever he's got planned?

"Mom?" says Tommy, voice thick, head lolling. "Is that you?"

Then I'm hugging him, holding him tight to my breast, and for once he does not protest. "Mom, my throat hurts," he says, slurring his words. "They stuck something in my throat."

Holding his precious face in my hands, I search his eyes. He's been drugged, no surprise, and I can see him fighting to clear his mind. His fingernails are torn up and he's thinner than he should be, and he stinks of sweat and pee, but other than that he seems to be unharmed.

A miracle.

"This is Tomas," Lyla says gaily, waving the spatula. "Tomas is Jesse's brother, isn't that nice? I figured if my Jesse likes pancakes, so would he."

"Is your husband here?" Shane asks her.

Lyla shrugs prettily. She's wearing a face borrowed from television, the Happy Housewife making breakfast for the kids. "Oh, he's around, I guess. Up to something, as usual. Wanted me to think that this boy was Jesse, isn't that silly? Swore to me. But a mother knows. A mother always knows."

My plan is to roll under the table with Tommy if the moment comes. Shield him with my body.

"Mrs. Cutter, is that the basement door?" Shane asks.

"Yes," Lyla says. She won't look at the door, as if she knows that something bad is down there. Something that will ruin her fantasy of being normal and happy.

Shane eases the door open, revealing a slice of shadow, stairs going down. Holding his finger to his lips, he gives me a look and then descends into the basement.

"Pancakes?" Lyla says, setting a plate on the table. "There's real maple syrup from Vermont."

Shane's voice comes up from the basement. "Hold it right there!" he orders in his best cop voice.

That's when I remember that Randall Shane doesn't have a gun. He's unarmed. Went down those dark steps with nothing but his courage.

Shane, Shane, Shane.

In my precious son's ear I whisper this: "Can you hide if you have to?"

Tommy nods. I kiss the top of his head and go to the basement door.

Shadows. Stairs going down. A single light at the bottom. And there in a pool of light, the man in the mask, unmasked. Wearing his army uniform, crisp and clean and perfect.

Gun in his hand. A big, ugly, black thing. Aiming at Shane, who stands a few paces away.

"Take two steps back," the man says. "That's an order."

Shane takes two careful steps back.

The man looks up the stairwell, spots me.

"Hello, Kate," he says. "You have a beautiful son, you know that? When the moment came, I couldn't do it, can you believe that? Couldn't kill one for the other. Thought I could, but my own beautiful son was gone, so what did it matter if his heart keeps beating?"

"Put the weapon down," says Shane.

The man in the perfect uniform shakes his head. "Can't do that," he says, and he raises the gun to his own head.

A clap of thunder and he falls.

When Shane comes up from the basement I reach for his hand and pull him to me and kiss his battered face and thank him, again and again.

A few minutes later the men in the flak jackets and the assault rifles burst through the open door and find us sitting around the kitchen table, me and Tommy and Randall Shane. Lyla, too. She's pretending nothing bad has happened. At her insistence we're eating pancakes with butter and real maple syrup. Not as good as my pancakes, of course, but not bad, all things considered.

EPILOGUE

one year later

One Year Later

The Fairfax Yankees finally got a new manager. Me. Figured this was my son's last year in Little League, I wanted to share every moment. Selfish, I know, but I can't help it. He'll grow up soon enough, turn into a surly teenager like all the others, and decide that the worst experience in life is appearing in public with his mother. But for right now he's my twelve-year-old miracle boy, and he's coming up to bat with the game on the line. Snapping and tugging at his gloves like his hero, A-Rod.

A-Rod is short for Alex Rodriquez, did you know that?

We've got a couple of new coaches, too. At third base, throwing hand signals like soft brown grenades, is one of my new partners, Sherona Johnson. When she signs for a bunt, you better believe the players obey. Connie, my other new partner, declined a coaching position by pleading overwork, but we all know she doesn't give a fig for baseball. That's okay, she and Mr. Yap attend the big games, and she cheers at all the wrong moments while he barks punctuation, and we love her for pretending to care who wins.

That tall, rangy galoot coaching first base is Randall Shane. He's still doing his thing, finding lost children, but shows up as often as he can. The kids love him, no surprise, and whenever I hear them shout, "Shane! Shane!" it reminds me of Ted's favorite movie, and I know he would approve, which makes me feel easy in my mind, and leaves my heart open.

The big news is, Shane recently got his driver's license. That sleep-disorder thing has improved to the point that he often gets several good nights' sleep in a row. The doctors think it had to do with a blow to the head, but I like to think it has something to do with us. Tomas and me, making a place in his life.

We've talked with Tomas about searching for his birth mother, but he says he's not ready, maybe when he's sixteen—like all twelve-year-olds, he thinks sixteen is practically grown-up. Whatever, I'm in no rush to deal with that particular problem. Time will take care of it or it won't.

Truth is, I'm not sure where all this is going. Or if it has a happy ending. All I know is we're taking it one day at a time, and finding joy in the smallest things, all three of us.

So far so good.

Now you'll have to excuse me. My perfect, precious, truly gifted son is stepping into the batter's box.

"Come on, Tomas! Clean stroke! Good at bat!"

I have no doubt.